A BORROWED MAN

A
BORROWED
MAN

GENE WOLFE

A TOM DOHERTY ASSOCIATES BOOK
NEW YORK

A BORROWED MAN

Copyright © 2015 by Gene Wolfe

A Tor Book
Published by Tom Doherty Associates, LLC
175 Fifth Avenue
New York, NY 10010

www.tor-forge.com

Tor® is a registered trademark of Tom Doherty Associates, LLC.

The Library of Congress Cataloging-in-Publication Data
is available upon request.

ISBN 978-0-7653-8114-9 (hardcover)
ISBN 978-1-4668-7799-3 (e-book)

Our books may be purchased in bulk for promotional, educational, or
business use. Please contact your local bookseller or the Macmillan Corporate
and Premium Sales Department at (800) 221-7945, extension 5442,
or by e-mail at MacmillanSpecialMarkets@macmillan.com.

First Edition: October 2015

Printed in the United States of America

0 9 8 7 6 5 4 3 2 1

For my British friend, Nigel Price

A BORROWED MAN

1

FROM THE SPICE GROVE PUBLIC LIBRARY

Murder is not always such a terrible thing. It is bad, sure, sometimes awfully, awfully bad. But only sometimes. I have been lying here on my shelf trying to figure out why I wrote all this, and I think maybe that is it. The law is not perfect.

You kept reading! All right, here we go.

I am really a young guy behind an older guy's face; you must understand that or you will not understand half the stuff I am going to tell. I was a mystery writer, a good one. You must know about the truckloads of his memories I am carrying from all his brain scans; so please keep them in mind all the time, just like I have to.

I live here, on a Level Three shelf in the Spice Grove Public Library. Our shelves are sort of like furnished rooms, if you have ever lived in one of those. About like furnished rooms, only three walls instead of four. There is a roll-up bed and some chairs, and the little table I have got this screen I borrowed on. I am not supposed to have the screen, but when the library is closed we can do just about whatever we want. There are the 'bots, sure;

but sometimes they cannot seem to tell us from you fully humans. Sometimes I wish I could peek inside one and see how it thinks. Not that I believe that would really work. I know it would not.

Have I said there is a curtained-off part with a toilet and a washbowl? No, not yet. Well, there is; only when I want to take a shower I have to go to the shower room, and I am not supposed to until after six.

Unless we are checked out, or at least taken to a table for consultation, we cannot leave our shelves until the library closes. We sleep here, shit here, and wash here. You have caught on to that already, I guess. At first it is not as bad as you might think. One time I saw a girl whose tits read: EVERYTHING FOR/A PEACEFUL LIFE. All right, I have got a peaceful life. Also I will get a peaceful death, when they burn me and death comes again. Only after a while you want more, and death comes again way, way too quick for anybody who never gets borrowed. Just the same . . . Well, you know. Naturally having you, my reader, in the back of my mind so much worries me.

I have been borrowed twice, thanks to all this about Colette, the locked doors, and my old book. Colette will come back next year and borrow me again. I have seen to it. I am called E. A. Smithe, just like I was—I mean, the first me—and I am really just like you. I ought to say that before we get in too deep. We reclones are people, even if we do not count as human beings with you fully human ones. She knew that.

My watch had struck two when she stopped to stare up at me; I sat there trying not to grin and liked looking at her. She was at least as tall as I am, with coal black hair, dream-deep blue eyes, and that paper white skin that burns in five or ten minutes if it is not protected from the sun. When a whole lot of fun and daydreams had passed, she whispered, "You might be the card that opens the book for me."

I nodded. "There's only one way to find out, madam." It is not just that I look like him, I talk like him, too. Boy, do I ever! Really, though, I talk the way he wrote exposition. I have to. Only I could not write like that if I wanted to, or nowhere except here when they do not know. They will not let me, just to begin with. Someday I would love to kick the guy who worked out all this business of bringing back writers but not letting them write.

Colette took my hand and I jumped down off my shelf. Then she took me to a table. You can guess how happy that made me. Being consulted is not nearly as good as being checked out, but it is good, too; and in three years I had not gotten consulted more than three or four times. It was July, and so far that year it had only been once, for maybe fifteen or twenty minutes. In my dreams I could see the flames and feel the heat.

"Do you know about books?" Colette asked. She sat down, which let me sit, too.

So play it cool. I shook my head. "I don't. I fear you've got the wrong man."

"Yes, you do!"

"No. I know something about men. I know more about women than most men do, which really isn't saying a great deal. I know a little about children, rather more about dogs, and much less about cats. I'm afraid that's as far as my knowledge goes. Nothing worth mentioning about books or music or cooking or ten thousand other things."

"I've researched you, Mr. Smithe. You wrote *The Lantern in the Library*, so clearly you know a lot about books."

Hoping I was teasing her along, I shook my head.

"There's a book that holds an enormous secret."

I said, "There are thousands upon thousands of books that hold millions upon millions of secrets, madam. A few hundred of those secrets may be enormous. I won't argue the point."

"Not like this."

"I see." I waited; and when she did not speak, I asked, "What is this secret you seek?"

"I don't know," Colette said; she should have looked put out at the question, but she did not. She just smiled at me, and I felt she sure as hell knew.

So try something else. "What's the title of this mysterious book?"

Still smiling she said, "I'm afraid I don't know that, either."

"You're being very close-mouthed; I can only hope you have a good reason. With no more information than you've given, do you expect me to tell you the title?"

"No, I don't; but I expect you to help me ferret out the secret."

"I will—if I can. I am a library resource, after all." I was still not sure I would be able to wrangle a checkout from her. "Knowing no more than you've told me, how can I be of help?"

"A man wants to change one page of a certain book to incorporate information he needs to conceal. Am I making myself clear?"

So spy novel stuff; I tried to keep a straight face as I nodded. "Perfectly."

"Very well. How can he do it?"

"In any of a dozen ways, or so I would think. To begin with, paper books are now printed exclusively on demand. You can buy a download from a company that is selling the book you want and have one printed for you. You must know about that."

"Tell me about it." Colette was concentrating, so she had stopped smiling.

"There are machines. One can be bought or rented. You download the text. You may design the cover. If you do not, the machine will design its own. Those are very plain, for the most part, and you can save a bit of money by specifying two colors instead of four."

She nodded, impressed; and silently I blessed a couple of librarians whose conversation I had overheard eight or ten weeks ago. "Say that I want to conceal my information in a standard reference such as *Common Deciduous Trees of Our New America*. I'd download a copy from the publisher, carefully scan the text and illustrations, then insert my information at an appropriate point. That done, I would rent time on a demand printer and binder." I shut up and waited for a question or a comment, but she did not say a word.

"I would not have to go where the machine was, you understand, just rent the time. I would download the text I had prepared and specify one copy. The machine would print and bind the book in something less than a minute. The exact time would vary, depending upon the length of the text and the number and difficulty of the illustrations. The company that owned the machine would send me the book, with a bill for machine time and postage." I waited for a question before I added, "In most cases, it would offer to print me additional copies at a reduced price, if I were satisfied and wanted more."

"You said there were a dozen ways, I believe."

"There are. Here's a simpler one. Books—books other than textbooks particularly—often contain errors. When they do, the publisher may include an errata sheet correcting the error. 'On page two twenty-one *store age* should read *storage*.' This library tips those sheets into the back of its books."

Colette nodded.

"If the information someone wanted to hide were brief, he could easily print up his own errata sheet. 'On page two twenty-one, the formula such-and-so has been omitted.' Do you like that one?"

She smiled. "You really are the person I need. I don't know how I knew it."

That was flat-out encouraging. It sounded like she might actually borrow me; so I smiled, too, hoping to hit the next question out of the park.

"Give me another. You said a dozen."

"I feel sure you've thought of the simplest. He could write something on a flyleaf, or in the margin of a certain page."

"I don't think it's as obvious as that."

"There are chemical formulations that will disappear into the paper when they dry, only to reappear if the paper is warmed. When it cools, the writing vanishes again. Say that he writes his secret on a flyleaf. Conceivably it might be warmed by accident and some reader might notice it. But that would be extremely unlikely."

"I didn't know about the chemicals."

"A great deal will depend on the nature of the information. The longer it is, the harder it will be to hide. If it can be expressed in text, that's one thing. If it requires diagrams . . ." I pushed my shoulders up and let them drop.

"Suppose it's solid. A physical object."

I was not ready for that one, which was limiting and pretty crude. I said, "Ouch!"

"Yes, exactly. But suppose it is."

Thinking hard, I said, "It would have to be quite small."

"And flat, right?"

"Wrong. A pin might be pushed into the binding of a cloth-bound book and go unnoticed. A leatherbound book would be worse still."

"Most books have plastic bindings, like this one." She got a book out of her shaping bag and held it up.

"Of course, but almost anything is still possible. Is it information? Basically?"

"I think so."

"Then it might be encoded in a microchip, which is a tiny physical object that can hold, well, a lot. A chip like that can be inserted in a mouse's ear and used to locate and identify the mouse. If you really want me to help you, you're going to have to tell me a great deal more than you have so far."

"Not here," she said.

"Where, in that case?" Here I was afraid she was going to suggest someplace in the library; I would have to counter that somehow.

She shook her head. "I doubt that we're being bugged here, but it's possible. If we are—let's just say that anything we say may put us in danger."

That sounded paranoid; I decided to play up to it for the time being. "They would bug the place you named before we got there."

"Something like that. Yes. Come with me." She had decided, and she jumped up fast. "I'm going to check you out."

That was exactly what I had been hoping for, but I managed to hide my grin before we got to the front desk. Colette showed her library card to the 'bot we called Electric Bill, and it got us a fully human librarian who told her, "I'm afraid your card hasn't been approved for reclones."

Colette nodded. "I want to get it approved so I can check out this one."

"We need a deposit. It's quite substantial." The librarian's tone said Colette could not possibly have enough money.

Colette nodded again. "I suppose it must be. I'll return him."

"It will be refunded when you bring him back, assuming he's not damaged. How long?"

Colette pursed her lips. "Let's say I'll keep him for ten days."

The librarian looked skeptical. "For a period in excess of a week, I may be able to get you a special rate; but it will still be a great deal of money."

Electric Bill asked, "Will we give her the long-term discount, ma'am?"

"With undemand."

Electric Bill hummed. "My figure is forty-seven hundred for ten days, ma'am."

Colette took it calmly enough, but to me it came as a pretty stiff shock; I had hoped the library valued me more highly. The librarian merely pulled out another card and waved it at Bill, who promptly coughed up a couple more. The librarian took them and passed one to me, saying, "July thirtieth."

I said, "I'll remember."

"Not that we wouldn't like to hang on to your money, Ms. Coldbrook." Smiling, the librarian handed Colette the other card.

Maybe I should stop right here and explain that up until then I had not known Colette's name. As we were going out of the library I said, "It will be quite a treat to be in your company for so long, Ms. Coldbrook," and she told me to say Colette.

A hovercab came at her signal. I had seen hovercabs before, but I had never ridden in one. There is nothing scary about them—or anyway I was not scared when it seemed pretty clear that Colette had ridden in them a lot. The whole thing should have been a lot scarier than it was; of course Colette's not being scared helped. "Taos Towers, please," she told the sim who'd showed up in the hovercab's screen.

It touched its cap, and the hovercab, which had been floating up like a bubble in still water, picked up speed enough to push us back in our seats.

"It's quite a run," the sim remarked. "Takes a load of energy, ma'am."

"Which will be covered by your charge."

It nodded thoughtfully. "I'll have to deadhead back, though."

"Unless you pick up another fare there. Which you probably will."

"These exclusive places . . ."

I believe she ignored him. I was looking down at New America, something I had seen before only on maps. We flew from twilight into day while I watched. The mountains were much nearer now.

Colette leaned forward, whispering to the hovercab, and I felt it make a change of course. "Another thirty-four thou and I can buy out," the sim told us.

Colette did not speak; so I said, "I suppose you'll go humanoid?"

"'Course I will. That what you are, sir?"

Colette laughed.

I shook my head. "I'm flesh and blood. Almost the real thing."

"Sorry, sir. I didn't mean nothing by it."

I was looking up, mostly. Also down and around.

"You have a wonderful face," Colette told me.

My eyes left the sky; when I looked at her, I had to catch my breath. As soon as I could, I said, "No one else has ever thought so."

"Of course they have! You mean they haven't said so. You can't possibly know their thoughts."

"There must be machines for that."

"There are. When I was still a student they took us to Long Lawn. They have one there to help them treat the patients. One of the other students volunteered, and they let us look into his thoughts. Imagine an anthill, but instead of just seven kinds every ant is different. Then they let us listen to them. It was like listening to the whole city talking, everybody talking at once."

"You have an enchanting face," I said to her. "Any number of men must have told you that. Please don't be insulted."

She laughed. "Half a dozen men and three or four women. The women were trying to sell me clothes and the men were trying to get me to take them off."

"I'm not. Believe me, I know what I am."

"A less-than human who contemplates the sky." Said with that tender smile, it did not sting.

"How can anyone not? This is a lovely world, and until a few minutes ago I didn't know how lovely it is. People are wonderfully fortunate to be born now. I remember a world whose sky was gray with smoke or black with dust."

"That's right, you have his memories. I'd forgotten that."

I nodded. "Wonderful memories. Back in the library, on my shelf, that was what I did most of the time. For day after day I read and remembered."

"We're down to about one billion now. I'd halve that, if I could." Colette paused, thinking. "It must have been lonely there in the library. Did you tell yourself your own stories?"

"Sometimes. Stories help, sometimes. When I tire of stories, I daydream about Arabella—Arabella Lee. Perhaps you know her work?"

"I'm afraid not."

"She was a poet, and a fine one. Her poetry was lovely, although not half so lovely as she. We were married. . . ."

"Yes?" Colette pronounced the word in a way that made it seem she might really be interested.

"Only for two years; then she divorced me. I mean the original me, back in my own time. The me who wrote all my books."

"How old are you? Not him, but the living, breathing reclone sitting beside me."

When I did not answer, she changed it to, "How long has it been since you were published?"

I shrugged. "They told me, but I've forgotten."

"You're lying!"

"Yes. Am I that transparent?"

"Certainly. All men are. Women lie and lie—do you know that?"

I said, "I suppose I do now."

"It's one of the things men tell each other, and it's true. We women lie and lie, because we're good at it. Men generally tell the truth because they're not."

"I have nearly half a century of memories. Doesn't that make me old?"

"Certainly not. I'm a good judge of age. Shall I tell you how old you are?"

I nodded and tried to smile, although no smile came. "I wish you would."

"You're twenty-one or twenty-two, but you could easily pass for thirty or more. Most people wouldn't believe that you're only twenty-two."

Although Colette would and did. And it was not quite true, I decided, that I had an old man's memories and a young man's mind. That was what they had taught me to believe, but it was not really that simple. How old was my judgment? I think your judgment depends on both those things, but it depends more on something else, something I cannot put my finger on. On insight and this other thing. Only I am a lot younger than Colette thought.

I could study the mountains in the middle distance when we landed in what looked like the ruined garden of some abandoned estate. There were trees like towers of bells, and patches of golden-green sunlight. A waterfall roared about a hundred paces away. "This grass is fresh and very soft," I said when our hovercab had lifted off, "but I wouldn't think you'd want to sit on the ground in that skirt."

Colette nodded and waved her hand, leading me to a couple of stones about a hundred steps away. I dusted off both with my handkerchief, which got me a really great smile, and I sat on mine after she had sat down.

Opening her shaping bag, she took out the plastic-bound book she had shown me before. "Books like this are almost obsolete now. Did you know it?"

"The librarians have told me so. I would hate to believe it."

"You must, because it's true."

I wanted to walk. That was a new feeling for me, or maybe only an old buried one coming back, one so old I had forgotten it. I got up and walked up and down, not fast but not slow. Books—real books printed on paper—were the heart and soul of a whole culture that had been mine. Cultures are like people, it seems. Sure, they get old and die; but sometimes they die even when they are not very old at all.

"I can see you're trying to keep this age straight." Colette herself was trying hard not to laugh.

Still dizzy with thought, I nodded.

"That's good. Do it. I'll stop talking until you sit again."

Without paying much attention to what I did, I had gone to the edge of the waterfall. I guess it was pretty small, no higher than some of the belltower trees, but really pretty. I must have watched it for ten or fifteen minutes. Maybe more.

At last I went back to her. "You told me that books are almost obsolete, yet you carry that one in your shaping bag. That must mean that this secret you're looking for is in there, or you think it is. You were afraid of our being overheard—afraid there were hidden listening devices in the library."

She nodded, looking grim.

"Why would the police be snooping our conversation?"

"They wouldn't be interested—not as far as I know, or at least not seriously." She shut up for a long look at the book. "You may be right. I . . ."

"Yes?"

"I'll certainly consider it. Probably for quite a while."

I sat down again. "Are you yourself a scientist?"

She laughed and shook her head. "What makes you think I might be?"

"Our earlier conversation. I didn't ask about a map that might give the location of buried treasure. I talked about formulas and diagrams, none of which you challenged. So it's a scientific secret, or at least you think that it might be."

"Yes, it might."

"But you yourself are no sort of scientist. What are you, then?"

"What do I look like?"

I shrugged. "A wealthy, well-educated young lady."

"Close enough! Let's leave it at that." She had been reading the book. "You mustn't ask me how I know the secret's in here."

"In that case, you'd certainly lie if I did." I smiled, remembering something she had said.

She nodded.

"So I won't. Tell me this, please, and don't lie. Is it in all copies of that book, or only in that one?"

"You . . ." She hesitated. "I don't really know. What difference does it make?"

"A great deal, or so I think. If it is in this one alone, we need only look for a difference between this copy and the rest; but if it's in all the copies, that approach would be quite useless."

"If it's in all the copies, it must be in the text."

"Correct," I said.

"While if it's only in this one, there could be some difference in text. Or else something physical, like the chemical ink you talked about, or the errata sheet."

"Exactly. Are you good with modern screens? I knew next to nothing about the wonderful computers of my own time, and I know less than nothing about the screens you use now."

"No, not at all." She paused. "Some people are fascinated by them."

"You aren't, I take it."

"No." She opened the book and closed it again. "I'm not. Those people are mostly boys, and they get into the mathematics— all sorts of things that machines can handle much better than we can."

"We may have to enlist one of those boys, in that case. Millions of books are available in digital form, or so I've heard."

"Several digital forms, really." She smiled. "I see I've let the helium out. I'm sorry. Really, I am."

"Not necessarily. Why several forms?"

"Sometimes people want to see the author's original text, prior to editing. In other cases there are several forms. Suppose a Chinese book has been translated into English. There could be three or four translations, and arguments about which translation is best."

"Is that a translation?"

She shook her head. "I've researched it, and it was written in late English—in the language we're speaking, in other words."

"Is that the only language in use now?"

She shook her head again. "There are dozens of others."

"In time—"

She nodded again. "Yes. I know what you're going to say, and I agree: there may be a planetary language. But it hasn't happened yet and perhaps it never will."

"Since we don't have to worry about translations, what do we have to worry about? The author's original text?"

She smiled. "You should know."

"What do you mean by that?"

"You wrote it." She handed me the book.

I glanced at the title page and shook my head. "I see I did, but this one must have been written after my death. I don't remember it at all."

"Oh, come now!"

"I meant almost. After my last scan, in other words, and nobody thought it was worthwhile to make another. I suppose I wasn't selling all that well. As to the author's—as to my original text . . ."

"Yes? Tell me!"

"I don't think we have to worry. I wasn't generally edited a lot. You couldn't hide an enormous secret in minor corrections of punctuation and the like, or I don't see how you could."

"And it would have to be something you, the author, *could* see."

"Which is why you thought I might be the one to help you?"

"Exactly. I've talked to experts on codes and ciphers. Nothing they told me seemed to lead anywhere; then I thought of you. Are you sure you don't know what you put in this book?"

"I am." I opened the book and read a few paragraphs. "It seems to be in my style, or something very near it, so I doubt the title page is lying. I don't recall writing it, but the copyright date must—"

"What's the matter?"

"I just thought of something, that's all. You knew where these stones were."

She nodded.

"So you've been here before. Isn't it possible that the hearers you fear are listening to us? That they've bugged it?"

"I doubt it. It's been almost three years since I was here last."

"You sat on these stones."

She nodded.

"And he sat on this one I'm sitting on."

"Oh, stars! Now you'll want to know who he was, and whether I still care about him, and how much I cared about him when I did, and whether we slept together a lot, and if he and I—"

I had raised my hand. "No!"

"You don't have to shout at me."

"I wasn't shouting, but if it seemed like that to you, I apologize most humbly. All I'm saying is that this site could be bugged. Perhaps it's unlikely, but it's certainly possible."

"How about over there?" She pointed across the stream.

I agreed.

The stream was narrow and deep, with a fast current. The land on the other side was rough with broken building stones. We walked slowly, I wearing the one pair of low shoes that was all I had, and Colette in screw-heeled fashion boots. I wondered how soon she would want to stop. Now I think she was probably thinking something like that about me.

After a while she said, "Not all the animals here are harmless, you know."

I shook my head. "I didn't."

"Some of the dangerous ones have been killed off; but they keep coming back, bears and wolves, and panthers that look like big Siamese cats."

"Were they less dangerous near the waterfall?" We were still walking.

"Yes, because there was no scent trail for the animal to pick up. We're leaving one now."

I nodded. "Then let's stop and talk here."

"There's no place for the hovercab to land."

"We can go back."

"If anything's tracking us, we'll meet it. You realize that, I hope."

"In that case, the sooner we start back, the safer we'll be."

"Not if they're listening." She paused. "I know you're right—they might have found out about that spot."

"Who are they? Do you know?"

"First I want to sit down. Isn't that terrible?"

I shook my head. "We've walked quite a distance, and you're wearing screw heels. I didn't think we'd come this far."

We went back to the stream. The water was well below ground level there, and we sat on the bank. We hadn't been there long before she pulled off her boots and splashed the water with her feet. I pulled off my shoes and stockings, and did it, too.

2

COLETTE'S STORY

I had a brother named Conrad, Mr. Smithe. He was two years
older than I, and although he had teased me as a child we
were on very good terms as brothers and sisters go. He was always kind and protective of me, and I loved him for it—even
when it was a trifle embarrassing." Colette sighed. "We played
together as children—played screen games, and ran footraces.
All sorts of stuff. Eventually he became an engineer and I a
teacher."

She paused, looking thoughtful. "I hope I don't look like a
teacher, but perhaps I do. Do you know about the eds in our
schools?"

I nodded and said that I knew they existed but little more than
that.

"They're excellent—wonderful—if the student really wants to
learn. If she doesn't, they're worthless. The teacher's task is to
light that fire and puff it into a blaze. You'll think I'm being
melodramatic, but I'm not; that's what it's like. That's what it is!
Sometimes you can see it catch, by just watching their faces.

Sometimes you don't know how hot it is until it burns you a little. The student asks a round dozen good questions, you have to admit you don't have answers to most of them, and your student goes off searching sites and diskers and even looking into what we call the physical texts sometimes. Usually it's next to impossible to get anyone under the age of twenty to open a real book."

I nodded to show I understood.

"I'm going on too long about teaching, I know. I'll try to cut it short. My mother died. I got leave to go home and attend her funeral; I did and hurried back to my students."

I said that I was sorry, and that it must have been terribly hard.

"Here I'm supposed to say that it's all right and I'm over it." Colette's eyes flashed. "It's the polite thing to say and I know it—but it isn't all right! Not one filthy bit all right! Death is a horror, an atrocity and an injustice, and I wish to heaven we could kill it, for a change. I went back to work, but I still miss my mother terribly. Now that I've got the money, I'm going to have her recloned." She drew breath.

"A few years later my father died, too. You'll have a lot of questions about him when I'm finished, so I want to tell you right now that I won't be able to answer most of them. He was a brilliant man." Colette paused, staring away, her violet eyes cloudy with thoughts. "Brilliant, but brilliant in ways most people didn't appreciate. Brilliant and—and horribly secretive."

I nodded, feeling that every word she said increased the likelihood that she would check me out for a second time next quarter or next year.

"When I was a little girl he lost job after job. Eventually I realized what was happening and came to dread it. He'd last a year in a new job, possibly two, then be out of work again. When

I was in my early teens, he stopped looking for new jobs and started doing things on his own, giving financial advice, managing investments for other people, and so forth. Consulting. All sorts of things. He put out a little newsletter, just one screen each week. It cost more than most of them do, but before long he had over a thousand subscribers. He made investments of his own, investments that prospered. He never talked about any of those things to me, you understand, or to my brother. If he talked about them to my mother, she never told us anything about it. I doubt that he did; he wasn't the kind of man who confides in his wife—who confides in anyone. What little I know about him I learned from people outside the family, from other teachers and from the parents of my students, mostly. All I knew at the time was that we moved into a big house and suddenly there was more than enough money for college for Conrad and later for me. Two flitters, then another for me. Very few families can afford one flitter."

I nodded again.

"I went home for his funeral, of course. Just before I came back here my brother showed me Father's laboratory. It was a fourth-floor complex in our house, a suite that was kept locked any time he wasn't in it and often when he was. There is an office in one room, desks, screens, and keyboards, diskers and even file cabinets—all the things you'd expect, and that's just one room in the suite. There is a chemical laboratory—I suppose you'd call it that—with a thousand different chemicals. Burners, ovens, and scopes. There was a workbench in another room, and machine tools I don't know the names of. You program them with a screen, my brother said, and then they work on and on in a sort of trance. All kinds of things. My brother took down a screen in the office so I could see the safe set into the wall behind it. It was quite large and looked as strong as a bank vault. He told me he was going to hire an expert in to open it and asked if I wanted to be there when they did it. He didn't expect me to trust him, you see. I told him that I didn't have to be there, that he should just do it." Colette paused. "We talked for a long time after that."

I said, "I imagine so. Did you refuse your brother's invitation because you didn't want him to think you didn't trust him?"

"Not really. It was because I did trust him, and I was afraid Father had confessed some dreadful secret. He was that kind of man, or at least I thought he might be. I was afraid he'd been blackmailing someone or had recorded a confession to some dreadful crime. If he had, I didn't want to hear it. My brother might or might not tell me about it, but either way would be better—far better—than hearing my father saying it. I . . . I knew the pain that would be in his voice, and hearing it would hurt me as badly as telling us about it hurt him. Lonely people like my father keep everything locked inside them, and often they suffer terribly because of it." Colette's soft white hands writhed in her lap.

"Only that wasn't it at all. My brother came to me a few days ago, when I had practically forgotten about the safe. He told me they had opened it the day after I left." Still watching me, she groped the soft green grass for her shaping bag and took out *Murder on Mars* again.

"He said he knew I'd been expecting bundles of bearer bonds or gold and emeralds. Something of that kind, but there hadn't been anything like that. Just this book. That this book was the only thing that was in there. He wasn't lying. That's what you have to understand. He was not lying."

I said, "I know you knew him very well."

"I did. We'd grown up together, and I knew him almost as well as I knew our mother. If he'd been lying, he'd have made up something more plausible. That the safe had been empty and he thought someone must have gotten to it before we did. Or that there had been private papers in there, and he had burned them. Anything. But he said there'd been nothing at all in it but this book, and he was desperately afraid I wouldn't believe him. I knew him, as I said. Even though he didn't lie a lot, he was a better liar than most men; and when he did lie, his lies were always smooth and plausible. This wasn't."

I held out my hand, and she handed over the book for the second time. I opened it. "Your father's name was Conrad Coldbrook?"

"Yes, and that's his signature. I've compared it to every other example I had, and they all match. Or if it's a forgery, it's probably good enough to fool an expert. Conrad was my brother's name, too; perhaps you remember. My brother was Conrad, Junior, while my father was alive. When father died he dropped the Junior."

"That's what one does." I handed the book back to her.

"You don't remember writing this? *'He was neither angel nor devil, but something for which we have only bad words or none, a being young and ancient, neither good nor evil, who knew too well the roads to the farther stars.'* That's how it begins."

I had read that, too, and I was about to say I hadn't when it hit me that the words were really a little bit familiar. I took the book again and had another look. It was print-on-demand; but the cover picture might have been lifted from some publisher's edition: two planets, the larger one mottled blue and white, the smaller one dark red, scarred, and choked by a snake.

Colette remarked, "The serpent represents evil, I suppose."

I was thinking of a dozen other things, but I nodded. "I don't suppose you've read it."

"No. No, Mr. Smithe, I haven't. The important points are that it was in my father's safe, the only thing he kept there. And that you're listed as the author. Look at the title page."

I had noticed my name there already, but I checked it again anyhow. It had not been a collaboration or a fix-up of some dead man's unfinished manuscript. On the back of the title page, the copyright date was thirteen years before I died.

Sighing, I opened the book at random. "*Eridean had called them the sewers, but they were enormously larger and more varied than the term implied, tunnels and cellars and subcellars and worse, far beneath the city. There were animals in them, he knew. Animals, men more hostile and more fell than any beast, and plants that throve without the sun, pale growths that feasted upon the living and the dead. Yet what first Apolean met was none of these, but a woman.*"

Talking mostly to myself, I said, "I remember it now."

"Wonderful!"

I turned back to the copyright page. "They give the original publisher." I held up the book so Colette could see it. "Pixie Press. It was a small press, just one woman and her husband, with a part-time volunteer who was paid mostly in books. My regular publisher didn't want it. My agent tried a few others, then gave up and handed it back to me. Handed it back metaphorically, I mean. Pixie published a limited edition of . . ."

I stopped to think. "Three hundred and fifty copies. That was it, I'm sure. One hundred signed and boxed, and the rest just hardcovers on acid-proof paper with Zistal dust jackets. This looks like one of those."

Colette smiled. "I hope it sold for them."

"It did. The entire edition sold out in a good deal less than a year, Jen told me. She was quite happy about it. It was the first time they had ever had a book sell out in under one year."

"Now you remember writing it. You must."

"I do. It was one of the sideline projects I did now and then. When I was stuck on *The Ice-Blue Kiss* I'd work on this for a while. At first it was meant to be a short story."

Colette smiled and gave the water a little extra splash.

"It kept growing and growing. I didn't mind, but sometimes I felt guilty about working on it. I knew it would never make any money."

"Was that all you cared about, Mr. Smithe? Making money?"

I flipped through the pages while my brain took care of the heavy lifting; it was sort of like petting a dog. "Obviously not, since this didn't."

"And so the money's still in the book, still locked up in there. Money or power, and they're the same thing at bottom. If you've got money you can get power, and if you have power you can get money. Matter is energy and energy is matter. I always put a question or two about that on the final."

"The interchange of matter and energy is a pretty big leap from the paltry fact that your father had locked this copy in his safe."

"It isn't just that." Colette was not smiling.

"I didn't think it was. What's the rest?"

"I've told you a little about my poor brother. About Conrad, Junior."

"You've told me that he gave you this book. Almost nothing beyond that."

"And I told you he was the one who had Father's safe opened. He went straight to Spice Grove to tell me about it, gave me this book, and went back to New Delphi. I think he must have been murdered that same day."

Maybe two or three times in your whole life you feel the chill, and that was one of those times for me. I asked, "Someone killed him?" The minute the words came out, I knew how stupid it must have sounded.

Colette nodded. "The police told me the killer had gotten him as soon as he stepped into the house. His bag had been opened and searched there on the floor of the reception hall. The rest of the house had been searched, too. In the bedrooms, dresser drawers were pulled out and dumped, and so forth. The policeman told me all about it. Do you want his name? I've got his name somewhere."

I said, "Not now."

"He said they were looking for something, and it seemed as if they hadn't found it. All the books in Father's library had been pulled off their shelves and thrown on the floor. Two or three hundred real paper books. It must have been an awful mess."

I had gotten on top of the chill by then. "You didn't see it?"

"No. The police told me about it. This one policeman did, mostly. Of course I was tempted to tell him about that book you're holding, but—"

"It didn't seem wise. You were probably right."

Colette nodded gratefully. "Later I called Bettina Johns; she's an old school friend and lives near there. She went over and looked at everything, and it sounded just dreadful. She—"

I interrupted. "How did Bettina Johns get into the house?"

"The maid 'bot let her in. The 'bots are still there, I think four of them. Anyway she told me about a company called Merciful Maids. They specialize in cleaning up the homes of dead people. Those homes are often disorganized and dirty—this is what they told me."

"I understand."

"The late owner is ill and unable to take care of things for weeks and weeks before she dies. Often, they said, her friends and relatives steal things, anticipating the owner's death. All Merciful Maids' employees are bonded, and there will be half a dozen or so in the house at the same time, one waxing the floors while another cleans up the kitchen and two more dust. One or two more—these are upper-level employees—make an inventory. I hired them to straighten the place up."

"Do they use 'bots? I've been told they have certain disadvantages, but they wouldn't steal."

"I don't know," Colette said. "I never asked."

"Did they send you the inventory?"

She nodded. "Now you'll ask if there was anything missing. There wasn't. Or if there was, it was something I didn't know about. Now tell me, please. What do you think we should do?"

I know that nobody who reads this is going to believe it; but right then was the first time I really and truly understood myself, what I was and what had been done to me, and how unreal all of it had been. I was not the man I thought I was, the one whose name I used—whose name I still use right now, for that matter. I was somebody else, a kid who had been grown from that guy's DNA and loaded up with his memories, phony memories of things that had never happened to me and never could happen to me. "Implanted" was what they said; but all it really meant was that years and years of dead stuff had been read into me while I lay in a sort of coma.

I was a kid who had no real memories of his own except the library, dumb memories of sitting on my shelf until the library closed, of moving around a little then, running up and down the stairs, doing push-ups, arm wrestling, eating and talking over dinner with other twenty-first-century people who were just as phony as I was. Of thinking and thinking about Arabella and the day they would discover her, clone her the way I had been cloned, and shelve her in Poetry . . .

> One by one across the desert
> Until our boots grow too heavy with
>   The sands of time.

I carried the memories of ten thousand decisions big and small, but I had never made a real one. Sitting there, holding—sometimes—Colette's hand, I knew I did not even know what intercourse was really like. I had touched the hands of a few women. Nothing more than that! Now I kept smelling Colette's perfume, her perfume and the freshness of the cold water our feet splashed. Lovely, flowing water. Clear, cold water that could never, ever, wash away the sands.

Not that I had accumulated a lot, or that they were apt to fill my boots really soon. We are bound to last a long time, we library people. That is a joke we make, and I have never understood why so many of us laugh at it.

I had never had a real childhood.

"What should we do, Mr. Smithe?" Colette repeated.

I wanted to tell her I did not know, but the words stuck in my throat.

3

WHAT WE DID

"Honestly," Colette said, "I don't know. What do you think?" I sighed, hating to leave the water and the grass, scared half to death to end the moment. "Surely that's obvious."

"Not to me." She sounded sincere. "Oh, I'm so glad I checked you out!"

"We talk to the expert who opened the safe for your brother. But first"—inside I was jumping up and down at having thought of it—"you tell me the other reason you're so certain *Murder on Mars* is valuable." I had laid it down on the bank beside me. When Colette just sat there without saying anything, I picked it up, riffled the pages, and handed it back to her.

She took it, looking thoughtful. "I could throw it in this creek, couldn't I? Doing that now might save a lot of trouble."

"Suppose they captured you, tortured you? Do they know you have it? They'd never believe you'd thrown it away."

"I suppose you're right. As for their knowing I've got it, perhaps they do—or they may just think it's likely. They must have known somehow that my brother had it, but he didn't have it when somebody murdered him. They must have thought he had it on his person then—in a pocket or in his traveling bag. But of course it wasn't there; he'd left it with me. Why do you want to talk to the man who opened the safe?"

I took a deep breath, really sucking in the air. This was chancy and I knew it. "First, to verify your brother's assertion that there was nothing else in there—also to get a lead on what the other contents may have been, if there were other contents. Second, because the people who are after the book must have learned about it in some way. There are at least half a dozen ways they might have found out, and maybe more. You may have told them yourself, for example. Or they may have overheard you telling someone else. But—"

Colette interrupted. "No, they couldn't! I've never told anyone but you."

"Good! Your brother may have told someone, and so on. But highest probability—or so it seems to me—is that they learned about it from the locksmith. If so, he must have seen them. In my day, one could call others on many telephones without being seen. Now, screening—well, I suppose it might be possible to fake a face in some way, but you'd have to be very good with screens to do it. Or so I imagine."

Colette nodded. "I've been using screens since I was a little girl, and I don't believe I could manage it. I wouldn't even know where to start."

"Besides which, I doubt very much if a simple screen from a stranger would do it. You could explain that we need to know, that your brother is dead now, and so forth. They wouldn't have that advantage. The locksmith could say, why do you want to know? And he probably would."

"They may have bribed him."

"You're right," I said, "money always works—if it's enough money. Offered more, he might describe them and his conversation with them. That information might be vital to us."

She nodded again. "Knowledge is power, if it's the right knowledge."

After that she screened for our hovercab while I dried her feet—a real blast—with my handkerchief. Then I helped her with her boots and put on my socks and shoes. I kept looking for animals as we made our way back to the clearing where the hovercab had let us out, but I never saw a one.

After fifteen minutes or so, the hovercab came back. It had a bill on its screen that was a lot larger than it had been when it left. Colette ignored that, got the sim, and for the second time told it to take us to the Taos Towers.

Then she turned to me. "All right if we go straight there? In a hovercraft the trip will take two or three hours and it's getting dark here already."

I shrugged. "You've checked me out for ten days. May I assume you'll at least put me up for the night?"

"Only if you'll sit with me, sip a little wine while we watch something, and whisper clever compliments. Then be content to sleep in my guest room."

I should not have grinned, but I believe I did. "I'll do them all very willingly indeed."

"Fine." She smiled. "I've five rooms and a bath. The lounge and the dining room are open to you. The lounge is the biggest room, and it's where the couch is. The bathroom's available whenever you need it as long as I'm not in it, but the kitchen and my bedroom are private property. If you want something to eat, or a glass of milk or something, I'll bring it. There's wine and beer and who knows what all under the bar in the lounge. Ginger ale, peanuts, crackers, and so forth. Take any of that stuff you want. Understand? Just stay out of the kitchen and my bedroom. It's my apartment and those are my rules."

"Which I will certainly follow."

"You won't go in the kitchen? Or my bedroom?"

"Absolutely not."

"You'd better mean that. If I find you in either one, you'll go back to the library just as fast as I can get you there."

Later, in her suite, she said she had expected me to want to see her father's house in New Delphi as soon as I could.

I shook my head.

"I won't ask why not."

"Good."

"You've been awfully quiet."

I told her, "I've been trying to compose dozens of clever compliments."

She smiled. "Any luck?"

"No. You're marvelously beautiful, but I've told you that before and there's nothing clever about it. Every man who sees you must think the same thing. You're as brave as a lioness, but women don't like being told how brave they are."

"Then why did you tell me?"

"Because I value honesty above diplomacy." Putting a finger to my lips, I tiptoed over to her shaping bag, took out the book, and carried it off. When I returned to the lounge, Colette raised her eyebrows. I put my finger to my lips again.

She nodded, went to the screen, and ordered food. While we ate, she murmured, "Eventually you're going to have to explain."

I figured she was probably right, but I whispered, "No."

"Suppose it's cameras?"

I shrugged.

After dinner we watched *April and Its Spotted Lilies* and *Twice Terror*. As I told her, I had heard of roundvid but I had never seen those dramas or any others. *Twice Terror* was working up to its big scene when they came. My watch struck eleven just as her screen flashed VISITOR A-1, and she muttered, "Oh, stars!" I asked what was the matter.

"The building just let someone in." She had gotten up and was striding toward the door. "Two someones. It's supposed to show them on my screen, and turn them away if I don't approve them." She tripped the night bolt.

I asked, "Why didn't it do that?"

"It said they were A-1. That means they're guests I've designated who get in automatically, whether I'm here or not."

"Then we may assume they are. It may be a pleasant visit." I was trying to soothe her; she looked frightened and angry.

"Cob was the only one I ever designated—and he's dead."

I had been expecting a knock, but we did not get one. Colette's door swung open without a sound, and two men sauntered in. The second shut it behind him. The first, a stocky man in dark clothes, said, "We're not going to tell you who we are or who we represent. The less you know, the safer you'll be."

I nodded and put my arm around Colette, the first time I had taken the chance.

She had the controller, and she held it up. "One stroke gets the police."

The second man took two quick strides toward her and

snatched the controller. "I'm sorry, officer," he told the uniformed sim whose electronically faked image had joined us in the lounge. "My little boy got hold of it. We've told him a thousand times that he's not supposed to play with it." He pressed a key and the SGPD sim disappeared, uniform, badge, and all.

"I don't have a lot of money." Colette's voice sounded steady, but I could feel her trembling. "You can have it all if you'll only go."

"You've got the book." That was the second man. He looked younger than the stocky guy, wore a hat, and was a good head taller. "You've got it and we want it. Hand it over."

"I have several books," Colette told him. "I'm a teacher. Perhaps you know."

The stocky one farted with his mouth.

"You know the book we mean," the tall one said. "Give it to me. As soon as you do we'll go, and you'll never see us again."

I said, "Will someone please tell me what you're talking about?"

"Ms. Coldbrook had a brother," the tall one said; his voice reminded me of a library 'bot about to use its prod. "He stole a book that belongs to us. We want it. Now!" As he spoke, he dropped Colette's controller into a pocket of his jacket.

I stood up. "This doesn't concern me, and it seems to me that it doesn't concern Colette either."

"We know it does," the stocky one said. He said it like he was telling me the time, but his face said he'd tear the arms off babies.

The tall one asked, "Just who the fuck are you, anyhow?"

"Simply an admirer of Ms. Coldbrook's. This would appear to be a private matter, one in which I have no wish to intrude."

Colette's hand found mine. "Don't go, Ern! Please don't!"

"If you don't want me to, I won't." I tried to make my voice reassuring. "If I can be of any help to you here, just let me know."

The stocky one said, "I'll give you your last chance now. Do you have the book?"

Naturally I said, "What book is that?"

"The book Conrad Coldbrook gave his sister here."

I shook my head.

"But you know about it."

"I believe she mentioned a book. *The Lantern in the Library*? I think that was the one. An excellent book! I've read it."

That was when Colette tried to run to the door. She nearly made it, but the tall one grabbed her from behind before she could get it open. Somebody jumped on his back and got an arm around his neck—and that is all that I remember.

I said "somebody" because I cannot remember deciding to do it. I cannot remember doing it, either, but I know somebody did. Somebody, not me. I was standing nice and quiet in front of the couch.

By and by my arms were behind me. I could not move them forward no matter how much I wanted to rub the side of my head. Colette was off to my left, her hands tied with white stuff and held behind the back of her ebonite dining-room chair. She was naked. When I finally looked away, scared that she could see my reflection and I was embarrassing her, it soaked through to me that I was naked, too.

I am not sure what I said then, but this is close. "It was nice of them not to gag us. I don't suppose it will do much good to shout for help."

Colette did not say a word. As far as I could tell, she was staring straight ahead, and tears were trickling down her cheeks.

"Soundproofed, no doubt. Otherwise they would have killed us."

"Yes. It's very good." She spoke so softly that I could scarcely hear her.

"Have they gone?" I was taking care not to look at her anymore, afraid that she would be looking right at what might happen if I did.

"Yes. They ransacked the whole place. Where did you put it?"

"I didn't put it anywhere. I thought you intended to destroy it."

She worked her chair around until she could stare at me for a moment, then managed a brave smile. "I suppose you're right."

"I don't believe I can free myself," I told her, "but if you'll permit it, I may be able to free you. I'm afraid I'll have to break this chair to do it, though."

She stared.

"Have I your permission?"

"Can you? Go right ahead, if you can."

My legs had been tied to the legs of the chair, and the chair legs were not braced with rungs. I could not describe all the contortions I went through trying to put as much stress as I could on the spindly front legs of my own chair, but eventually one snapped. Five minutes later I got the other one. That was the only time in either life that I have wanted to be fatter than I am.

With them broken, I was able to shake free of the rest of the chair and walk into the kitchen. They had searched it, and their search had included throwing a set of ceramic-bladed steak knives onto the floor. I found one whose blade had not broken, and by kneeling and bending down I was able to grab the figured naturewood handle between my teeth. I had not expected it to be easy to cut through the strips of stout cloth that held Colette's hands; but that steak knife was sharp, and it was not as difficult as I had been afraid it might be.

She rubbed her hands and slapped them together, muttering cuss words (including a couple that were new to me) and rubbed and slapped them again.

"You cut me a little." She stopped to lick one of her cuts.

I said, "I couldn't help it."

"I suppose not. You couldn't see what you were doing, could you?"

"No. Not at all."

"They're listening to us. Maybe watching us, too. How long will it be before they come through that door again?"

I shrugged. "I don't think they will."

"Really? Did they find it?"

I shrugged again.

"You went into my kitchen."

I admitted I had, and explained that I had forgotten her rule.

"We'll forget about that this time, but not next time." Colette paused. Then, "I think I can get you loose now."

And she did. We found our clothes and dressed, and after that she wanted me to help her move the furniture to barricade the door. I told her to wait.

Half to herself she muttered, "I suppose you want to screen the police."

I shook my head. "They'd want the book, and arrest you when you couldn't produce it."

For a few seconds, she digested that. Then she said, "I don't see how they got around that lock. Those locks are terribly sophisticated."

"So are our friends." I sat down on the divan and rubbed my head.

"I suppose."

"Five hundred years ago, you would have had an iron bar you could drop into brackets. Anybody who wanted to get in would have to demolish your door with an ax. Today we're very clever, but someone more clever still can get in easily."

"Are you sick?"

I shook my head. "Just tired. I want to take whatever you've got for headaches."

Leaning very close, she whispered, "Where did you put it, Ern?"

I shook my head again.

"I know I gave you a bedroom and a bed, but can I get you to sleep out here? And make noise if they come in to wake me up? You'll have to sleep on the divan."

"They won't come back, but I'll be delighted to sleep here if it is your wish. I need to ask you about laundry facilities, however. In the basement?"

"That's right, and you'll need a card. Would you like me to take you down?"

"That won't be necessary. Or at least, I hope it won't. Can you lend me a robe?"

"One of mine? I'll be happy to, but I'm going to come with you; I'd have to lend you my card—you'll need a card to get into the laundry room and operate the universals. Are you going to clean that suit?"

"Not unless you think it needs it."

"It doesn't. That shirt doesn't have to be pressed, does it?"

I shook my head.

"Then the whole thing should take ten minutes or so. You'll want to strip in your room. Wait a minute and I'll find a robe for you."

I waited, then retreated to Colette's spare bedroom carrying a woman's filmy robe with white roses and purple morning glories all over it. In there I took off my shirt, undershirt, socks, and briefs. I put my trousers and shoes back on, slipped into the robe, and told Colette I was all set to go.

As I had expected, each tenant had a locked bin for dirty clothing. "Now I have to borrow your card," I told Colette. "I hope you don't mind."

"Of course not." Unnecessarily, she pointed out the bin with her apartment number. "Your things should be in there."

"No, yours." I unlocked the bin.

"Some of mine, yes; but I usually do laundry once a week. There's no need to do mine now."

I was reaching into the bin. When I found *Murder on Mars*, I held it up.

Colette's eyes widened and her mouth shaped a little round O.

I touched my finger to my lips. Her mouth formed the words "the chute," and I nodded. The woman's robe she had loaned me had a big pocket on each side, each of them plenty big enough to hold the book.

She shut her door that night, but she did not block it with furniture the way she had wanted to block the door of her apartment; doing it would have made a good deal of noise, and even though I listened for it I heard nothing. When I was dead certain she had gone to bed, I stripped again, took a shower, and moved the thin cushions from the couch onto the floor. That made it as much like my shelf in the library as anybody could want. Probably you know that after the library closes, we sleep on mats that we roll up and push to the back of the shelf during the day.

Right here it would be handy to say that I was dog tired and fell asleep at once—handy but a big lie. This new softer mat, with me stretching from corner to corner, was too new. Ditto the long lending. Colette had checked me out for ten days, which I had thought hard-rock unlikely. I had never been checked out for more than a couple of days. I had heard a few of us talk about a week or even two weeks, but I had never more than half believed any of it. Rose Romain the romance writer once told me she had kept tabs on three of her friends, and none of them had ever been out for more than five days. Now it seemed like Colette's estimate had been crazy short. I got up and got my jacket out of the closet to look at the card I had put in the pocket: July thirtieth. Right. Before six o'clock that day, I was supposed to say good-bye if I could get away and go back to the library.

But tomorrow both of us would leave Spice Grove and flitter southeast to New Delphi to look at the Coldbrook house and quiz the expert who'd opened her father's safe. Sooner or later we would come back here—or anyway, we had better.

What if we were grabbed again? Would we ever get loose? Both of us? Alive?

After worrying about all this and a couple of dozen other things for what seemed like an hour, I got up, got my book from the pocket of the robe Colette had loaned me, and read myself to sleep.

Only to dream about wrestling a monster with a man's head at one end and an ape's at the other end, and one hell of a lot of arms. This desperate struggle was in a grave thinly disguised as a wormhole through Mars. A wormhole that was already starting to flood. I guess they have a lot of water on Mars, when you are dreaming.

When I woke up it was nearly morning and I was soaked with sweat.

4

HER FATHER'S HOUSE

Somehow I had assumed a city house. It may only have been that in my time—I mean in the time of the earlier me, in my first life—there was not much land where new building was allowed. Anyway this house where the Coldbrook family had lived was not even close to the actual city of New Delphi. When Colette pointed it out, I asked her to circle it a couple times so that I could get a better picture of the house and the country-side around it. The house was supermodern and shiny as a new ground car, but you could see it was not really all that new. Built forty-three years ago was what she said, and added to and altered ever since. I counted four floors in some places but only one or two in a couple of additions. Scattered around it were a hangar, a barn, a garage, and some other outbuildings that were anybody's guess. There was a walled garden, too. Seeing it from the air like that I did not realize how badly the garden had been neglected.

"You and your brother grew up here?" I asked.

"Not exactly." She banked and dipped, bringing our racy little flitter closer to the house. "I was fourteen, I think, when we moved in. Conrad, Junior—we generally called him Cob or Cobby back then—would have been about sixteen, I suppose. Sixteen or seventeen."

"Did you like it?"

"Not as much as Mother did. My father really bought it for her. She was . . . not social. Not a bad person or even an unfriendly one; but other people, even people she knew and liked, stressed her out." Colette paused. "Do you understand what I mean?"

I had to admit that she had lost me.

"Well, after dinner the men would generally sit around the table, have another glass of wine, and talk. And the women would clear things away and feed the dishes to the washer. Sometimes Cob and I would help with that. Then they'd go into the music room or in nice weather out into the garden. Only Mother wouldn't be there. It would generally be half an hour or so before anybody noticed. Nobody'd know where she'd gone or when, but she wouldn't be with the others."

"What about you?" I was trying to picture it. "Would you stay with the women?"

Slowly, Colette nodded. "Pretty often I did, or else go up to my room to watch some show or do my homework. My room was on the second floor. So was Cob's, and I've been trying to decide whether I could bear seeing it again. All right if I land now?"

She did. The little red flitter's cabin split, spreading its little red wing; and we drifted down on the wind like a maple leaf in the fall. I had never flown a flitter or even flown in one back then, and I had a hunch that I was going to have to fly that one before long; so I had been watching everything Colette was doing and trying to learn, following every motion. Once we had landed and recombined, and were taxiing over to the hangar, I asked, "Wouldn't the autopilot do all that for you?"

"The screen? Yes, of course. But if you only do the easy parts, it takes a lot of fun out of flying. I like knowing that if the screen failed, I could do everything myself. I—well, sometimes I teach my students myself, Ern. The eds could do everything for me, all the teaching, but my job is to make them want to learn, and sometimes my own teaching helps. Then they know I know it— or that's how it seems to me. Since I've learned it, they can, too, and they should. Do you understand? Understand a little bit at least?"

I said, "We're like that, I believe. I mean people like me, people who belong to libraries or museums, or to you fully humans." For a minute I shut up, trying to spit my foot out of my mouth. "Does it bother you when I call us 'people'? If it does, I apologize."

"Not in the slightest." She stopped our flitter in front of the hangar, and its engine ceased to purr. "What are you getting at?"

"You fully humans have our books already, and our books are better than we are. Better than we can be, really. But what the books give you is one thing and what we can give you is another. You've got A Christmas Carol and Oliver Twist, The Old Curiosity Shop, and a lot more. David Copperfield and Bleak House and in fact just about everything Charles Dickens wrote. But you don't have Charles Dickens. You would spend a lot now if you could get his DNA and one scan, but if you were willing to spend a hundred times that much you still couldn't get them. You'd like to ask him how he really felt about Kate, and about that actress. How he had intended to finish Edwin Drood—and so would I."

She grinned at me as she pulled up in front of the hangar.

"You understand what I mean, or at least I think you do. I could make love to a joyboy. It would be warm and handsome and do everything I wanted, and it would tell me over and over how beautiful I am and how much it loved me. But they're not the same as a real lover." She got out easily and skillfully, and I followed. "They're for women who can't get a real lover, or at least can't get one they like."

I had heard of joyboys, and I nodded. "There must be a lot of those."

"There are." We got out in front of the hangar. "I'd put our flitter in here if it weren't locked, but it's sure to be. There may be a card in the house. Keep an eye out when we get inside."

"I certainly will," I promised. I pushed the button next to the door. "You have a card for the house, don't you, Colette?"

"To get us in? Of course. I wouldn't have come here without one."

"Is it possible that your card might open this hangar, too?"

For a moment, she stared. "You know, I never thought of that. The hangar was hardly ever locked when all of us lived here."

"I've never seen the interior of a hangar," I told her. "I'd like to see it."

"I'm not certain this will work." She was rummaging in her shaping bag. "It won't open the fourth-floor doors, but it's worth a try."

She waved her card at the lock, and the green light flashed; I pushed the button again, and the big hangar door slid smoothly upward.

"Well, I'll—you'll have to move, Ern. I want to taxi in."

I did. There were two sleek flitters in the hangar already, one shiny black and the other bright yellow; both were quite a bit bigger than Colette's. Peeking through their windows I could see they had six seats instead of two, and I believe they may have had a longer range and that they could carry more baggage. How much money had it taken for a family to have three flitters? The black one for Colette's father, the yellow one for her brother, and the little red one for Colette? I did not know then and I do not know now, but it must have been a lot.

"Come on. I'm glad you find this interesting, but I want to show you the house."

"And I want to see it." I followed her out of the hangar and closed the door.

A broad, paved path led from the hangar to a rear door of the house. "This is the kitchen," Colette said as she stepped inside. "The 'bot can fix us some lunch after we've seen the house."

I remembered a great many kitchens, but I had never learned my way around a modern one. The room was wide and bright, with butter-yellow walls and a faint odor not so much suggestive of food as of vegetables and fruits laid out for sale. Somehow I had thought I would recognize the stove, the refrigerator, and so forth, which shows you just how dumb I can be.

Colette wanted to know whether I was hungry, and I shook my head.

"I doubt that you'll find anything in here," she said, "and the 'bot will whip up something when we want to eat." I did not reply, and she added, "You can look around if you want to."

I said I might do that later, but right now I wanted to see her father's study. I did not tell her how badly I wanted to see it, but it was a lot.

"And the safe, I'll bet. It's in there."

I nodded and kept my mouth shut.

"We can go this way or that way." Colette pointed to the doors. "This way's the formal dining room. It's two floors high, with skylights, very impressive. It seats . . ." She paused to consider. "Twenty-two, I believe. That was where we entertained two or three times a year."

I nodded to show I understood.

"The other way's the sunroom. That's where the family ate, mostly. It's long and kind of narrow. An artist told me once the proportions were off, but I like it. All windows on one side—it faces south—and a long wall on the other with framed family pictures. You can tap them and get a lecture, and sometimes the people will start talking. You know the kind of thing, I'm sure."

"Not intimately," I told her.

"Which way do you want to go?"

"The sunroom, of course."

She nodded and led the way. It was long, bright, and cheerful, as she had hinted, with a small table for meals—four chairs—and other chairs with side tables scattered around for reading or conversation. Here was Colette's father, unsmiling, with a bony, unhandsome face and intelligent eyes.

Here was Colette herself, smiling, beautiful, and athletic, in a bra that would have let her fence or play softball, a university skirt, and low-heeled high-laced shoes that might have served for almost any sport. Girls actually look sexier when you cannot see the whole breast.

Close beside her, Cob—Conrad Coldbrook, Junior—handsome, but oddly reflective of his father.

And here all four, even Colette's mother, her shoulder gripped by her husband's right hand; his left was on Cob's shoulder. For a moment I thought that none of the rest was touching another member of the family; then I saw that Colette and her brother were unobtrusively holding hands.

"I'm glad you like the pictures," Colette told me. "May I show you the lift tube now? It will take us to the fourth floor and Father's lab."

I followed obediently.

"Two doors, you see," she said after opening one for us. "One on each side. If you went out that one, you'd be in the formal dining room." She added, "Fourth floor!" and the door through which we had entered closed swiftly and silently behind us before we began to rise.

5

ON THE FOURTH FLOOR

We flew up to the fourth floor in the lift tube. "This whole floor was my father's place," Colette told me. "If he was going to be away for any length of time, he disabled the lift tube—reprogrammed it or something. When he was gone, it wouldn't take you higher than the third floor. Of course we could still climb the stairs, but all the doors on this floor would be locked."

Looking around the laboratory, I said, "This isn't the only place up here, in that case."

"You must've seen the other doors on the landing. Cob and I were always curious about them, but—well—Father never spoke of them; and we had learned very early that it was dangerous to ask him questions."

I nodded to show I understood. "Three doors. There could be three suites up here, or one door might belong to a closet."

"I've always assumed there were two more suites, that's all. Maybe there's nothing more important than brooms and mops in them, but why would Father keep unimportant things locked up?"

"You're right, of course." Just to make certain, I asked, "You've never been in the other suites? Not in either of them?"

Colette shook her head.

"Not even when you went to look at this study after your brother's death? With both your father and your brother gone, there could be no valid reason not to."

"But I didn't. I suppose that makes me guilty of something."

"No, not at all. I'm just a little surprised." I smiled, hoping to take the sting out of what I was saying. "Women have a reputation for curiosity."

"Father didn't want us on this floor. Not ever. I felt unwelcome here then, and I feel the same way now." Colette got quiet, beautiful white teeth gnawing at her crimson lower lip. "I was always a good girl, Ern. Well, nearly always until I started to . . . You know, womanhood. Breasts and curves and all that comes with them. You men mature slowly; it rushes on us like a storm, and I wasn't always good after it came. Can I tell you something about Cob?"

"Your brother?" I was itching to have a long look around the laboratory and explore those unknown rooms, but I nodded.

"This happened one time when Father was gone. He used to go away from time to time and be gone for a few days—for a week or more, sometimes. Mother may have known what he was doing on those trips, but Cob and I certainly didn't. Anyway, we took the lift tube as far as it would go and climbed the stairs to get to this floor. All the doors on this landing were locked. Neither of us had a card for any of them. I told you about that."

"Yes, you did."

"We went back down the stair, and Cob went into one of the guest rooms on that floor." Colette paused. "That's what we called them then, even though there were never any guests. He opened a window and stuck out his head, looking up and all around. I tried to find out what he was doing, but he wouldn't tell me. Finally we went into another guest room, and he did the same thing. The third or fourth room was a corner room, with windows in two walls. He looked out them both, then he told me he was going to climb up. He said I didn't have to wait for him."

Thinking of the gleaming walls I had seen from the flitter, I shuddered.

"Well, I waited for him anyway, walking up and down and wondering if he'd be killed. Cob and I were very close."

I nodded.

"When he finally came back he was frightened. Badly frightened, although he tried to hide it. He wouldn't tell me what had frightened him, and eventually I decided he must have nearly fallen. I kept thinking that if he had gotten into one of the fourth-floor suites, he would have come down the stairs—that he could open the door from inside, so why not?"

Thinking aloud I said, "Wouldn't that depend on the lock?"

"Yes, but there aren't very many of that kind, and I don't believe I've ever seen one in this house." Colette went back to the door by which we had come into the room. "Look at this one. If it's locked, you have to show a card to get in; but if you're inside, you can flip this and it will let you out, then lock behind you every time it's shut. That's why Cob propped it open."

"So if your brother could get a window open, he could have

gone into the suite beyond it, had a look around, and left through the door. That would certainly have been less risky than going through the window again and climbing back down to the third floor."

"Exactly."

"Now it would appear that you no longer believe it was merely the fear of a bad—quite possibly fatal—fall that frightened your poor brother so much. That was a simple, entirely reasonable explanation. May I ask why you abandoned it?"

"I told you he brought me up here and showed me the safe, and told me that he would engage someone to open it for us."

I agreed that she had.

"Well, while I was up here I wanted to look in the other rooms. He said we couldn't, that they were locked. And I said that since he'd found a card for this room we could probably find one for them. He said he hadn't really found the card for this one, that it had been on Father's body, and a woman at the mortuary had given it to him." Colette paused. "They had given us, given Cob and me, a big envelope marked 'Conrad Coldbrook effects.' I asked him where that card was, and he said he'd put it away— that he'd left the safe open." She gestured toward it. The thick metal door was wide open. "And he'd left the door of this room unlocked, too."

I had glanced at the empty wall safe before; now I went to it and peered into its dark interior. Above the main space were two rather small black metal drawers. Neither one had a lock. I opened them both—both were entirely empty.

"Find anything?"

I turned back to Colette. "No, nothing. Surely it has occurred to you that the card that opened this door might open the doors of the other suites on this floor as well. From what you say, your father welcomed no visitors up here."

"I suppose you're right. All of us carried cards for the downstairs doors. I mean, the same card opened all of them, and all of us had one."

"The front door and the kitchen door, the one by which you and I entered the house."

Colette nodded.

"Are there any other doors?"

"Yes, the side door. That's the shortest way in if you've parked in the garage."

Thinking out loud again, I said, "Your card opened the hangar, too."

"Right, and it will open the garage. I'd forgotten that. We didn't lock it much, but when somebody did our cards would open it."

"If the card for this room was on your brother's body, the people who killed him presumably have it now."

Colette nodded. "I'm sure you're right. The police didn't give me anything. They must have taken everything."

"You attended his funeral, didn't you?"

"Yes. You're thinking of the morticians. They didn't give me any cards, either. All right if I sit down?"

"Of course." I moved aside, and Colette took the chair in front of one of the screens. I said, "What about another relative? Might not the morticians have given a few of your brother's possessions to someone else?"

She shrugged. "I doubt it. I was paying them. It cost a lot."

"Who paid for your father?"

"Cob and I." Colette sighed. "That one cost a lot, too. Cob picked out everything, but I paid half. It was before I got my inheritance, and it took almost everything I had."

"Did he receive as much as you did?"

"More, really. A lot m-more. H-He got . . ." She had started to cry and was rummaging in her shaping bag for a handkerchief. I gave her mine and apologized.

"Oh, it's all right. Talking about it just made me think of— can I tell you? I need to tell somebody and there's nobody else."

"Certainly. I wish you would."

"We got the same amount of money, and it was a lot. A lot more than I'd expected. Not the stocks and bonds until we're thirty, and not the real estate except that Cob got this house, too. I suppose it was because he was a son and I was just a daughter, and he was older. He was still living close by, too; but I'd moved away and so forth. I really don't know why Father did it that way, but he did. I didn't say anything, but Cob saw how I felt. I'm no good at hiding my feelings. I'm sure you've noticed." Through tears, her lovely violet eyes stared up at mine, seeking understanding.

I said, "Not at all."

"Anyway, he came to me after it was all over, the reading of the will and the transfers, and he said he didn't think it was fair for him to get the house, too, so he was giving half to me. We'd see the lawyer again and have him arrange it. I said he was w-wonderful, which he was, and kissed him."

I said her brother must have been a fine man.

"He was, only that wasn't the end of it. We went out to dinner together, after. While we were eating he said, 'Now that you own half the house, Colette, I'd like to buy it from you. How much do you want?' I thought that he was teasing me at first, but he was completely serious. He was giving me half the house, but he wanted to buy it back. I—well, I said for him to make me an offer, but he wouldn't do it. Finally I said I'd have to think about it."

"That was wise, I'm sure."

"So I paid an appraiser to look at it. He gave me a valuation of two million five hundred thousand." Colette paused. "Don't look so surprised."

I managed to tell her that I knew nothing about real estate.

"There's the house and the hangar and the garage with space for four ground cars in it, and the barn for horses, and the greenhouse, and so on, and almost four square kilometers of pasture. The house doesn't have a ballroom, or even a private theater, but it's quite large and rather nice."

I said I felt sure it must be worth at least as much as the appraiser had said and more.

She nodded. "So at first I was going to ask a million two hundred and fifty thousand. Then I felt bad about that when I remembered how generous Cob had been to me. So I made it one million even. Of course he took it and sent me the million."

"Now you'll have the whole house, I suppose, and your brother's fortune as well."

Colette nodded again. "I suppose so. I'm the only one left. Except that really we're all family, aren't we? Even you. All we humans have got to be related, however distantly. Humanity can't have evolved twice, or at least I wouldn't think so. I'll give some of Cob's money to charity. Quite a lot, I believe."

I said it was good of her and went over to a file cabinet. "These are yours, too. Do you mind if I look?"

"Not at all. Please let me know if you find anything interesting."

As I pulled out the uppermost drawer of the nearest file cabinet, I said, "I'm surprised that your father still had these, and all these papers to put in them. Isn't everything on screens now?"

Colette shrugged. "There are still things we've got to have paper for, stock certificates, for example. Deeds and affidavits and everything else that requires an actual signature."

I was still thinking about the stock certificates. "Couldn't the company record your ownership?"

"It does, of course, because they have to know where to send your dividends. But suppose their screens were hacked?"

"There's still hacking?" I was surprised; no doubt my face showed it.

"Yes, quite a lot of it. I'm told—don't ask me to do this, I don't know how—that you can program your own screen to hack someone else's and alert you when it's gotten through."

I pulled out a file. "Perhaps that's why your father had these."

"What are they?"

"Articles from the *Hanover Journal of Astrophysics*. They look as though he printed them out. They aren't whole issues, simply individual articles he must have found of particular interest."

Colette said, "He wasn't a scientist by training—or at least I don't believe he was. But he was interested in just about every science you could name. Physics was only one of them. Chemistry, too, and geology."

A moment later I said, "Thus far I've found six pieces by a K. Justin Roglich. Can you look in that screen's address book for his name?" I spelled it.

I was reading one of Roglich's articles when Colette said, "Here he is, Ern. He's a Ph.D. and so forth. A full professor, too. He's on the faculty at Birgenheier, over in Owenbright. Are we going to voice him?"

"No, you are." I had found a paragraph in one of his articles that had been highlighted. "Tell him who you are, and explain that your father's dead. Say that you believe—no, let me rephrase that. Tell him that you know your father consulted him, and that you'd like to consult him yourself. Say you'll be happy to pay him for his time and trouble."

"All right, if you say so. I just hope you know what you're doing."

I took a deep breath. "So do I."

"You have a nice smile. Want to explain?"

"Not now. Voice Dr. Roglich, please, if you can get him. Leave a message if you can't."

She did, and looked to me for further instructions when she had done it.

"One more thing. No, several more. First, I want you to turn up a list of print-on-demand sites. Pick one, and place an order for a copy of *Murder on Mars*. Will you do that, please?"

"By E. A. Smithe."

"Correct. Tell them to send it here or to your place in Spice Grove. It doesn't matter."

Colette did as I had asked, watched by me. I was nervous and trying not to show it.

There was a pause that seemed terribly long. Then a reply: *No such title.*

She looked to me for further instructions. "They can't find it."

I said, "Try another site, please," and turned back to the filing cabinet and its many crowded drawers. I was not looking for anything in particular, just doing something to keep myself from staring at Colette and making her nervous. There were handwritten receipts for uncut gems, so I read a few of them.

She said, "Same thing, Ern. Apparently they haven't got the text."

"That's not exactly the same. The first one said it didn't exist, which we know is wrong. Try the National Library in Niagara. See if they have a copy."

That took a good twenty minutes. "They say they don't."

I thanked her.

"Why are you smiling?"

"So I won't cry. I thought your father's locking up your copy of my book meant there was something in it that was exclusive to that particular copy. Now we've found out that it may be in all the copies—assuming that there are others. It's simply a rare book, in other words."

Slowly, Colette nodded.

"Someone strangled your brother as he returned to this house. Is that correct?"

Colette nodded. "I told you about that. I . . . well, I'll never get over it. I'll never stop missing him."

"Have you any reason to suspect that your father was murdered, too?"

"No, none. If—there was a medical examination. I'm told one's required whenever the dead person is under the age of one hundred. My father was only a little over half that."

"I see. What was the verdict?"

"A blood vessel in his brain had burst. Isn't that what they call a stroke? I don't know the medical term."

"Not exactly. Let's avoid the grim details. The point is, I think, that the people who visited us last night—the people who may be listening to this now—did not know that the secret of the book existed until after your father had died. Your father was afraid someone might find out, clearly; otherwise he would not have put it in his safe. Presumably no one did. Let's see . . . your father died, and you attended his funeral and the burial. How long after that did your brother die? It doesn't have to be exact. A quarter? A year?"

"Not that long. The reading of the will was a week—no, six days—after the funeral. Cob was murdered about two weeks after that."

"Plenty of time."

"For what?" Colette's eyebrows were up.

"For him to find something in this house. Something he didn't tell you about because he felt sure you wouldn't believe him. That could be it." I was as puzzled as she looked. "Or because you might want to do something he felt would be dangerous. Or even because he was afraid you'd tell someone who couldn't be trusted."

"I see. Only . . ."

"Only you can't imagine what it was he found. I think perhaps I can, a little. But we need to find out a great deal more. Plenty of time, too, for your brother to tell the person who betrayed him. It could've been idle gossip. Did he drink?"

Colette shook her head. Hard.

"In that case it was probably someone he consulted. Someone he confided in to some extent."

"Don't you think . . . ?" She cupped a hand behind her ear.

"Yes, I do. Not always rightly, but I think. I can't help it. Come with me."

I left the overfurnished room that had been her father's office, went to the lift tube, and held the door open until she came.

The lift tube let us out in the long bright sunroom that ran along the south side of what appeared to be the oldest part of the house. Earlier, we had come into the house from the kitchen. Now we left through French doors. Without the least idea of where I was going, I walked off over the lawn.

"You're trying to get away from the listening devices, aren't you?"

"Certainly. But a little fresh air may do both of us good. It clears the head."

"You did a whole lot of talking up there."

"I did, with a purpose. Your father's secret is hidden somewhere in that book. Do we agree on that?"

"Absolutely!"

Colette was hurrying to keep up, and I slowed my pace accordingly. "Suppose we find it. Suppose we open those two doors or break them down. Suppose we learn exactly how your father gained his sudden wealth. What good will it do you if the people you fear have planted all these listening devices—the people who strip-searched us in your apartment—are still at large? I want to get them out into the open. If I'm guessing right about them, they won't dare kill us until they have the secret. But once we learn it, their learning it will be a snap. Capture either or both of us. Use drugs, torture, or brain scans. Any of the three ought to work quite well."

"And I'm just a woman." Colette's smile was a trifle bitter.

"They could wait until I'm back in the library and check me out." I pointed. "There's a gate in that wall. Where does it go?"

"To the garden. Would you like to see it?"

"Not particularly, but we're approaching a fence. Perhaps we'd better go in."

We did. There were trees and shrubs that probably bloomed in spring but now (at the dry height of summer) looked half dead. The flower beds were choked with weeds and the grass uncut. We sat in the shade on a granite bench in front of a marble fountain that no longer played.

"I'm going to fix this," Colette declared. "I have all this money. I'll hire our old gardener back and tell him to find a couple of assistants."

"Good. May I ask who cuts the lawns? Do you have a service?"

"No, the 'bots do it. They're based in the barn. They'll water and weed this if I tell them to, but they're not real gardeners. No planting or planning or anything like that. Do you want to talk to them?"

I shook my head. "The police will have questioned them. I know there's a 'bot in the house. What about human maids?"

"Not until Mother died. She couldn't stand them and Father didn't want them. People who've never had servants think you can just pay them and leave everything up to them, but in the real world they take a lot of supervision. Humans steal, gossip, drink, and snort dope. 'Bots are sick half the time. Besides, they do crazy things and think they're just fine. Have you ever argued with one?"

I smiled. "Once or twice."

"Then you know how it is. If it's what they were programmed to do, they think it's perfectly fine no matter what the situation is. A friend of mine who survived a crash told me the steward kept passing out refreshments when their flitter had lost power and was headed for the mountains. I believe her! They can be exactly like that."

I said, "Has anyone ever told you how beautiful you are when you're angry?"

"Yes!" Colette raised her fist. "Usually it's just before I hit them."

"Seriously now, 'bots are capable of a great deal of intelligence, and they make devoted workers. They're so complex that they're frequently in the shop; I'll grant you that."

"Nice of you. But the more intelligent they are, the more they cost. That's up-front cost, and my father said you can often spend as much up front as you'd pay a human employee over ten years. When your human gets sick, the government pays. When your 'bot gets sick, you pay. There was a cleaning company that came in once a week; I don't know the name. Now don't tell me that this argument was what you didn't want those people who tied us to chairs to overhear."

She had me. I shook my head.

"All right, what was it?"

"Simply this. You're afraid our enemies will visit us again. Understandably so."

Colette nodded.

"I'm afraid they won't. We need to make them show their hand. That's why I gave you K. Justin Roglich's name aloud and even spelled it. We might like to kill them, but that isn't really necessary. Even if all we can do is draw their fangs, that will be enough. But the worst thing we can do, the thing that would increase our danger tenfold, would be to discover the secret while they're still intact, listening, and waiting to pounce."

"I see what you mean. You may be right."

"You think I may be right. I devoutly believe I am. Can you show me why I may be wrong?"

Colette nodded. "I think so. The money. My father was a minor executive without a job. He became a wealthy investor very quickly. I told you how his little newsletter, just one page of advice a week, was an overnight success. Not literally, but in just ten or twelve weeks. A lot of that was his personal reputation. When I tell people who my father is—was, I mean—some of them are awed."

"You would have a great deal of money with which to defend yourself, in other words."

"Right!"

"From what you've told me, you have at least two million now, and probably more than that."

Slowly, Colette nodded again.

"Rent a combat 'bot and hire four human bodyguards. The 'bot will be there all day and all night, every day. With four humans, you can have at least one on duty at all times—Saturdays, Sundays, and holidays. Day and night, twice around the clock."

Colette sighed. "And if the people who killed Cob were able to corrupt them, they would be right on the spot, overhearing anything I said to you and anything you said to me. Ready to turn on us whenever Cob's killers gave the signal."

"Why wouldn't that be so if you had ten times as much money as you have now?"

"Don't bully me!"

"I don't intend to bully you, I'm trying to save your life and my own."

"You think the two who tied us up are all there are! Those two men!"

I shook my head.

"That's it! Or at least, that's a part of it. We don't even know how many there are."

"You're right, we don't; and because we don't, we're prone to think their numbers are infinite. Once I read a quote from a wise old general that has stuck with me. He said there's always a temptation to believe your enemy commands an infinite army with infinite munitions, but it's never true. As far as we know for certain, we face only two individuals. There may be more, possibly five or even six; but have you any idea how difficult it is to keep a conspiracy secret? It's terribly hard, and each additional conspirator increases the risk."

"There could also be a dozen," Colette said, "and there's one number I'm absolutely certain of. There are only two of us."

"You're wrong," I told her. "The law is on our side. We're committing no . . ."

I shut up because Colette had clearly thought of something; or if I finished the thought, she didn't hear it. To tell the truth, I did not either.

I rose, stretched, and walked a dozen steps down one of the little paths that wandered away from the fountain. When I had returned and resumed my seat, I asked why she looked so happy.

"Because you're right. I was smiling because I've lost the argument. Want to hear the whole thing?"

"Yes," I said. "Very much."

"All right. You were unconscious when they undressed you and searched your clothes. They searched you, too, felt around in, well, in your mouth and all that. Then the young one told the mean one that he was going to tie you to that chair. He did while the mean one watched, talking all the time about how they were going to torture us. Pull out fingernails. Burn our feet. There was a lot of that."

I said, "I'm glad I missed it."

"I wish I had. Then the mean one started pulling my clothes off. I yelled and hit him." She paused. "I know I can't use my fists like a man, but I can hurt you even so, and I hurt him. He knocked me down."

"I'm sorry. Terribly sorry!"

"He started to kick me, but the other man, the young one, grabbed him and pulled him away. He helped me up and told me to take off my clothes. He told me I wouldn't get hit again if I did it. Then he searched me and made me sit in that chair, and tied me up. The mean one was afraid the rags weren't tight enough, but he tested them and they were."

"This is interesting." I was thinking hard. "The young one— that's the taller of the two, correct?"

"Yes, and I think he's not as bad as the other one, and he might even come over to our side if there was enough money in it. Or if we got them arrested like you want—I know that was what you were getting at—he might testify against the others."

I nodded. "I wish we had some way of contacting him."

"So do I. So we're back to what you want, getting them to come out of the woodwork again. If you're right and there are only a few of them, he may be one we'll see. Are we going to visit this Dr. Roglich?"

I nodded again. "Just as soon as we can arrange a meeting with him."

6

BACK ON THE SHELF

I'm Colette Coldbrook." Smiling, Colette held out her hand, which Dr. Roglich shook even more carefully than I would have. I was looking around his office, which was a trifle larger than I had expected and saturated with the mixed smells of pipe smoke and money.

"An honor, Ms. Coldbrook. A great honor and a real pleasure." He had a high, tremulous voice. His two-hour lectures must have been a blast. "Please be seated, both of you."

"This is my friend, E. A. Smithe." Colette was still standing. She smiled. "Perhaps I should say my dear friend and advisor. Mr. Smithe is a veritable fountain of information."

Dr. Roglich and I shook hands; his was a damp hand, though bigger and more muscular than I expected. I sat, waiting to wipe my own on my trouser leg.

"I can explain my situation," Colette continued, "but you probably don't want to hear all that. Let me just say it's difficult and complicated."

"Please do sit down." Dr. Roglich seemed to be talking to the bookcase in the corner.

"Of course." Colette took the big leather chair with arms, I having left that one for her. "I suppose you're afraid I'm about to burst into tears. I won't, I promise."

Dr. Roglich sat, too, looking relieved. "First, let me offer my condolences on the death of your father." He glanced at the bookcase. "A great loss, I realize, and not only to you."

I said, "Colette finds herself alone in the world, I'm afraid."

"I do." The smile had vanished. "My mother passed away a few years ago, and my father only a little over six weeks ago. Here I'm tempted to dance around the truth, Dr. Roglich, but I must not. I won't! You knew my father, I know. Did you know my brother Cob, too? Conrad Coldbrook, Junior?"

Dr. Roglich had gotten out a handsome briar; he began to fill it, then laid it down. "I did not have that honor, I'm afraid. From the way you speak of him—from your tone . . ." He looked toward the bookcase. Only its lower shelves were protected by notint. "I take it that . . . I hope I'm wrong. . . ."

Colette blotted her eyes.

I nodded to Dr. Roglich. "He's dead."

"That's what I meant by dancing around the subject." Colette sighed. "My brother was murdered, Dr. Roglich. You could easily uncover that fact, and—and others. A thorough search might tell you that he'd been away from home for a day or two. It's possible that it might not also tell you that he had gone to visit me in Spice Grove, but he had. His killer—"

"Or killers," I added. "We have reason to believe that there may have been more than one."

"His killers or killer had broken into our childhood home and were waiting for him to come back. Or at least that's how it seems. He did, and someone strangled him as soon as he walked in. A 'bot discovered his body in the front hallway. I've questioned it, but—"

"It never saw his murderer?" Dr. Roglich was trying to sound sympathetic.

Colette shook her head. "His suitcase was nearby. Next to his body, I mean. It had been opened and searched. His body had been searched, too—that's what the police say. I realize you don't want to hear all this."

"I want to hear anything and everything you want to tell me," Dr. Roglich said.

"Thank you." Colette took a deep breath. "Please don't think we're meddlers, needlessly prying into your affairs, Doctor. That's not it at all. But you're an astrophysicist and my father consulted you. Will you tell us about it?"

I said, "First, we'd like to know how he got in touch with you, and why. After that, well, he was a financier. What was it he wanted to know, and what was it you told him?"

Dr. Roglich nodded absently. He was fumbling some mutated herb or other from the potbellied humidor on his desk into the bowl of his pipe. "Are you investigating his son's death, Mr. Smithe?"

"No, that's a job for the police. Perhaps they'll be in touch with you, although it seems to me there's no reason why they should." I cleared my throat. "As Colette will confirm, her father's business interests are being looked after by his executor. He is an attorney and presumably he can be relied upon to handle routine. However, there's a great deal that neither he nor we understand. When Colette reaches thirty, everything will be turned over to her—stocks and bonds, a money market account, and various real estate holdings. Some of the things her father did, and some of the records that have turned up, seem inexplicable. I doubt that she and I will ever get to the bottom of everything. But total ignorance? That would invite disaster."

There was a second or two of silence before Colette said, "My late father was a financial genius, Dr. Roglich. I most certainly am nothing of the kind, but I'm not willing to admit that I'm incapable of comprehending what he did or why he did it."

Dr. Roglich nodded. "I understand. Furthermore, I agree. I can tell you what he wanted to know, but I have no idea why he wanted to know it. He was interested in the fundamental nature of space. Our physical universe exists in space. In that respect, it differs from all the others. Take the mathematical universe, for example. The ancient Greeks discovered that there was an invariable relationship between the diameter of a circle and its circumference. Please note that I did not say they invented it, I said that they discovered it. Was it their thinking about the possibility of such a relationship that brought the actual relationship into existence?"

Colette shook her head.

"What do you think, Mr. Smithe?"

"No. Certainly not."

Dr. Roglich smiled. It was a faint smile and looked to me like a painful one, but it was a smile just the same. "I ask you both, why not?"

Colette said, "Because thinking about things doesn't make them happen, or make them true either. A teacher told me once that chewing up autoraser would make my eyes fall out."

"If we admit that principle, the fixed relationship between circumference and diameter must have existed long before any human being thought of it. Before there were humans, and indeed before there was life. Where was it, Ms. Coldbrook?"

"I have no idea," Colette said.

"Then let us give that place a name. We'll call it the Mathematical Universe. I'm sure you're familiar with the Big Bang. Everyone learns about it before puberty. Matter and energy— lots and lots of both—appearing like rabbits from a magician's hat. We astrophysicists suppose, some of us, that it is a property of mere vacuity to call matter and energy into being." He opened what must have been a lighter of a design I'd never seen before and tried to light his pipe with it, then fumbled it and dropped it on his desk.

Colette's eyebrows were up. "Is this what you told my father, Dr. Roglich? Is this what he came to you to talk about?"

"In our first chat, yes, it was." His small cough sounded embarrassed. "Your father was deeply interested in the fundamental nature of space. He grasped the problem intuitively, if I may phrase it thus. The quality we call intelligence today is merely verbal felicity. Your father was a major intellect, if I may put it so, in way that our psychologists do not even understand exists."

Colette said, "Thank you."

Tried again, the gold lighter flamed and went out. "He explained—perhaps I should not say this, but it is at least true— that he could not pay my consulting fee but that he was eager to discuss the essential nature of space. He promised to pay me later, if he could—as in fact he did."

Colette said, "I'll be happy to pay any reasonable fee. I feel sure I told you that when I screened. Would you like me to pay now?"

"No. No, that won't be necessary. Please don't feel that I'm going to bill you so much an hour." Dr. Roglich glanced at his watch. "I have until five. Until then I'm at your service."

Colette thanked him.

"Does the universe have boundaries, Ms. Coldbrook? Could a space probe leave our galaxy and travel outward and travel in a straight line indefinitely? Or would it reach some boundary it could not pass? Would it perhaps enter hyperspace? If it did, what properties would we expect it to encounter there?"

I told Colette to take whichever she liked; I'd take the rest.

"I seems to me," she said thoughtfully, "that it can't go on forever. Nothing really does." She looked to me for confirmation.

Dr. Roglich said, "No doubt my example seems overly fantastic. Keep in mind, please, that light moves in a straight line unless it is curved by a strong gravitational field. Our theoretical spaceship is in sober fact a photon."

"It won't go on forever. I can't believe it does."

Dr. Roglich nodded. "In that case, space must have existed previous to the Big Bang. The Big Bang can hardly have constructed distant walls at the moment of the explosion. Any such walls, any such boundaries, must have preexisted. How did they get there?"

I said, "I don't think there are any."

"The universe extends to infinity in every direction? At no time did it not exist?"

I nodded. "Precisely."

"If that is true, and if mere vacuity somehow calls matter into being—thus violating the familiar maxim that matter and energy cannot be created or destroyed—there should have been an infinite number of Big Bangs, whereas we see evidence of only one." Wetting his lips with his tongue, Dr. Roglich gave the bookcase a worried glance. "The night sky ought to be an almost uniform blaze of light. Will you agree?"

I said, "I suppose I must."

The pained smile returned. "There remains another question, little noted but more difficult than the first. Where did all that space come from? All that emptiness? It can hardly have summoned itself into being. Let us say that in the beginning there was nothing. Nothing at all, anywhere. Had there been nothing forever? Endless ages of nothing stretching infinitely into the past? If that were so, what prompted creation after endless ages of infinite and utterly empty intergalactic space? Notice that space is something we generally have to create. You ask your friend how she likes her new apartment. She tells you she loves it, but there isn't enough closet space. If space somehow created itself, wouldn't her closets grow bigger and bigger?"

Colette laughed, shaking her head.

"You offer her a solution. Build a new wall here, making the living room a trifle smaller. Doors here and here. Presto change-o! Additional closet space has been created."

I said, "Not without losing space elsewhere."

"Exactly. Space has been moved from the living room to the new closets. Now suppose I had some means of moving space without employing walls and similar indirect methods. I open my window. Let us say my apartment is on the fifth floor. There is plenty of space out there, I decide. No one will notice if I take a few cubic meters. I will move a little of it into my apartment. My lounge, let us say, is ten meters long, six meters wide, and four meters high. I set the controls for three meters, three meters, and five meters. I activate my equipment, moving forty-five cubic meters of space into my lounge. When I turn around, I discover that my lounge has become pleasantly larger. It is ten meters sixty centimeters long and six meters thirty-six centimeters wide now. Nor is that all. It has a four meter twenty-four centimeter ceiling. My wife will buy new pictures. Big ones." Dr. Roglich mopped his forehead with his handkerchief.

Colette asked, "What about the carpet?"

"A penetrating question, Ms. Coldbrook. It occurred to me as well, and solving it required a good deal of investigation. It became longer and wider, just as the walls grew higher. The temperature of the room plummeted abruptly. The architecture of the building became somewhat odd, and possibly weaker; but all that had to happen if my lounge was to contain the additional space that had been thrust into it.

"Nor is that all. If I have not frozen to death, I will eventually discover that the building across the street is nearer my own. How could it be otherwise when space between the two buildings has been removed?"

"It sounds crazy," Colette murmured.

"Believe me, Ms. Coldbrook, far crazier facts are met with every day in astrophysics. I'm no particle physicist, but I know enough about the field to tell you that the same thing is true in that discipline. Could we but reclone him, Lewis Carroll would be delighted."

"You can't actually do this?"

Briefly the ghost of a smile appeared on Dr. Roglich's perspiring face. "No, Ms. Coldbrook, I cannot. Nor could the equipment that would permit such an operation ever be constructed, in my opinion. Still, it is theoretically feasible. I—I . . . C-could you bring me a copy of my book, Mr. Smithe?" Dr. Roglich pointed to the bookcase. "A th-thin book in a b-b-blue binding. If you would be so kind. There are s-s-several copies in there."

I rose, went to the bookcase, and ran my fingers along the underside of the top.

"N-not th-there. Second shelf. On the s-second shelf!"

The thing my fingers found was round, smooth, and black. I tore it off, and discovered, as I had expected, that it had been mounted with double-sided tape. I dropped it to floor and crushed it under my heel, picked up its broken pieces, tore them apart, and dropped the fragments into the wastebasket beside Dr. Roglich's desk.

Colette said, "Was that—" and fell silent.

"You're right," I told her. "That was one of their listening devices. Dr. Roglich knew it was there, and his eyes and voice told me. They must have frightened him badly, then let him see them plant it." I dropped back into my chair.

"They won't like this," Dr. Roglich said. He looked relieved.

"Tell them the truth. Tell them I did it."

"Are you sure?"

"Yes. But they probably know already." Rising again, I took a slender blue book from the second shelf of the bookcase and flipped through its pages. They were filled with equations.

"You may keep that copy, if you wish," Dr. Roglich told me.

I thanked him.

Colette said, "Are you going to read it?"

I shook my head. "I don't know enough math to follow this, but eventually we'll find somebody who can." I tried to make that sound more confident than I felt.

Back in my chair I said, "Describe them to me. You saw them. What did they look like?"

"I'd really rather not."

"You allowed their listening device to be destroyed," I told him, "and they may try to kill you for it. They can't hear you now, and Colette and I are fighting them. What did they look like?"

It took a while to get descriptions, but we did. The men sounded like the two who had tied us up. The third was a woman.

When my watch struck five, Colette rose. "You've been extremely helpful. You must have billed my father at his home. That's where he worked."

Dr. Roglich nodded.

"You may bill me at the same address."

Outside, Colette said, "You want them to show themselves."

"Yes. That's the idea. I wanted to find out why your father had consulted Dr. Roglich, and I believe we did. I also want to get our opponents out into the light. If this doesn't do it, we'll try something else."

"Apparently they got here before we did."

I was too busy with my thoughts to reply.

"Either that, or they've got a branch office here. Somebody in New Delphi may have voiced them and told them we were coming."

"A branch office?"

Colette grinned. "All right, I was just joking. But it could be a secret society, couldn't it? Something like that?"

"That's certainly possible. Not as likely as the first possibility, I would say, but entirely possible. It's also possible that they're simply watching Dr. Roglich because your father consulted him."

"What do you think?" Colette was looking up, hoping to hail a hovercab.

"The first—that they learned what we planned and preceded us. When we see them, we'll know."

"Is that why you want to stay here overnight?"

"That's part of it. Yes."

"What's the rest?" Colette was waving.

"I want to give them a chance to break into your father's house. We won't go straight in—in fact, we may not go in at all. We'll look for a strange vehicle and have a talk with those 'bots in the barn you mentioned. If they cut the grass and so on they should have noticed any strangers. If it appears that the people we're talking about are in the house, we'll call the police. I assume you have an eephone?"

Colette nodded.

"Fine. Or we could use the screen on your flitter."

"It might work," Colette said thoughtfully.

"'Might work' is good enough for me." A hovercab was settling onto a lawn to our right. Seeing it, I said, "Now we'd better watch our tongues."

On my advice, Colette declined the first hotel the cab suggested and took the second, renting us a small suite with a lounge, two bedrooms, and two baths. We left her overnight bag on the bed that was to become hers and went shopping for clothes for me—underclothes, socks, pajamas, shirts, and slacks. It was generous of her, and I thanked her most sincerely.

Back at the hotel, we decided to change before dinner. I went into my bedroom and she went into hers. I took off the clothes I had worn, bagged them for the hotel laundry, showered, and dressed again.

When I left my bedroom, Colette was gone. Naturally I thought that she was simply in her own bedroom or bathroom.

I waited for about an hour listening for some sound—for bath-water running, a toilet flushing, drawers opened and closed . . . Anything.

There was nothing.

Finally I knocked on her door. By then I didn't expect her to answer.

I called, "Colette! Colette!" There was no reply.

Finally I opened the door. Her bedroom was empty and her overnight bag was gone. A lamp had been knocked over, and her bed was rumpled, although it had never been turned down. When I saw those things, I knew that she had been taken, prob-ably while I was in the shower.

Two things hit me straight off. The first was that I had better screen the police. The second was that I could not check out of the hotel, since I could not pay.

I got the police on the hotel's screen, talking to a sim in police uniform who looked intelligent but let me down with a thud.

"You need to understand first, sir, that the lamp proves noth-ing and the bed proves nothing. Second, that we do not inves-tigate missing persons until the person has been missing for twenty-four hours or more. When your friend Ms. Coldbrook has been missing for that length of time, a relative or other family member may report the fact. We will keep an eye out for an ad-ditional twenty-four hours and then, provided that the missing person has not turned up, we begin our investigation."

The sim paused until I began to speak, then started up again. "As I understand, you are neither a relative nor a family member. You're a library reclone? A borrowed man? Is that correct? Not fully human?"

"Ms. Coldbrook is fully human," I insisted.

"Her status does not concern us at the moment. Yours does. A relative or family member must report her missing after the passing of twenty-four hours."

"Twenty-four hours from when?"

The simulation stared at me for several seconds. "I'm not sure. From when she went missing, perhaps. Or from when someone saw she was missing. Or now, from the time of your first try to get us to look for her. I think that's probably it. You ought to have tried sooner."

I agreed.

"Only I'm not sure this counts, because of you being a reclone and not a family member."

"They're dead," I told it. "Father, mother, brother—all dead."

"That doesn't matter, any of them will do."

I terminated.

The people who had taken Colette had left her shaping bag. There was zero chance that I could go around with a woman's bag like that, so I took out everything that looked valuable, putting it into various pockets and leaving the bag hardly more than a leathery envelope. I had taken her money, to start with, a card to her apartment in Spice Grove, another for the house in New Delphi, two pairs of diamond nipple rings, and some other stuff.

When I left the hotel, I wanted to take the clothes I had bagged for the laundry, but I did not. For one thing, there had been no wardrobe on my shelf in which to store additional clothes. When the lights are about to go out, our clothes are collected by 'bots for laundry or dry cleaning, and robes and slippers are passed out. We wear those until we go to bed, and wear them when we get up, too, until our day clothing is issued to us just before the library opens at ten. I knew things would work about the same way in another library.

As I walked, I looked at all the tangled ways I could try to find Colette. I could hire private investigators, but they would want a lot of money upfront. I should at least notify the executor, the attorney she had talked about; but I was not in New Delphi, and I did not know his name. I could tell the school in Spice Grove where she had taught, but what could a school do? The people who worked there were no more relatives or family members than I was. All these black thoughts were interrupted five or six times by short pauses while I asked strangers for directions to the Owenbright Public Library. Usually they did not know.

Discouraged and dead tired, I eventually found it. I showed my card—July thirtieth—and explained what I was and why I had come, first to a 'bot and afterward to an unsmiling librarian.

"We'll have to send you back when the truck comes," she said.

I nodded.

"There's an empty shelf in the fiction section, I believe. Two, perhaps. I'll shelve you in there until something can be arranged. No checkouts, of course. You may be consulted but not checked out."

I told her I understood.

Our shelves were three high in Owenbright, each shelf being 190 centimeters high—high enough for me to stand up, though there were a few of us who could not. As you can imagine, the lowest shelf is always the best and the highest shelf the worst; shelves are numbered down from the uppermost. In Spice Grove, the shelves are four high, so that my pretty nice shelf had been a three. In Owenbright I got a one, which was what I had expected. You get into all these high shelves by climbing narrow ladders.

I climbed, reached my shelf, waited for half an hour or so for the library to close, stripped, and slept. Once, as if I were dreaming, I heard what seemed like a familiar voice. For a while I lay awake, listening. It did not come again.

Eventually I turned over and slept once more.

7

"Where's E. A. Smithe?"

Next morning a watchbot woke me by poking me with a light pole. With its legs extended like stilts it was a pretty tall 'bot, but not tall enough to reach that shelf in Owenlight. "Get up and get dressed! Open in half an hour!"

It did not have to tell me I had almost missed breakfast. I yawned, got my new clothes back on (it was clean stuff now, since it had been taken up for washing and dry cleaning the night before), brushed my teeth, shaved, and so forth. You know. After that, following my nose took me to breakfast, a pretty long table in a wide aisle of the reclone section; I was late but not too late to get a bite to eat.

Most of us do not fancy creamed chipped beef on toast or cheese grits. I am lucky there. I like creamed chipped beef and I love good cheese grits. I was helping myself to my second ladle of grits when I heard a woman's voice at the far end of the table say, "Is that newbie Ern Smithe?"

All right, I ought to have recognized her voice, but I did not. I just said, "Here!" and went back to eating.

Pretty soon I smelled perfume, felt a little hand on my shoulder, and turned to look. I said something, I know, but it did not make much sense. I stammered, too, and that did not help.

I believe it must have been the stammering that got me kissed long and hard.

"I was just getting up." That was Johnston Biddle, the historian.

Then he was gone and Arabella was slipping into his place. "You," she announced in her iron lady voice, "are the world's most irritating man."

"And you have the sweetest voice in the world," I told her. "Goes with your face."

"You mean in poetry." She knew darned well exactly what I meant. "I could write terrifying poetry, too. I just don't choose to. Or not mostly."

"In poetry," I told her, "and also in conversation, but especially conversation. No matter what you say, your voice is always music."

"You'll be bringing me chocolates next."

"I've apologized a thousand times for those stupid sucking chocolates. I'll do it a thousand more, if you want me to."

She looked pensive. "Actually, I enjoyed them. They just ruined my diet. Greased the skid to hell, as a matter of fact. I put on eight kilos."

"One lousy box of chocolates on Valentine's Day couldn't possibly make a woman gain eight kilos." Nobody else at the table was talking, and I was so conscious of it that it hurt.

"Well, it did. It started me eating horrible junk that I should never have touched. Candied watermelon rind, macaroni and cheese, devil's food cake, preserved turnips. Every kind of awful stuff."

Preserved turnips? "I don't believe you."

"More chocolates that I bought for myself. Lovely chocolates as dark as sin, and saltwater taffy. I remember the saltwater taffy vividly—the seascape on the box, the red, blue, and green wrappers, everything. If you still imagine my voice is sweet, you should taste that taffy. I . . ." Arabella shut up.

I leaned nearer, lowering my voice and wishing I could risk a kiss. "What is it, darling?"

"I was just thinking. . . ." She let it trail off, looked at me, and looked away.

"Yes? Tell me."

"You can't buy me chocolates here, can you?"

"Here in the library? It certainly wouldn't be easy, but it might not be impossible."

"We don't have any money." Her hand found mine. "No money at all, Ern. And it's against the rules and we can't leave the library."

Somebody ought to do a study on how long a man can talk to a woman without having to lie. I said, "Certainly I don't have any money now, but I might get some. If I did, I might be able to buy your chocolates while I was checked out."

"You get checked out? Really?" Arabella turned to stare at me.

"Sometimes." The terror that had befallen Colette filled my mind and, I am afraid, my voice, too. "Sometimes I do. Recently I was checked out for forty days and forty nights, but I've become separated from my patron. That's why I came here."

"You don't belong here?"

The others were beginning to talk again, the kind of quick embarrassed talk people use to cover up the fact that they have been eavesdropping.

I shook my head. "I'm the property of the Spice Grove Public Library."

"They'll send you back there."

"I know. That's why I came here. The lady who checked me out lives in Spice Grove. She's a teacher."

"You're property. Property this lady borrowed."

I nodded.

"Don't you think that's horrible? Really now, Ern. Don't you think it's criminal?"

"It's worse than criminal. It's factual."

"I suppose you're right. There's no use talking. Eat your eggs."

"They're cheese grits." I took a bite. "Wouldn't you like to taste them?"

"I did once. Will we ever be free?"

I shook my head.

"Why would they do that? Why reclone me? They won't even let me write."

I sighed. "If I try to explain, will you resent it?"

"Yes! No. Oh, I don't know!"

"Then I'll try to explain. They won't let you write because there would be no point to it. Few people would appreciate your poetry, and new poetry from you—written tomorrow—would only cheapen the wonderful work you did a century ago."

"They'll burn me! If nobody checks me out, they'll burn me."

I put my arm around her, and she pressed her face against my chest. We sat like that until three 'bots came to clear the table and made us leave.

Arabella stepped away. "I got your shirt wet."

I told her it would dry.

"I know. But it won't be comfortable until it does. Will you take it off?"

I shook my head.

"You're afraid they'll punish you. We're not supposed to do those things."

"They wouldn't do anything serious, just make me put it back on or bring me a new one. But . . ."

"What? What is it, Ern?"

"We'll fight. Or I'm afraid we will."

"I'd like that. Fighting, I wouldn't be so down, just mad. Mad's a lot better. 'Great wit is unto madness near allied.' Who said that?"

"Shakespeare probably. It sounds like him."

"He's lucky." It sounded serious.

"Because he can't be recloned?"

Arabella nodded, her black curls dancing. "They'll burn me. You've been checked out how many times? Honestly now."

"Three."

"Once for forty days. You said that."

"I was lying. It was really ten days. One and a half weeks, if you want to look at it like that."

"And now you're separated. You've lost the woman who checked you out."

I nodded. "She left me behind in a hotel room."

"That's not as bad as being burned. I can't bear to think about that."

"Then don't. Someone will check you, probably several some-ones. And before they burn you, the library will offer you for sale at a very low price. Somebody will surely buy you then."

"And have me burned as soon as I begin to show my age. You're not a woman! You don't know. We do!"

"This is the fight I knew would start. I wish you'd come up onto my shelf, so we could fight up there. This is terribly public."

Arabella hung her head. "They'd tell me I was going to be burned. They'd only mean it a little bit, but it's a little bit more every time they say it. Oh, Ern! Can't you get me out of here?"

"I'll try. You probably know what I'm going to tell you now, but I'm going to tell you anyway. Maybe reminding you will help. The world population is down to about one billion, but a lot of people want it lower still—a few hundred million. Reclones add to the population. Not a lot, but we're different and stand out. There's political pressure against recloning. To escape the pressure as much as possible, the libraries have to treat us like things, like books or tapes, and destroy us in some fashion when we're no longer useful. Burning is painful, but quick. They could starve us to death or see to it that we died of thirst."

"You're taking their side!"

"No, I'm explaining why they act as they do. If we want to live, we've got to understand why it is they think we've got to die. All right if I change the subject?"

"That depends on—the library will open in a minute or two."

"And a 'bot will come around to shoo us onto our shelves, but you won't be shooed if you'll join me on mine."

"I won't!"

"Then I'll join you on yours."

"Damn it! I—I knew this was going to happen. I'm terribly, terribly sorry that it happened so soon. We're not married anymore."

"Arabella . . ." I tried to find words. Maybe I said something sensible. If I did, I can't remember what it was.

"I know what you want, Ern. Our divorce is final, and you're not going to get it." She turned and walked away fast, heels clicking on the floor tiles.

I called, "All I want is for you to love me!"

She was climbing the ladder to a high shelf when I shouted that, and if she heard me she gave no sign. It was one of those times when I wish to God I could talk the way I think.

Back on the shelf where I had slept, I walked up and down. Four steps one way, and four the other. What had I done right, and where had I screwed up? For sure I had tried to rush things, thinking—assuming, really—that she would understand that I just wanted to hold her, to kiss her a dozen times and get kissed by her. Maybe she had, but I do not think so.

Time passed, and the same old thoughts, the same old regrets, came back again and again. When they were stopped by somebody's calling for me, I was glad to get away from them. He was young, blond, and quite a bit smaller than most men, dressed in a faded blue chore smock that did not even come close to going with his culottes and pointed boots.

He waved. "Come down, will you?"

I was happy to do it.

"You're E. A. Smithe?" He offered his hand. It was softer than I had expected. "I guess there's a lounge here somewhere. Someplace where I can buy you a nerbeer?"

I shook my head. "I doubt it."

"Kafe maybe? Something like that?"

"I'm a stranger here myself, but it doesn't seem likely. We might ask."

We did, meaning he did.

"Out on the patio," he said when he came back. "It's out into the hall, two lefts and a right, then through the double doors, but I'm not supposed to buy you anything to eat."

"Then don't," I said.

"Maybe they'll have hot chocolate. You like hot chocolate?"

Here it was again. I nodded, mostly because I was too dumb not to.

"Great! We'll find out. I'm not supposed to borrow you. I guess you know."

"Correct." We were walking, and walking damned fast. I wondered what had got him so nervous.

"Why nothing to eat?"

"There is a rule to that effect." The truth was I had never thought about it. "If you checked me out, you'd be expected to feed me if you kept me more than a day. Here in the library it's forbidden. I suppose it must be to keep us from begging, not that we would. Or at least only a few of us would." I was trying to remember the name of the boy Dr. Johnson had talked about, the young genius who had choked to death on a sweet roll. It would not come, and that boy had lived hundreds of years too early for recloning anyway.

The blond man stopped. "Hey, would a couple of yellowbacks help?"

I tried to remember if anybody had offered me creds before.

"Maybe you don't have a lot." He was getting out his wallet.

The truth was that I had quite a bit, the money from Colette's shaping bag. I knew what would happen if the librarians found out about that, so I said I did not have shit, adding, "We're not paid, you understand. One doesn't pay property, and most of us belong to some library. It's the Spice Grove Public Library in my case."

"Sure. You're slaves."

"Not exactly. Slaves are fully human and can be freed. We aren't and can't be. Besides, slavery is currently against the law. We just require a license."

"I got it. Here's a couple—three hundred. With my compliments. All right?"

I took the money, telling myself I did it because I did not want to piss him off.

The Owenbright Public Library had this screwy patio covered with a wide tent top of semitransparent film. There were potted palms, tables and chairs of the outside kind, and a counter (under its own little roof) where you could buy kafe and doughnuts—stuff like that. A couple of the tables were already getting leaned on by patrons reading diskers they would probably get all spotted with kafe.

The blond man picked a table and told me to sit down. "I'll get us somethin'. Chocolate if they got it. Just wait here. How about a san'wich?"

I knew the rule, but I had not gotten much breakfast, and it hit me that this library'd probably be too chicken to punish another library's reclone. So I said I would like one and thanks.

"I'll see what they got."

He came back with a little stack of sandwiches and two mugs of hot chocolate. He set a mug and a sandwich in front of me, looked around to see if anybody was watching, and pulled a flask from a pocket of his loose blue smock. "Swan-n-Sweetheart five star. Pretty good, too." He decanted a healthy swallow into my chocolate and helped himself to one.

My sandwich turned out to be tuna salad on rye.

"Listen. S'pose I could get you out of here. Would you play along?"

I shook my head.

"Hey, I been nice to you, right?"

I nodded.

"I got you that san'wich you're eatin'. I gave you a few 'backs. I even got you chocolate and gave you a shot of my dog. So why not?"

"Because another library's reclones not on loan cannot be checked out. We would be violating the law. You would be prosecuted. I would probably be burned." That last was really stretching it and might have popped into my head because of what I had told Arabella; I would sure as shit be punished somehow, though.

"'Spose I was to pull my friend on you. You know what I mean? My one-eye friend. These big pockets on this coat ain't just for show. Get me?"

"I do. But I wouldn't come. First, because I like you. If you shoot me, you'll be getting yourself into trouble. But if I were to go with you, I'd be getting you into trouble. I prefer not to do that."

"Yeah, right. What's the second one?"

"The doors here are alarmed. I know they must be, because they're alarmed in all libraries. When someone borrows a disk, a card is inserted in the box. It gives the date on which the disk is to be returned, and it's automatically scanned as the box passes through the door. If there's no card, or the card is invalid, the alarm goes off. There is no security 'bot at some doors, but one is always nearby."

"You ain't no disk!"

"Correct. I am a human being, even if other human beings refuse to consider me human. Still, I've got a card." I took it out and held it up. "My card, however, is for the library in Spice Grove, whose property I am. It would not permit me to go out the door here."

"You can put that away."

I did.

"Want another san'wich?"

"Yes, if you don't mind." I sipped kafe, wondering about the Swan-n-Sweetheart. Brandy or whiskey?"

"Okay. I got ham and cheese. Or chicken salad. Up to you."

"Ham and cheese, please."

He tossed it. "You won't come, huh? That's firm. Only maybe you would if you knew who sent me."

I shook my head, feeling sure he would say Colette and just as sure it would be a lie.

"The tall man. You know him, right?"

"I don't believe I do."

"Good-lookin' guy, a lot taller than me. Wears a big hat."

I had a strong hunch, but I said, "I don't believe we've met."

"Well, he knows you." The blond man stood up. "So do I, now. See you 'round."

I wanted to thank him again for my hot chocolate and the food he had bought, but he was gone before I could get the first word out.

Thinking hard, I finished my second sandwich. I did not want the third, but it seemed to me somebody might ask questions if I just walked away and left it. Two tables away, a fat girl was reading one of the broken novels some people like now. I went to her table, smiled, and offered her the remaining chicken salad sandwich. "My friend bought too many, and I don't want it. I doubt very much that they'll take it back."

She gave me a smile a lot warmer than mine and thanked me.

Back in the reclone section, I stopped to look up at Arabella. She sat prim and silent, her face full of thoughts. A minute or two passed before I saw one hand twitch, fumbling for a pencil. Finding there wasn't any, she came to, shrugged, and returned to her silent stare into space. It would be super cool, I thought, to move that space of hers into some museum; but I had no idea how to do it.

Then I remembered something I had forgotten a hundred years ago, grinned, and finally laughed out loud.

Arabella looked down. "It's you. Am I that funny?"

I shook my head. "I am, darling. I was laughing at myself."

"Well, there's a 'bot looking for you. I suppose they're going to send you back."

8

ON THE ROUTE TRUCK

The back of the truck was dark and crowded. What was worse, that truck was dead set on shaking the fillings out of my teeth. Since I didn't have any, it looked like it was going to jolt all the way to Spice Grove. Of course it might decide, I decided, that the best technique was to run into a tree. Up front the driver had springs or something. Shocks, maybe. The seat beside him probably had them, too; but the books and I did not.

Someplace I ought to mention that it was about three o'clock when I got on the truck, and after seven when it stopped for dinner. The driver let me out then and locked up.

"That's where we're goin' to eat." He pointed. "It's not too bad. I only get six creds per meal to feed you, though. You want to order for yourself, or should I do it for you? You'll get a bowl of soup and a glass of milk if I do."

"I'd prefer to order, of course."

"Then you got to remember six, 'cause I'm going to have to cancel if it's more than that. Six has got to cover the works. Taxes. All that shit."

"But you have the six creds for me."

His nod said he knew I was going to hit him with something, but he was ready for it.

"In that case I propose a better plan. I will order what I wish, and you may order what you wish. I will pay for both dinners, yours and mine. In return, you'll allow me to ride in front, as if I were fully human. You'll of course have gotten a free dinner—anything you like—and you'll be six creds to the good, plus the cost of your own meal. What do you say?"

He pursed his lips. "What about tomorrow?"

"I ride in front until we reach Spice Grove."

"You got to sleep in the truck."

"I will. On the front seat."

"You pay for your own breakfast tomorrow, and mine, too. If you'll do that, it's a deal."

"I ride in front and sleep in front for the entire trip."

Slowly, he nodded.

It was way too cold that night in the front of the truck; so when we stopped for breakfast, I told him I was going to walk to a nearby store and buy myself a good, warm blanket. He hesitated, then said he would have to go with me. I agreed, and he did. Afterward, I paid for our breakfasts, just as we had agreed.

When we were under way again, he said, "You're not supposed to have money."

"While you," I told him, "aren't supposed to have as much as you do."

He nodded thoughtfully.

"If you inform on me, I will of course inform on you. But if you do not, you can rely upon my silence."

He thought about that, too. "I won't, only they wouldn't believe you."

"Will it profit you to make the experiment? I can be persuasive, I warn you."

He nodded again. "We'd be smart not to talk too much about it."

"In which case, I won't."

"You were a writer, right? They're all writers or artists is what I hear."

"Correct." I waited, not knowing where he was going with this.

"Travel books, maybe?"

"No. Mysteries. Mysteries and crime novels." A thought hit me then, so I said, "*Murder on Mars*? That was fantasy murder. Perhaps you've read that one."

"Not me. I read travel. On my doodle, y'know? I got one of the waterproof ones, so I can read in the tub." He laughed. "Shakes the wife outa her tree."

We stopped at the library of some tiny town. I do not remember the name. I told him I would help carry books, but he waved me off—there were only two. Back in the truck, I said I was surprised he had made the stop for just a couple of books.

"I got to. If there's books to drop off or books to pick up, I got to. Even if it's just one. If there's nothing either way, I can skip it. Only that don't happen much."

I said, "Couldn't they simply mail them?"

"They'd lose too many. Most books, nobody's got new copies. Either they never been scanned, or the scans are lost. You pay through the nose if you can find a copy for sale, too."

"Couldn't they scan everything?"

He laughed. "You trying to put me out of business? Sure they could, only it would cost the world and take about a hundred years, and put them out of business, too." Suddenly, he became serious. "Besides, if one guy could control all them scans, he'd have a lock. Pretty soon, nobody'd know anything he didn't want 'em to know. You think that one over."

I said I would; and I darned near added that I had been underestimating him, which I had. If I could talk the way I think, I probably would have. It got me to thinking maybe he had been underestimating me, then about what makes us underestimate people. It is mostly them underestimating themselves, or anyhow that is what I finally came up with. Sure, I talked fancy. I cannot help that, but what about what I had been saying?

Pretty soon I got to thinking about Colette and her problem. There were things about it that bothered me quite a bit, and I sort of turned those over in my mind while we rode along and I looked at the scenery, which outside the ruined towns was mostly pretty good.

For one thing, she had said she was going to get her mother recloned. What about her father? He had been the financial genius, right? Alive again, he could make her a lot more money. After I had thought that over, I decided that she figured she could not control him, not even if he was a reclone and did not count. That was something to keep in mind.

Another thing was that sometimes she talked like he had been dead for a quarter before her brother died. Only other times it sounded like he was hardly cold. That second one seemed to me like it made a lot more sense. Her brother had lived right there in New Delphi, so why would he fiddle around for weeks and weeks before he got somebody to open that safe? I felt like he would get it opened as soon as he could.

Then there was the tall man. Colette seemed to think he was not such a bad guy. A nice crook? Nice crooks are only in books. I used to write the books—or anyhow the earlier me had written a bunch of them—and I knew. Real crooks are sons of bitches.

They had stripped her naked, just like me. Only they had not tortured her. She was a living doll, but they had not raped her. They hadn't even smacked her around for laughs. She would have talked about it if they had done it, and been bruised and maybe cut up; and she would probably have cried when she thought about it. Only she had not. All right, maybe—just maybe—no cuts and no crying; but she would have had bruises for sure, and I had not seen any. The more I thought about it the surer I got that there was something funny going on, but I could not even guess what it was. A lot of guys say that women are always mysteries; but it seemed to me, jouncing along in that truck and looking out at all that was left of one of the old cities where I used to live, that Colette had gone way over the limit.

Then there was the little blond guy with the pointed boots and the work smock. Sure, little guys carry big guns and big guys carry little ones. A plainclothes cop I had talked to one time when I—the first me, that is—was getting background for *Men Who Kill* had told me that, and he generally knew what he was talking about. Besides, it made sense. The big guys figured they did not really need a gun much. Guns are heavy, even if they are mostly plastic; and forty or fifty rounds cannot help being heavy. But the little guys carry a big gun and maybe two or three. They might need them.

So the work smock made some sort of sense, but why did the little guy give me so much money? If he was one of the gang, the gang made even less sense than I had thought. If he was not, what was he up to?

"Life is crazy." Sometimes I say things out loud that I do not mean to say.

"For me, and that's for sure," the driver told me, "but not for you."

I am putting that in here because it shows the way they think about us. I wanted to explain to him that I was exactly the same as he was, sure I did; but I had been around long enough to know it would have me riding in the back of the truck again.

Anyway I asked about his problems instead, and he told me. So he talked about his wife as we rolled along, and how she spent all his money, and maybe she had another guy on the string while he was away driving the truck, and a whole lot of other stuff. None of it is worth telling here, and I would not do that anyway because none of it was really my business.

The next library we stopped at was different, a really big university library with gray stone wings running off in every direction and the main building covered with ivy. About half the books on the truck were either going there or coming back there. I helped unload and carry, and I was glad we did not have to shelve them, too; it would have taken a week. I was sweating, and tired, and really glad it was almost over when five 'bots wheeled in the books we would be taking away, bundles and bundles of them going to libraries all over the country. I said something about the stone of Sisyphus, and the driver wiped his face and said we would get lunch before we started on those. Then I said maybe we could get the 'bots to help.

The boss 'bot said, "We have other work, sir, but there is a reclone as well. It may be of help."

Here I expected the driver to explain that I was a reclone myself, but he did not. I had been underestimating him again, and it made me want to kick myself. What he really said was, "We're going off now to have some lunch. We'll be back."

"You must leave your truck here." That was one of the other 'bots.

He nodded and turned to me. "We'll walk. It ain't far."

It was not, and I found it was really nice to stroll though the campus to the cafeteria in the student center. The sun shone bright and a little warmer than I liked just then, but there were big trees on both sides of the paths and their shade made the whole walk a pleasure. When we got there, the driver paid for his own lunch, and I paid for mine. We did not even talk about it, that was just the way it was.

When we got back, Arabella Lee was sitting beside the loaded book carts waiting for us. I wanted to shout when I saw her, but she was in my arms and kissing me before I could catch my breath.

I guess some other driver might have broken us up, or tried to. And maybe I might have killed him for it, or tried to. I think probably this one grinned at us for a minute or two before he began loading books. I was not paying attenion. Right then, Arabella's kiss was all I cared about.

Eight or ten kisses later, she wanted to know what I was doing there. I tried to explain and she said, "Then let's help." Which we did. The driver told us where to put each bundle of books, so the ones we'd unload first would be nearest the back of the truck. We made some mistakes but nothing serious. While we were working, I asked if Arabella was on her way back to Owen-bright. She said she wasn't, that she belonged here and was going out on interlibrary loan. This was a different copy, of course.

So we kept working, and all the time I was hoping that Arabella was bound for Spice Grove. Only hoping, because I did not dare ask.

When we had finished and were ready to go, where we would sit started a big argument. Arabella wanted to ride alone in back. I said no way! She had to ride up front with the driver. The driver said that according to our bargain, I got to ride in front. There was nothing in there about her riding up front. For a new setup there would have to be a new bargain. I said that if she was going to ride in back, I'd ride back there with her. Great, except that once she understood the bargain I'd made with the driver, she swore up and down she'd never agree to that. I had to ride up front.

I began to argue, but then I had an idea and shut up instead.

The driver sighed. "You got more to say? I been hopin' you were finished."

"Dame fortune," I told him, "dashes our hopes to the ground with one hand while lifting them to the highest heavens with the other. I was about to say—indeed, I will say—that I know Arabella well. For two years she and I were wed, as she will doubtless confirm. I know her intimately and she is an angel, but she's as stubborn as a brass monkey."

"Ern!"

"Well, you are, you know." I turned back to the driver. "I will pay for dinner tonight for all three of us, but you must permit Arabella to ride in front, seated on my lap, for the remainder of the trip."

The driver got his thoughts going by scratching his head. "Here's the first thing. I'm not changing our route. That's firm. I'd be risking my job, and I need it."

"Agreed," I said.

"So she's got to get out at Inspiration. That's where she's bound for, the Inspiration Popular Learning Center. It's on her tag."

"That's right," Arabella whispered.

I wanted to swear and maybe spit, but I tried hard not to show it.

"Here's the second thing. You two got to sleep in the truck tonight. I know you're going to want to rent a cabin for you and her, or a room, or whatever. That won't wash. It'd be worth my job if they found out, so I won't allow it. You sleep in the truck and I lock you in."

Arabella said, "Agreed."

"Third thing. You got to promise not to fight. If you fight up front you'll drive me right over the edge, and I'm not going to stand for it. If you fight, you've got to do it in back. And no hitting, neither. If she's got a fat lip or a black eye when we get to Inspiration, I'll never hear the end of it."

I turned to Arabella. "We argued a great deal when we were married. Marriage does that, I'm afraid. Did I ever strike you?"

She thought for a minute before she answered. "There was that one birthday. You spanked me."

"Not hard," I said.

"Brutally!" She made it firm. "Absolutely brutally. I cried for a week."

I told the driver, "That's an exaggeration. It is only for decency's sake that I refrain from characterizing it as a lie."

He pushed me out of the way so he could stand directly in

front of Arabella. "What was he hitting you with when he spanked you? Was it his hand, or did he have a belt or something?"

"With his hand, but very, very hard."

"That don't count. Now quit fighting, or I'll dump the both of you, and tell 'em you run away."

"Peace," I said, and held out my hand to Arabella, hoping to God she would take it. She did, and in another minute we were both smiling.

"One more thing. When you sleep in back, you're going to have to lie on the books. Don't mess 'em up. Not any of 'em. You can use the bucket, like Smithe here did last night."

So that was what we did, more or less. Mostly we were both up front, with Arabella on my lap; now and then I rode in back, and once or twice she did. I am not about to pretend that I thought a whole lot about Colette or her brother's murder on that leg of the trip. I did not. A little bit now and then, but not very much. Arabella and I talked about how it was when we were married, and what we had done, and all the good, happy times. When I thought at all, it was mostly about those. That was what was really important as far as I was concerned. To you the important stuff is probably the rest of it, and that was sort of important to me, too. I kept wanting to ask Arabella why she had divorced me, what the real reason had been. Only I knew if I did I would get a whole list of shit, money, and I was cheating (that one was a lie and she knew it), and I wanted to screw all the time (only she wouldn't say that, just hint, and it was another lie anyway), money, and I was always telling the truth when I should have said something nice. There were a couple of dozen others, too, like kicking my dirty socks under the bed.

Only listening to her and thinking back, I believe I finally got it. I did not like it and I still do not, but here it is. Mysteries sell and poetry does not, or hardly ever. Not even great poetry. My editor was always after me for another book, another Red Searcher story or another Mrs. Jacoby story; but Arabella had to go from publisher to publisher and finally she just put her books out on the Internet and let it go at that—you could download them if you wanted to, only there were not any hard copies.

That was when she divorced me. Once I had figured it out I tried not to talk about any of that shit, and I think she did, too. We talked about the classes she used to teach, and a magazine that I had tried to start one time.

Another thing I thought about was how she would take this trip of ours and make a poem out of it. A good one, and maybe a great one.

"It's all so different now, isn't it?" Arabella said that, and when she did it hit me harder than it ever had before that she was right.

I nodded, thinking, and finally I said, "This is full humanity's retirement. I have sensed that ever since they brought me back, and now I understand what it is that I was sensing."

"You mean you have retired from writing? Ern, they made us. They are forcing us not to."

"No, it's not that at all. I mean real humanity has retired. That's what we're seeing, the meaning of all the new places we're being chauffeured through. They chipped flint and made fire and exterminated the short-faced bears with nothing but spears and clubs, even though those were probably the most dangerous animals real humanity has ever faced. They had children and more children, and those children spread out and did the same and more until real humans were everywhere. The artic was a waste of deadly cold, but they were there. There was no jungle so hot, so wet, so disease-ridden that they didn't live in it. Some of them lived in caves of radioactive rock. The oldest died in their thirties, but they were born and grew up and gathered and hunted and died there anyway."

Our driver rolled down the window and spat. "You sound like one of those professors on roundvid. You got to talk like that?"

"Yes." I tried to explain. "I do. I wrote mysteries and crime fiction, you see; so many of my characters used a great deal of slang and made egregious grammatical errors. To prevent any confusion between their conversations and my narration, I made the latter rather stiff and formal. One requires contrast to prevent vulgar speech from becoming ordinary. The authorities responsible for the creation of my reclones—of whom I myself am one—appear to have supposed that I habitually spoke in this style."

Arabella said, "Or they believed that your readers probably thought so, Ern. That could be it. They knew that no one would assume I spoke free verse, but that's only because the readership for poetry is so much more intelligent."

"No doubt. What I was about to say was that the real humans warred with one another and explored every corner of this planet. They built cities under the sea and flitters that would fly as fast as bullets—then space probes that flew still faster. Their robots explored every gas cloud and orbiting rock in this solar system. They stretched real human life over and over again, but this system's radiation makes manned interplanetary flight virtually impossible, and nothing they could build would reach even the nearest stars in a hundred stretched lifetimes."

"Go on," Arabella whispered.

"And when they had done all those things and reached their

limits, they found that they were old. That's all. I say 'they' because although you and I are human, we are not fully human. We're not real humans, or at least we do not count as such."

Our driver chuckled. "Well, there's times when I have a real tough time rememberin' that. Listenin' to you two, anyway."

Arabella and I slept in the back of the truck that night, spreading my blanket over the books and huddling together. Fortunately, the night was warm. We were not very comfortable; but I was happy and I believe she was, too.

About midmorning of the following day we got to the Inspiration Popular Learning Center. We unloaded a couple dozen books there, and Arabella turned herself in to the librarians. I went with her to look at the shelf they were giving her; and—hell, let's be honest about this—I wanted to see if there was another copy of me there, a me that I could turn her over to knowing he would take good care of her and even die for her if it came to that. There was not.

We kissed. The librarian did not like us much after that. For myself I did not care, but I worried about what it might mean for Arabella. I still do. Legally we cannot own tablets or eephones, or use screens, or even send paper letters by Continental Package Service. Even if I could get my hands on a tablet or something, which I probably could, Arabella could not get my message. What I really wanted was one from her, anyhow.

By the time I got off the truck, the Spice Grove Public Library was ready to close. So it had been about an eight-hour trip. Knock off an hour for lunch and two more for a stop between Inspiration and Spice Grove. So five hours of actual travel. Say that we averaged ninety kilometers per hour. That means that the distance by road from Inspiration to Spice Grove is roughly four hundred and fifty kilometers. In the yellow flitter, they would be practically on top of each other. Walking it might take me close to ten weeks or more.

I'm giving all that mental math because I started doing it as soon as I caught sight of the Spice Grove Public Library, and I was still doing it when I got out of the truck and we started unloading. Besides me, there was not much.

A librarian came up. I would give her name here, but we make a point of not learning their names and not using them even if we know them. You have got to keep your pride up somehow, or they will soon be feeding you out of a bowl on the floor.

"E. A. Smithe?"

The driver said, "Returned from interlibrary loan. You have to sign a paper."

The librarian shook her head. "He was never so loaned, only checked out."

Eventually she signed, but it was only after writing something on the paper and crossing out some other things. I could not see it well enough to read what she was crossing out, but I could see what she was doing perfectly.

"You're dirty, Smithe."

I said I had not been able to shower since leaving Owenbright.

"We're closing in another hour anyway. You'll bathe, won't you?"

I wanted to say no; but I knew what would happen if I did, and that the 'bots would keep ducking my head into the water and holding it there. So I told her I was looking forward to it, which I actually was.

"Good. There are two patrons waiting to check you out. I've promised to notify them when you're returned." She paused.

"That's unusual. It's usually disks or cubes. Hardly ever books or reclones." Another pause. "Do you like books? I realize you used to write them. He did, I mean."

I said, "Yes, very much."

"So do I." She hesitated. "Someday I really must read some of yours."

Of course I wanted to ask about the people who wanted me, but I didn't. In the first place, she probably knew nothing at all about them, not even their names. In the second place, it was certain to piss her off; and the less she knew the more pissed off she would be. The thing to do was to ask some of ours if they had seen anybody in there looking for me. So I did, after I had a nice hot shower and washed my hair and all that. I went around in one of those stupid hospital gowns they give you for the night sometimes and asked at least half a dozen people. Millie Baumgartner (yes, the cookbook lady) was the only one who had seen anything, a little guy in dark clothes and a tall guy in uniform. She hadn't recognized the uniform, but she told me she was not good on them. Just a uniform. Green, maybe. Or blue. They had been together.

The small one sounded like he might be the guy who had given me money. He might also have been any of a million other guys.

So that night I went to bed back on my own shelf. It was a lot more comfortable than the truck, but here's the funny thing. I would rather have been back on the truck. I do not know why, except that I had convinced myself by then that it was all over. I would never see Colette again or Arabella either. I would sleep there on my shelf until I burned, remembering plots, and reviews they had gotten, and the quotes on the backs of my books. Not eating too much because I would get fat and would not look right, and not eating too little either because I would get skinny and then I would look wrong.

With all that going on, I should have had a hard time getting to sleep, and maybe I did, but I do not remember it. All I know is that I was sound asleep when the 'bot came in and woke us up for breakfast.

9

PAYNE, FISH, AND PAIN

They came for me about ten or ten thirty, two big, strong guys. Neither of them was tall and neither was short. Both wore conservative jackets with a little bit of blue piping; neither one was in uniform. They looked to me like they were both in their midforties, but I could be wrong about that. These days, who knows.

Have I said they both wore sunglasses? I do not think I did, but I'm not sure how you back up on this. Maybe I ought to stop right here and explain what I'm doing, how I'm writing this. Only what I'm doing is not really writing, which my brain is blocked on. (Or not all of it is. Only some of it.)

Like this.

I have got to use formal English when I talk. You know all about that. Even before they fixed me so I could not have kids, they put this mental block on me; so when I know what I want to say, another part of my mind, a part I cannot control, turns whatever it is into formal phrases and sentences. Let's call that part the autospeech center. Then they put in a rule against writing: NOT ALLOWED. Only I can do it on the keyboard like now, so it comes out right, the way I think and not the way I talk.

Well, with this screen I am using (maybe I will tell you about that later) you can either type on the keyboard like this or just talk to it if you would rather do that, which a lot of people would because there are not a hell of a lot of people who can use a keyboard anymore.

So what I do is dictate when I tell you what I said, and use the keyboard for what I think. Neat, right? Only I do not know how to back up on this one. I know you can pull up a manual on the screen, but I do not know how. I need to find that out, too.

The first guy shook my hand and said, "Pain's my name. Wonderful to meet you, Mr. Smithe. I listened to your disks years and years back, all I could find. Meeting you now is a great, great pleasure."

The other guy just shook hands, and off we went. Out of the library into the sunshine and then into a big black hovercraft, with the first guy in the driver's seat. Later I found out his name was spelled "Payne." The quiet guy's name was Fish, or maybe Fisher. Something like that. They were partners.

We never flew very high, nowhere near as high as Colette's hovercab had gone. I asked Payne if we were going far, saying we ought to notify the library if we were. It was something I had just made up; but I thought it sounded good, and I believe he bought it. He said no, we were just going to a safe house on the other side of town; and by the time he had said it we were there, with the roof of the old garage folding back so we could set down into it. I didn't think "safe house" sounded good, and I was right.

We got out and Fish said, "We oughta cuff him. He might run." It was the first time I had heard him say a word.

Payne said, "He won't, will you, Mr. Smithe? You'd get rocked. Tell Fish you won't run." That was when I found out Fish's name.

We went out of the garage and along an old, cracked path to a big screened-in porch. I noticed that from the outside you could not see into it at all, but from inside you could see out like the screens were not even there. I said it was a nice place.

Payne told me, "You won't be here long, I promise. Just for a couple of days if everything goes well. And then," he clapped his hands, "back to your shelf in the library, safe and sound."

Fish said, "Only we got you for as long as we want you. If we need to work you over for a year, well . . ." He shrugged. "That's how it goes sometimes."

"Here's how it went," Payne explained. "We were nice and said we wanted to check you out, and they said we couldn't because you were already checked out by somebody else. She'd never gotten her deposit back, and her time wasn't up. So they couldn't let anybody have you."

I nodded.

"So we said fine, we're taking him as evidence. You go to court and explain, and if the judge likes you, you'll get him back in a year or maybe two. Then they said, okay, you can check him out. So you're checked out."

I said, "They were supposed to give me a card, in that case."

"I'll speak to them about it. It doesn't matter to us, but I don't think we could ever sweat anybody for a year. You'd die. I know I would."

"You won't have to," I told him. "I'll gladly tell you anything you want to know, provided I know it myself. That is my duty as a library resource."

"Great! That's great!" Payne smiled. His smile reminded me of an aunt of mine (the first me) who smiled like that whenever she had wrung the neck of one of her chickens. The harder the chicken had tried to get away, the bigger the smile.

We went into the house and into a room that had navy blue drapes over all the windows. Payne saw me looking at them, and held one up. "Soundproofing, see? The window's shut, too. Double panes in all the windows, glass and notint, and both panes are bullet resistant. It's so good you can scream if you want to. We won't have to beat you to make you stop, or stuff a rag in your mouth—nothing like that. Go ahead and scream anytime you feel like it. Want to try it out?"

I shook my head. I had the feeling that if I did, he was going to say he could make me scream better than that and break one of my fingers or maybe burn my feet.

"It's pretty much a standard interrogation room, only it's off in the 'burbs where the lawyers won't find it." The smile had not gone. "And if they did, they'd need a warrant to get inside—which they wouldn't get. Do you have a lawyer?"

I said, "I'm afraid not."

Fish wanted to know, "We goin' to tie him to the chair?"

Payne shook his head, motioned toward a big ponticwood chair in the center of the room, and told me to have a seat. "I don't see why. Mr. Smithe's going to cooperate with us fully—answer every question we've got. Right, Mr. Smithe?"

"Correct."

"Besides, it's more fun if they're loose. They get ideas. Make us some kafe, will you?"

I said, "Aren't you going to sit down?"

Payme smiled again. Same smile. "Not me, Mr. Smithe. I sit down too much as it is. Desk work and all that dog shit. Taking screens and making screens. I ought to walk more. How about a cup of kafe? I should've asked sooner."

I said sure—only it came out as "certainly."

"First question, describe your connection to the Coldbrook family."

I said, "I don't really have any connection to the family as such. Colette Coldbrook checked me out, and she's the only member of the family I've ever met." I hesitated, wondering how much Payne really knew. "As I understand it, all the other members of her family are deceased."

"She borrowed you?"

"From the library. As I said."

"Several times?" Payne leaned forward, interested.

"No, only once. Are you holding her?"

He smacked me so hard I just about passed out. "I ask, you answer. Anytime you ask a question, that's what you get."

My eyes were watering; I fought to blink it back. "That's a nasty way to treat a library resource in place of kafe."

"It's how we do it. Oh, and if you stand up it's more of the same, only worse. Tell me everything you know about the Cold-brooks. No detail is too small."

"It's not much, I warn you."

Payne laughed. "You don't rattle easy, do you? I like that. I should've known from your books."

"That's very generous of you, very flattering. But I fear it's not really true."

"We're going to find out. Talk about the Coldbrooks, and keep talking."

"All right. It was a family of four consisting of the father, the mother, and two children. The father's name was Conrad. I don't know his wife's name; Colette always called her Mother. The children were Conrad, Junior, and Colette. At the time she borrowed me, the other three were dead."

"We'll start with the mother. What do you know about her?"

"Nothing, beyond the fact that she's dead. At least Colette said she was."

"You never saw her? Not even her picture?"

"No, I . . ."

"You thought of something. What is it?"

"I saw her picture. Or rather I saw a family picture, and she was in it."

"Good!"

Fish came in, carrying a kafe server, mugs, sweetener, and so forth on a tray.

Payne handed me a mug spangled with yellow flowers. "You get this for cooperating. White and sweet?"

I nodded. "Both, please."

"Tell me about the picture and you'll get them."

Fish set his tray down.

"There's a long narrow sunroom or solarium running down the south wall of the house. That's where the lift tube is. We went into it from the kitchen. The outside wall is notint windows, but the facing wall's hung with pictures. One showed the entire Coldbrook family, the father and the mother, Conrad,

Junior, and Colette." I sipped my black kafe, which was fresh and good but way too strong.

"This was the family's house, the house outside New Delphi?"

I nodded. "Correct."

"You've seen it. Been inside."

"Yes," I said. "Colette took me there."

Fish made a little noise of satisfaction.

"We'll get to the house in a minute. Describe the mother."

"I'll try. I didn't stand there and study the picture, you understand. I just glanced at it in passing. She was the smallest of the four, although I doubt that she was actually as short as she appeared. At the time the picture was taken, I would say that she was an attractive woman just entering middle age. Seventy, perhaps. Her clothes looked a bit old-fashioned, I thought, though of course the picture had probably been taken several years ago. Blue-and-white skimmer, dark blue scarf about her neck. Do you remember when women wore those?"

That got me another blow, one that knocked the mug from my hand. I picked it up, apologized, and offered to clean up the mess as well as I could. Payne shook his head and whistled for a 'bot.

When it had completed its task and gone, he said, "The woman we were talking about, the mother. Jewelry?"

I said, "I didn't notice any."

"Hair?"

I had to think. "Dark, I'm sure. It appeared jet black in the picture. It may not have been, but it was certainly quite dark. Of course women's hair colors change with the wind."

Fish rumbled, "Don't get fancy."

"With the phases of the moon, in that case, and the tireless march of the zodiac."

For a minute there I thought Fish was going to smack me, and so did he; Payne waved him back. "You said she looked small. Talk about that."

"Correct, she did. On another occasion, Colette told me she was terribly shy. Would you like to hear about that?"

"What about the father?"

"Very tall, and thin. Considerably taller than his son and daughter, although they both looked tall, and Colette is certainly tall for a woman. I would say that he was at least a head and a half taller than his wife. He had broad shoulders and large hands. It was easy to see that he was the dominant member of the family, the decision maker. Everything about him showed it, his height, his eyes, his body language. He had one hand resting on his wife's shoulder and the other on his son's. He was the only one who was touching another member—no, that's wrong. Colette and her brother had joined hands, I think. Not obviously."

"Describe the father's face."

I thought about that for a moment. "Thin. Bony. Strong jaw. Prominent nose. Not at all handsome, but impressive."

"Clean shaven?"

"Yes. No beard or mustache. I couldn't see his hair because he was wearing a cap."

"He was bald."

"Was he?"

Payne's hand went up. "Aren't you ever going to learn? I ask, you answer."

"I'm sorry. I was surprised, that's all. They can cure baldness."

"Maybe he didn't want to be cured. Tell us about the brother. Describe him. Did he look like his father?"

"No, I don't believe so. There may have been some resemblance, but nothing striking. More like his mother, I would say. His face was more rounded and not as thin. He looked tall, as I said, but certainly not as tall as his father. Half a head shorter, perhaps. Dark hair. Quite handsome."

"Colette borrowed you from our library, you said. From the Spice Grove Public Library."

I nodded. "Yes. She did."

"For some reason she took you to the family place in New Delphi. Probably she was going there, and she brought you along for company. How long were the two of you together?"

I had to think about that one. "Two and a half days, perhaps."

"So you had plenty of opportunity to observe her. How she looked, how she dressed, the sound of her voice. All that stuff."

"Correct. I did."

Payne leaned toward me, intent. "Fish and I have seen her picture and seen her on trivid, but we've never seen her in person, neither one of us. What would you say was her most striking feature? Think!"

"Her eyes, certainly. She has large violet eyes, very beautiful. In her smooth, pale face, they were positively arresting."

"Did you ever watch her get dressed? Watch her putting on her makeup?"

"No. I never so much as set foot in her bedroom. She had forbade that."

He leaned back. "Could she have been wearing tinted contacts?"

I thought about that one; it felt wrong, but it was something I knew little or nothing about. "I suppose so. I don't believe she was."

Fish grunted.

Payne ignored it. "She wore eye makeup, I'm sure. A woman like that—she'd be bound to."

"Correct. Also powder and face cream and so forth. I would have been surprised if she had not."

"What about false eyelashes? Would you have spotted those? They tell me the best ones are very good. Really good, but they're expensive and they've got to be applied at a salon."

I thought about that, wondering how long this would go on and whether I had any chance of getting away. "I doubt that very much. She wore mascara—but not false lashes, in my opinion."

"I see." (This was still Payne, leaning back with half-closed eyes.) "Good figure?"

"Yes, very good. Not voluptuous, you understand. She's slender, with long legs and a small waist. I've never seen her dance, but I would imagine she would be a good dancer. She's really very graceful for such a tall woman."

"You fell for her."

For some reason I had one hell of a time explaining that I was a reclone just then, but I knew I had to do it. "If I were to have a romantic relationship with a fully human, I would lose my life, Officer Payne. Besides, I—well, I am romantically attached to Arabella Lee, a famous poet. She was my wife—subsequently my ex-wife—during our real lives."

Payne leaned over me. "Yeah, reclones are things, not people. That's right. But some people have certain things they care a lot about. A pair of shoes, a ground car, maybe just an old cabinet that's been in the family for a couple hundred years. Does Colette Coldbrook care a lot about you, Mr. Smithe?"

"Ask her, please. She ought to be a better source of information, and . . ."

"Yeah? What is it?"

"And please tell me what she says."

Fish snorted.

I sipped my kafe, trying not to show that I felt like the biggest fool ever. "Something was said earlier about whitener and sweetener, and I see both on that tray. I'd like some, if it's not too much trouble."

Grinning, Payne stood up to get them. "For somebody who's not a man, you're one hell of a man, Mr. Smithe. I wish I had you on our team."

I said, "I am on your team, Officer Payne, for as long as you have me checked out."

He took my mug and added rather too much whitener and rather too little sweetener to it, stirred it, and returned it to me.

Fish growled, "Ask him about the house."

"Not quite yet." Payne poured himself more kafe. "You wanted me to ask Colette Coldbrook how she felt about you, Mr. Smithe. Clearly you were hoping to find out if we had her."

I shook my head. "I assume you do, though I doubt that she's in this house."

"We don't have her at all. Someone does, and I think I know who. But it's not our department—not even close. Does she like you?"

"If you intend affection, I believe she does. She likes me as a friend, as she might like a good book or a small dog."

"You've never slept with her?" Payne was grinning, and I wanted to hit him.

"Of course not! We've never so much as kissed."

"Too bad. She's a rich woman, and she's sure as shit going to be one hell of a lot richer soon. You know about the brother? You told us he's dead, and that's right; but do you know how he died?"

I said, "Colette told me he was murdered. Strangled, I believe."

"Exactly. Choked to death by somebody with a lot bigger, stronger hands than she's got. She'll get what would have been his half of the old man's money; but that's held up, and it's going to keep right on being held up until the brother's murder's solved. Did you know about that?"

I sipped my kafe. It was too strong but decent and still hot enough to keep all the yellow flowers blooming and spinning, but I hardly tasted it.

"Answer me, damn it!"

"Sorry. I hadn't even considered the possibility, and it took me by surprise. No, officer, I did not know about it."

"Well, that's the way we do it now." Payne rose and walked to the window. "Nobody profits by the crime until we find out who committed the crime. Did you ever meet the father?"

"Conrad Coldbrook, Senior?" I shook my head. "No, I did not. I never so much as knew he existed until Colette told me about him."

"I didn't know him either." Payne sounded thoughtful. "Now I wish I had. Somebody said once that he could pull gold out of the air. He couldn't, naturally, but I guess that was the way it seemed."

"Colette told me that he was a financial genius," I ventured.

"He was. It seemed like everything he touched made money. Naturally the trick was that he knew which ones to touch. Only where'd he get all his capital to start with? I don't suppose you know?"

I did not want to tell any more lies than I had to, so I said, "Someone must know."

Payne shrugged. "Sure, but who? Does Colette know?"

"I doubt it. Here I want to say that I'll try to find out if you'll free me, but someone has her. That's how it looks, at least. She was abducted from our hotel suite. I suppose you know all about that."

"Hell, no. All I know is that she's disappeared. Tell me about it."

"If you wish. I'll make it as brief as I can. We went to Owen-bright to question an academic, Dr. Roglich. It appeared that Colette's father had consulted him several times and paid for his advice. Dr. Roglich was afraid that someone was spying on him, but he wouldn't say who it was. I found a listening device concealed in a bookcase in his office, and I broke it."

Fish asked, "What did you do with it after? Is it still there?"

"I doubt it. To the best of my memory, I dropped it into a wastebasket."

Payne said, "You'd like to get Colette Coldbrook back, right? And free?"

"Of course. If that's what you and Mr. Fish are doing, you may trust me to cooperate fully."

"By answering my questions?"

"Certainly. I'd do that in any event. In every other way, as well."

"Then answer this one. I know what Fish and I want with you.

We want to find out about the Coldbrooks and about Colette especially. The rest are dead issues, see? She's still alive, or we hope she is. What did she want with you?"

"I can tell you very readily, but I doubt you will believe me. She had a book, one that I had written. She thought there was a valuable secret concealed in it, and she wanted my help in learning it."

Fish muttered something and moved closer.

"In a book you wrote."

"Yes." I nodded.

"What book is that?"

"*Murder on Mars.*"

"You put a secret in there?"

I shook my head. "Perhaps I did, but to the best of my knowledge I did not."

Payne turned to Fish. "Get headquarters. Ask somebody there to dig up a copy for us. That's *Murder on Mars* by E. A. Smithe. Smithe with an *e* on the end."

He turned back to me. "That secret was in the book. Or anyway, she thought it was in there. What made her think that?"

"I can only guess. Her brother had given her the book. He may have said something to cause her to believe it held a significant secret. Or his behavior at the time may have implied it. You are the police. You and Fish—or at least I have come to believe you are."

Payne shrugged. "Have I ever said so?"

"No, you have not."

"How about placing you under arrest? Did I do that, or even say I might?"

"Of course not. Persons may be arrested. Taken into custody, and so on. I am a thing, an object, a library resource that you have obtained entirely legally."

"You got it." Payne looked around, presumably to see whether Fish was in earshot, then pulled up a chair. "You remember all that, see? All the stuff you just reeled off. This is Spice Grove, right? You know that?"

I nodded. "Certainly."

"Well, Colette Coldbrook was a schoolteacher in a private school here, only a teacher with enough cash and connections to live in the Taos Towers. That's very, very up-list. Flitters and furs."

I nodded again.

"And somebody snatched her right out of that damned hotel in Owenbright. How do you think we feel about that? Not just Fish and me, but the whole force. How do you think the chief feels? How about the mayor? Those planet-size politicians in the Department of Enforcement up in Niagara? How do they feel?"

"You must find it unpleasant, I'm sure."

"You bet we do. It's macro-red. If you can tell me anything that might help, I'll be your friend for life, and that's no chad, see? So come clean. You've been answering exactly what I asked. You don't have to admit it, I know it. Now just tell me something that might give us a little help."

I said, "First allow me to deal with the way I have responded to your questions. Having no wish to be struck again, I speak exclusively of the subject at hand. When you give me liberty to wander, I may do so—though not far."

"Wander all you want." Payne straightened up. "How about some more kafe?"

I nodded. "With a trifle more sweetener this time, if you would be so kind." I handed him my mug with its slowing yellow blossoms, and soon received it back restored to full bloom.

He sat in the chair he had pulled over. "Now talk. If it's helpful to us, I'll take anything."

"It will anger you and perhaps frighten you, which I fear may be worse. But very well. Colette believed that there were listening devices hidden in her apartment. I don't know why she believed that, but she did. After she checked me out, we went by hovercab to a ruined garden. I don't know where it was, but the hovercab company will presumably have records."

Payne nodded.

"We talked there for an hour or more. That was where she showed me *Murder on Mars*. She would not tell me what secret she hoped it contained, but we discussed several ways in which a secret might be concealed in a book. Do you want those?"

"No. Go on."

"Eventually she screened our hovercab. It descended, picked us up, and took us to the Taos Towers. We intended to spend the night there and go to New Delphi the next day in her flitter, as eventually we did. We were seated in her lounge when a screen told us that someone was coming in, an A-1. I assume you know about that."

"Sure," Payne said. "They're special guests, or else they've got a warrant."

"I see. I ought to have thought of that. Well, the door of Colette's apartment opened and two men came in. Their guns were of a type unfamiliar to me, but they were clearly guns. Soon they knocked me unconscious. When I regained consciousness, I was naked and had been tied to a chair. Colette was in the same condition."

"She was naked, too?"

"Precisely." I was growing weary of all the talk, but I tried not to let it show. "She said she had not been raped. I assume she told the truth. Certainly I have no reason to doubt her."

"Had they robbed her? Taken her money and her jewelry?"

"I don't know, but I doubt it. If they had, she never mentioned it."

"Did she tell you what they wanted?"

I nodded. "She said that they wanted the book. I had hidden it before they came, however. Colette had been very concerned about listening devices—about being spied upon; so I had thought it prudent."

"She didn't tell them where it was."

"She couldn't. She didn't know. I thought that was best. We reclaimed it before we left for New Delphi." I waited for Payne to talk, but he didn't.

Finally I said, "I have never been a policeman, but I did write more than twenty published mysteries; and it seems to me that the great question for us in this case is not who killed Colette's brother, but who has kidnapped Colette. Colette's brother is dead, and thus beyond our rescue. Colette herself may still be alive."

Payne nodded. "To hell with the brother. He lived in New Delphi and he died there. Let them worry about him. Colette Coldbrook lived right here, and fifty or a hundred important people knew her. Pictures on the society sites, all that. Hell, I've followed so many links and watched so many interviews I feel like I knew her myself. She worked on the Charity Committee, she taught rich kids in that school, she was an eligible heiress. The works. We'll be heroes if—"

Fish returned. Seeing Payne seated, he dropped into a chair himself. "No book. Nowhere. Nobody's even heard of it. He's stringin' us."

"I'm not," I insisted. "There was such a book, and Colette Coldbrook had a copy, which she said had been given to her by her brother on the day he was killed. Take me to New Delphi, and I'll retrieve it and show it to you. That is with the understanding that it is Colette's, and must eventually be returned to her."

"He's stringin' us," Fish muttered.

I said, "If this is a subterfuge, it is one you will find remarkably easy to unmask. Take me there. Challenge me to produce the book. If I cannot, do whatever you think best."

"That's what we'll do anyway," Payne told me. "You're showing a whole lot of guts, you are. You must be proud of yourself."

"For this? No, not in the least. Are we going to New Delphi?"

Payne shook his head. "We can't leave Spice Grove without the chief's okay."

"Which we'd never get for this dog shit," Fish added.

I sighed. To tell the truth, I felt like crap on the carpet just then, but I tried not to let it show. "All right, I can solve your problem if you'll let me. Buses must run between Spice Grove and New Delphi. I saw several big passenger buses on the road when I traveled here from Owenbright by truck. Let me have creds enough for a bus ticket. If you'll do that, I'll go to New Delphi, retrieve the book, and bring it back to you."

My offer was refused, as I knew it would be. The refusal was followed by blows and burns, and a great many more questions, few of which I could answer in a way that satisfied my questioners.

Eventually, I was locked in a windowless room. It contained

a narrow bed and a mattress without sheets or blankets. There was a stinking bucket in a corner. I pulled off my shoes, lay down, and went to sleep as fast as I ever have in my life. Maybe you think that's impossible, but you have never been beaten or burned like I had been. I had nothing left. Hell, I had nothing left an hour before they quit.

I had a dream in there; I think it was just before I woke up. I was back in the stacks, and I pulled a book off a shelf and opened it. Arabella was in it and stepped from its pages as soon as I did. In real life, all her poetry books had been thin, but this was a thick, heavy book. I can still remember how heavy it felt. She kissed me, and we were on a beach. The little waves came up and washed our feet; and they were warm, really nice and warm. I put my arms around Arabella, and she was warm, too.

Then I reached out and got her book back and opened it again. She stepped back inside, and I shut it. The books were between palm trees, I think. In the shadows.

I got another book and opened that one, and Colette came out. She told me something I could not remember when I woke up, and I tried to make her go back into her book, but she kept struggling and struggling, sticking out arms and legs so I couldn't close it properly.

Then I woke up.

It was still dark in my little room, but it had been dark when they put me in there. I found the door and groped the wall beside it. There was a switch there, but no light came on when I touched it; so I sat still for a while and listened. Pretty soon I could hear the wind outside. It was really faint, but I could hear it. Twice, I think it was, I heard a refrigerator purr. It would go for thirty seconds, maybe, then stop and be quiet for a long time.

The way I figured it, it was probably after midnight. Payne and Fish had gone back to the station and punched out, or whatever it is policemen do. They were in bed with their wives now, and sound asleep. Probably they had told their wives what a tough day it had been.

And they figured I could not break down the door or break down a wall. After the beating I had suffered, I would probably just lie down and groan. That is what they thought.

The outside wall would be the best of all if I could get through it, but I found out pretty quick that it was really bad. It seemed like neocrete. The wall across from the bed felt rock-solid the first time I kicked it. By the fifth kick I was feeling it bow. Pretty soon it made funny noises every time. I felt around, and little chunks of grainy stuff were falling out and hitting the floor.

The back of that was some kind of wire net. That was the toughest thing in there. It had been stapled onto the ponticwood uprights, and my fingers were bleeding before I got it loose. Once it was down, I kicked a hole through the rest of the wall in half a minute or less.

The next room was as dark as mine, but I found another switch, and when I touched it what I saw was an ordinary bedroom with two windows and two beds, a bureau, and a dresser. Probably I should have scouted around in there for something useful, but I did not. I just wanted to get out, to get away from the house before the 'bot came or I set off some kind of alarm.

So out the door and down a little hallway and from there into the kitchen. That had a back door. I went out fast and circled around the house to get onto the street and started walking.

10

Road Trip

Let me say right off that when I got out I knew where I was going but at first I did not know why. It was the bus terminal, and as I walked, I figured it out. There were just two things I could do. I could go back to the library and tell the director how I had been mistreated. What would happen then, most likely, was the cops would send somebody new to take me out, probably a woman. She might say she was a cop, but probably not. Either way, I would have to go with her. It might not be as bad as before, but it might be worse, too.

The other way was for me to go overdue, find out who had Colette, and try to get her loose. Just thinking about that made me walk faster. As I saw it, that other way had a lot against it but a lot for it, too. Let me cover the against first.

It might get me killed. Murder is the most serious crime, and the people who do it are either pretty damned desperate or crazy; only killing me would not be murder, just destruction of property. They would probably have to pay for me; but maybe not, depending. None of which would help me one bit—I would be dead.

Here is the nasty one. I might get Colette killed. Back when the real me was still drinking coffee instead of kafe and writing mysteries, kidnappers did that sometimes. In a dirty way it made sense. The victim knew a lot about them by then, most likely. If they had to beat it, they would have to carry her with them, and she would be looking for help every chance she got. So smoke her.

Last one, and this one is easy. I might not be able to pull it off. Say they never got me, but I screwed up the whole thing. I would feel like shit and probably I would never get over it. I would doubt myself for the rest of my life, and I might even hate myself. I had never failed big-time up until now. Only I had never succeeded big-time either. Maybe I had been playing it safe, but what I really think is that I had never had a chance.

All right, this was it, my big chance. It was hero time.

So let's get on to the good stuff. If you have been paying attention, you have seen the first one coming already. I would feel great about myself. Sure, I would still be a reclone, but I would know I was every bit as good as the original. Maybe better.

Second, Colette would be safe. I have put that one second, but it had to be the main thing, the grand prize. Maybe she would think I shit ice cream and maybe she would not; but we had been friends, Colette and me, this lovely fully human woman and a reclone; and I was the reclone. Heck, fully humans can be friends with a cat or a dog, right? Cool, I was the cat. She had fed me and taken care of me and one time put her arms around me, and even told me how great I was and how glad she was she had checked me out. Now it was Puss in Boots time, and Colette was the Marquis of Carabas. If I was half as good as she thought I was, I could pull it off.

Third, it would get Payne and Fish off my back. They were like the drunk looking under the streetlight for his wallet because the light was better there. Colette had been kidnapped in Owenbright and they were Spice Grove cops and could not look around in Owenbright. All they could do was work in Spice Grove and hope that she was there or they could turn up something that would help the Owenbright cops and turn the heat off. If you asked me, it was more likely she was in Owenbright. Only then a hunch hit me, and it hit me hard: she was in New Delphi!

Had to be! No wonder I had known I had to get to the bus station.

I mean, look at it. What was all this about, really? A whole lot of money Colette's father had gotten from who knows where. Where was he when he did it? In New Delphi. That is where he and the family were living before he bought the big house outside town, and the big house was really in New Delphi, too. Where had the bad guys showed up first? In that big house outside New Delphi! That's where they had murdered Colette's brother. (All this is the way I was thinking then.) Where were the mystery rooms? In that same house, the big Coldbrook house in the country outside New Delphi!

So where was Colette now? Well, of course. Somewhere in New Delphi.

About then I caught sight of the bus terminal. I walked faster, you know I did, and the first thing I did when I got there was check on the next bus for New Delphi. There was a screen three

times the size of a bedsheet with the schedule; and there was a
'bot waiting beside it to answer questions. I told it I did not
necessarily want the next bus that would take me to New Delphi; what I wanted was the one that would get me there fastest.

"They are the same, sir, number one-oh-nine leaving at
five. That will be in two hours and thirty-four minutes precisely,
sir. I shall be delighted to vend you a ticket, if you wish."

I said how much and could I reserve a good seat, and all that
stuff. The answers were a lot, no, it was first come gets the seat,
five a.m. sharp and no waiting for anybody for any reason ever,
and a bunch more including the suggestion that I go into the
men's room and freshen up before time got tight. Which I did as
soon as I had my ticket, or anyway as much as I could. My face
was beat up and I had a cut under my left eye. Also my clothes
were a mess; in the men's room I did the best I could, which was
not a whole heck of a lot.

So I waited. There were screens spotted around the station
with shows on them, most of them pretty raunchy. I watched one
for a while, but that stuff is only interesting the first time you
see it. Here are things a guy can do if he can get her to hold still
for it. Here is what three women can do with one guy. (Try and
find them.) Two girls with three guys, only I had guessed most
of that one before it happened. After a while I wondered if the
people were reclones and started watching for that. Finally I decided the women were and the guys weren't. I don't really know, it
was just my guess, something about the way the women acted
and something else about the way the men did; and after that I
quit paying attention.

I do not think I really fell asleep, or anyway not completely;
but pretty soon my watch struck five and a lady driver was walking

around shaking shoulders and telling people that trip 109 was boarding. I got up and yawned, and then hustled over to the bus to claim a good seat because a bunch of other people were already getting on.

You will think that I am stretching it, but this is the stone truth. I got the best seat there was anyway. It was for one person, right behind the driver; and that one person business is why I got it. The ten or fifteen people who had gotten on before me were all couples or families, plus three guys who were traveling together. That seemed to be some kind of a sales crew, but I never did find out what they were selling.

For a minute or two I sat there looking back and forth between my watch and the bright red numbers changing on the dash. Both told me that five o'clock had come and gone, but the driver was still outside telling people. Twelve past five, and she got on and woke up her bus.

Fifteen after five, and it rose about half a meter and began to glide forward. As soon as it moved it said, "Trip one-oh-nine now departing for Rapid Rivers, Hapigarden, New Delphi, and Quinoafield. All abound! All abound! Don't be left!" I heard it because the doors were still open and there were speakers on the roof.

After that there were ten or twelve people yelling and trying to climb on. We were barely crawling there in the terminal, so most of them made it. Then when our bus was halfway out into the street, it had to wait for a break in traffic; and when it did the last ones got on, even the old couple that I had figured did not have a prayer. All right, I went over and grabbed the old lady's hands; her husband pushed her from in back, and the two of us were enough. So sue me.

Before I go any further, let me say that as soon as I had seen the other passengers I stopped feeling bad about my messed-up clothes. Some were clean and some were dirty, but even the clean ones were wearing cheap stuff, and a lot of it had been mended and patched and probably ought to have been thrown away. There was even one who looked like Payne and Fish had worked him over; if he had won his fight, the loser must have been a real mess. The world having a lot fewer people is supposed to mean that nobody's poor. Right. The politicians who peddle that stuff never rode 109.

Except for making a couple of friends I am not going to say a whole lot about the bus trip, what I saw and what I thought about it, because those things do not really have much of anything to do with the emeralds or cutting Colette loose from the guy that had taken her. Or anyway, not much of it does. We sailed on out of the city, gliding down an endless hill of air. Those ground cars and trucks we had to wait for before we could get out onto the street were the early birds, plus a few that had been up all night. There are always people working the night shift here and there. Nobody likes it, but there are certain things that have got to be done twenty-four seven. So somebody stays awake to watch the screens in the firehouse, or else they have a 'bot do it. Cops walk beats and ride around in ground cars and fly overhead in hover-craft. Burglars are night workers, too; and nurses go from bed to bed all night giving pills or shots to people who have trouble get-ting to sleep. We passed an all-night deli on our way out, and a bunch of businesses that were opening up or else getting ready to open.

Then we were out on the high road, with the turbine purr-ing and the wind whistling and the bus on autodrive. The close-packed buildings got smaller and smaller, and farther and farther apart. Most of them became houses, and there were evergreens and rosebushes. I will say this for our airbus, it went a lot faster and a lot smoother than the truck had on ten rubbery wheels.

In back of me, people were talking without making a whole lot of noise, and one man who must have been pretty close was singing softly, just singing to himself. *"Where has she gone, and why should I care? A woman's a snake, a woman's a snare; today it's a kiss, and come into my bed; tomorrow's a hiss, and you're better off dead. Where has she gone?"* It wasn't loud enough to bother anybody much, and I kind of liked it.

After a while I found out my armrest opened up. There were a pair of listening plugs in there, and the credits rolled for me as soon as I took them out. So I watched various shows for an hour or so, mostly a romantic comedy. One was a writer and one was an editor, only neither of them ever seemed to do any work. Pretty soon I caught on to the ending. The editor would confess he was really a woman in disguise and the writer would confess she was really a man in disguise. Did Shakespeare write one like that? If he did not, he should have—the girls in his plays are always pretending to be boys.

When it was over, I just looked out at the scenery. Silent woods and peaceful fields now. Old ruined towns, and starved-looking children in rags who just stood beside the road and stared. Once in a while you might see a 'bot doing some work, only not often. Pretty soon I went to sleep.

A little before noon we stopped at Rapid Rivers. Our driver got out to use the women's room and her bus told us we could get out, too, if we wanted to buy something to eat or view, or just to stretch our legs. I had missed dinner the night before. (When you check out a reclone, you're supposed to feed it if you keep it overnight. Right, please tell that to Payne and Fish.) Nothing in the morning while I waited for the bus either. I suppose I was too sleepy then to be hungry, or too tired, or hurting too much. Heck, the burns still hurt.

But I was about half starved. I had not had to use any of the money I had taken from Colette's shaping bag, but the other was nearly gone. Only I was hungry like I said, and I figured she would want me to use her money to bust her lose. Besides, she had checked me out and fed me while I was with her, so no harm. I got a bunnyburger and a big bag of air-fried peppers, two things I had heard a lot about but never eaten myself.

When you are as hungry as I was, everything tastes good, and after a while I decided bunnyburgers really were about half as good as people said they were, which was plenty. Various people had told me various things about air-fried peppers, some good, some bad. I had just decided I liked them when I happened to notice the woman sitting behind me. Her mouth was moving, then she licked her lips. Actually, I had not turned to look back at her. What I really saw was her reflection in a panel of notint that separated me from the driver.

Anyway, I turned halfway around in my seat and held out my bag of peppers. She smiled thanks and took a little handful, and the man with her said, "Thank you. May I have some, too?"

I said sure, so he took some. He was middle-sized and middle-aged, and looked kind of big without looking fat.

"You must excuse Mahala. She would thank you if she could. Unfortunately, she is mute."

"But grateful, as I saw." I really had not known what to say, but that came out. Things like that happen to me sometimes; I want to talk like everybody, but it comes out stiff and oh so formal. I try to pretend it is from being in the library all the time. Anyway, I was trying to look at the two of them without looking like I was doing it—you know what I mean.

"She understands everything we say, however. She is not un-intelligent."

I asked, "Can she write notes?"

"Yes." He smiled, and his smile made me feel about as sorry for him as I ever have for anybody. "She can indeed, but we haven't got a pen now, or paper. She used to have a tablet. . . ." He let that one trail away.

It seemed to me there had to be something we could do, but by then the bus was pulling out. I said, "I'm not sure what they carry in these stations, but I'll try to get something for her."

"And a few more peppers?" Smiling, he offered her the ones I had just given him; she took one and pushed the rest back.

"As I understand it, we've got another stop before New Delphi." I was thinking, and thinking hard.

He nodded. "Hapigarden. Mahala and I have never been there."

"I haven't either," I said. "Is that where you're going?"

He shook his head. "My name's Fevre, by the way. Georges Fevre." He spelled it. "The s really shouldn't be pronounced. Just call me George."

"Ern A. Smithe, and you can call me anything you want to. I'd shake hands, but mine's greasy."

"Mine, too." Georges ate a pepper. "For which I thank you from the bottom of my stomach."

We talked a little more after that, and I got Georges to spell Mahala's name for me. Only I am not going to give all that.

When it was over, I just turned around, watching the scenery and reminding myself to grab napkins next time if they had any. The reason I turned was that I wanted to ask Georges about a hundred questions, only it would not be polite. On top of that, he would feel like he could ask me a bunch of questions, too. Like where are you going? And why do you want to go there? And what happened to your face, Mr. Smithe?

Besides, I had the feeling that pretty soon he was going to figure out I was a reclone. They do not make us wear striped pants or orange shirts, or tattoo it across our foreheads; nothing like that. Only pretty soon most people seem to know.

So did I, for that matter.

When I first got to the Spice Grove Library I never had any trouble telling the librarians, the patrons, and the reclones apart. I just knew. And I had seen and heard enough of Georges to know that even if he was broke he was not dumb.

So I just looked out the window and kept my mouth shut. I would guess it took us another two hours, maybe a little less, to get to Hapigarden. Same drill as before: we would be there about fifteen minutes and you could get off if you wanted to. So I got off there; and so did Georges and Mahala, I think just to use the toilets. I looked around at the souvenir stuff they had in the station and found a little notepad and a pencil. I bought them, and a lady who worked there showed me where I could sharpen the pencil. It was smaller and a lot faster than the sharpeners I remembered but the same basic idea.

When I got back on the bus, the guy with the beat-up face

was sitting in my seat. My feeling has always been that it is best to start off polite. You can always get mean later if that is what it takes, but it is hard to go the other way. So I said, "Excuse me, but I was sitting there."

He would not look at me. "I'm sitting here now."

I said, "I know, and I'm asking you to leave and go back to where you were sitting before. Please."

I had expected him to smart off, but he did not. He just kept his head turned, looking straight ahead.

That gave me a free one at his right ear, and I took it. If notint were not tougher than glass, his head would have broken the window.

He turned around, I guess because he was going to get up; but my right got his nose and drove his head back into the window again. After that I shoved my thumbs into his eyes, but he never even yelled. It was the first time in either life I have ever knocked anybody cold, but that guy was out like a match. After that I pulled him out of my seat and kicked his head half a dozen times just because I felt like it.

When I got tired of kicking, I dragged him to the back of the bus and asked the people there where he had been sitting. Everybody who answered said they did not know; but there was an empty seat back there and I got him up onto it. When I turned around, the driver was standing up front and looking back at me. After a moment or two she decided the fight was over and there was no point in her getting involved. She sat back down in her seat, and the bus said, "Trip one-oh-nine will depart in five minutes. Trip one-oh-nine departing in five minutes sharp."

When I got back to my seat, I gave the notepad and pencil to

Mahala, and she wrote "THANK YOU!" in big letters on the first sheet.

Then Georges said, "We're getting off at New Delphi, Ern. We're going to miss you."

"Not as soon as you think," I told him. "I'm getting off there, too."

"No shit? Why, that's the best news I've had in a week! You live there?"

I just shook my head and turned so I faced forward, wishing the bus would get going. In back of me Mahala was clapping softly.

"We don't either. It's bigger than Spice Grove, or so I'm told."

I wanted to nod, and to turn around and ask him a few questions. It was hard not to, but I didn't.

Also I wanted to ask the driver at least one question, but there was a sign on the back of her seat warning that anyone who spoke to the driver while the bus was in motion would be put out.

That could have worked in my favor, if I had been quick enough to catch on to it. As it was, I just glimpsed the big Coldbrook house on a hilltop; then, before I caught on that fate had already handed me a way to stop the bus, it was gone.

"Please don't stand up while we're in motion." That was the driver.

I dropped back into my seat, thinking bitterly about the unfairness of a system that let her talk to me when I was not allowed to talk to her. That got me off on a hundred other things, like the ragged kids in those ruined towns, the old couple, and the guy with the beat-up face who had tried to take my seat; and when I looked up again, rain was pattering on the windshield.

"This is bad," Georges muttered behind me. I think he must have been looking past Mahala through the window at the rain.

I saw Mahala's reflection nod, and I turned to face them. "For me, too. I don't suppose you know anything about public transportation here."

"Nothing, really. Although . . ."

I waited.

"There's a—a place for distressed citizens here, or at least I've been told there is."

Mahala gripped his arm, squeezing hard.

"We're not going there. We have reasons for that." Georges stopped and cleared his throat. "I wouldn't mind telling you, but I'd rather not get into them in public." He was keeping his voice down.

I said, "Don't, in that case."

"My informant told me that they sometimes send out a van. You have an eephone, don't you?"

I shook my head.

"I thought everybody had them."

"In that case," I said, "you've got one yourself. Or you can borrow Mahala's."

"She couldn't speak into it."

I shrugged. "She could sign into it, and look things up."

Georges was quiet for a moment; then he whispered, "How did you know she could sign?"

"I didn't, but she seems intelligent and she can't speak."

"Keep your voice low, please."

I nodded.

Georges whispered, "Do you have a place to stay in New Delphi, Ern?"

I guess I'm not really strong on planning ahead. Anyway, I had been thinking how hard it might be to get a hotel room; and when he said that I realized how dumb it would be and dropped the whole idea. For a few seconds there, I was thinking as fast as I ever had in my life. Finally I said, "Can you drive, Georges?"

"Yes." He got out his wallet and handed it to me with a twisted grin. "Have a look, Ern. While you're doing it, check my license; but if you find any money in there, we'll divide it equally."

Of course there was no money at all. His picture and a retina scan were on the license, which would be valid for another twenty weeks. I returned his wallet.

"I'll look for work when we get there," he told me. "I can drive, so I might drive a cab. They can't all be self-programmed."

I don't believe I said anything then. I was thinking.

Georges said, "Sometimes people want a driver who can help them with their luggage and so on. Or I could drive a limousine."

"Wouldn't you need a commercial license?"

"They might be willing to overlook that, or help me get one."

"You're not going to the shelter."

He shook his head.

"Where will you spend the night, in that case?"

"In the bus station, if they'll let us."

I spoke to Mahala. "Can you cook?"

Surprised, she nodded.

We had turned off the high road and onto a broad street lined with office buildings and shops; it was raining harder than ever, beating down on the roof of the bus. "I think I can promise food and a place to sleep," I said. "I'll do that, and do whatever I can for you both as long as you do what I ask. What do you say?"

"That you're the answer to a prayer." Georges's smile was real. "I speak for both of us."

In the terminal, I found a 'bot who didn't seem to be busy. I explained that I needed the van from the shelter, and asked it to make the screen for me.

"From the New Delphi Rest for the Needy? It is coming already, sir. Just go outside and wait under the awning."

"Someone's already screened it?" I was surprised and I suppose it showed.

The 'bot said, "It meets all the buses, sir. There is always someone."

Georges and Mahala joined me after I had stood under the awning for five minutes or so. Mahala had written THEY WILL PUT ME AWAY on her pad. I read it and told her I would see to it that they did not.

Georges whispered, "We were hoping you'd stay in the station with us tonight." His voice was almost lost in the drumming of the rain.

I shook my head. "I promised you both I'd find you a better place to stay and get you some food. I will. Only I'm going to have to talk to the van's driver first. Trust me."

Georges did not say anything to that; I could see he was wondering whether he should. Mahala printed WE DO on her pad. I nodded and gave her a sick smile, worrying the whole time that the van would be self-programming or the driver would be a 'bot.

He was a human being, and he looked every bit as poor as Georges if not poorer. It was quite a relief. I got in, motioning for Georges and Mahala to stay right where they were. Smiling, I asked the driver, "Does this go to the shelter?"

The driver said, "To the New Delphi Rest for the Needy. Only we're about full up there." He hesitated. "They might take the lady. I dunno."

"If they're full, I'm surprised you came."

"For old people and kids. I'm supposed to bring those."

"Are you an employee of the Rest?" When he did not answer, I added, "Are you paid?"

"That's none of your business." The driver sounded tired.

"Actually, it is." I was reaching into my pocket. "How much do they pay you?"

"Why the hell do you care?"

"Since you won't tell me, I'll have to guess. You live there now, and you offered to drive for them. You have a license, so your offer was accepted. Because you drive for them, they let you stay, feed you, and perhaps supply some clothing."

For a moment he stared at me. "It's that obvious, huh?"

"It is to me, because I was in a similar situation for several years." I pulled out Colette's money, which had been folded up in a pants pocket, and peeled off a twenty-five. "This will be yours if you'll take us where we want to go."

He licked his lips. "Where's that?"

"The Coldbrook residence. I can't tell you how to get there, but I assume this van has guidance."

The driver nodded and pushed a button. "The Coldbrook house." He looked at me. "It's a house, not a flat?"

"Correct." I waved for Georges and Mahala to get in.

On the drive there, I thought hard, trying to make plans. There was nothing to see outside anyway, beyond the road and the rain. Georges would have resented it, I knew, if I had studied him the way I wanted to, or Mahala, or the two of them. Perhaps she would as well. From time to time I looked at them, though, and they were holding hands every time. Once they were looking at each other—staring into each other's eyes. I do not think any of the plans I made ever worked out. I was going to do this and do that; but things changed and changed, and in the end, they did not. Perhaps I ought to have slept. That might have been more productive.

A long drive between files of dripping trees led up to the house. There it branched, one branch looping, and the other leading off to the garage. We took the loop and stopped in front of the main entrance. There the three of us got out, and I gave the driver the twenty-five I had promised.

Mahala showed me her pad: YOUR HOME?

I shook my head. "Let's get out of this."

There was a small porch or covered stoop, almost absurd on that towering house. When we were there and so out of the rain, I told them, "I don't own this house or live here; it belongs to a friend of mine, but I have a card. She wouldn't mind our staying here for a few days, and simply by being here and looking around—observing whatever there is here to see—I may be able to find out what's happened to her. I may have to go into town as well."

Georges said, "She won't mind us, either?"

"When she learns you're helping me, I'm sure she won't." I stopped for a minute there, thinking about the ground cars in the garage, and maybe the house was bugged, and half a dozen other things. "If I go into town, you'll have to drive me."

The card I had taken from Colette's shaping bag was in the breast pocket of my jacket. I took it out and waved it at the front door, which swung noiselessly open.

Inside the house, I heard Colette speak, then scream.

11

A LONELY HOUSE
IN THE RAIN

We searched the house, naturally. Mahala wanted to go off on her own, but I had the gut feeling she would disappear and never come back. Maybe Georges felt the same way. He sided with me, telling her over and over that we ought to stay together. Which we did, first floor first, then second, then third, and by the fourth I saw it coming. Two doors were locked, and my card would not open either one of them. The door to what had clearly been Conrad Senior's office and laboratory was not locked.

Not so the others. Not either one of them. I tried to kick one open, and it was like kicking a neocrete wall. (I could tell because I had tried kicking a neocrete wall the night before.) Georges and I counted to three and hit it with our shoulders. Nothing. Naturally he wanted to know what was in there, and I had to tell him I did not have the faintest idea.

After that we tried the other one, and it was the same thing all over again. We might as well have been trying to break open the door of a bank vault. The door looked like ponticwood, but it was really something one hell of a lot stronger.

So we went downstairs and into the lounge and sat. We were all tired by then. I know I was tired enough to drop, and Mahala took her shoes off. Finally Georges said, "It's pretty clear what happened. They heard us when we came in. This girl you told us about screamed—"

"Colette Coldbrook."

"Thanks. She screamed and whoever it was who brought her here rushed her out the back door. It's a big house and we were at the wrong end of it to hear their ground car. You say the garage is off to one side."

I nodded.

"Well, that's where their ground car was. In the garage or parked in front of it. Didn't you say something about flitters?"

I dropped into a chair. "Yes. There were two in the hangar when I was here before. Colette and I came in hers. Presumably the other two belonged to her father and her brother."

"If the family had three flitters, there's a landing spot."

I nodded again. "Yes. There was."

"So whoever it is that's holding the girl may have a flitter, too. Maybe hers, maybe one of their own. If they do, they could be in Afasia before midnight."

Mahala showed me her tablet: IN HANGAR? When I had looked at it, she showed it to Georges.

I said, "She's right. They could be hiding in the hangar. Or in the barn or one of the other outbuildings. I know there's a barn and a greenhouse as well as the hangar. There's the garage, too; you just mentioned it. They could be in any one of those."

"Yeah, they could; but I think they've gone." Georges sounded stubborn.

"If they have, we can't possibly find them," I told him. "But if they haven't, we might. So I'm going to look. I'll check out the barn first. You two can stay in here and stay dry if you want."

Georges said, "I'm tempted to stay and try to force one of those metal doors upstairs. Pry it open, if I can find some sort of tool in that lab."

"So am I. Come with me while I look in the hangar and the rest, and I'll help you pry when we've searched them all."

"Later, maybe. All I really want to do is sit. No, go to bed. But you're going in alone to make trouble for a bunch of kidnappers? You'll be chopped meat."

It was still raining hard, and Georges and I ran as we went out the back door; then we saw something that stopped us dead. It was a ground car, parked in the rain at the back of the house. I tried to open a door, but it was locked. They were all locked. Georges told me that when you lock one, you lock them all. That was when Mahala caught up with us. I had thought she was not going to come; she may have thought the same thing.

We were soaked to the skin by the time we got into the barn, and in there we found something else that stopped us dead, just like the ground car had; only this time it was something I should have expected. So call me stupid; I had not. And just in case you would prefer not to, *should have* should not make a spoonful of difference. There were five 'bots sitting around in there, four grimy gardeners and a shiny little maid with a white lace cap and a lace apron.

"You are wet, sir," the maid 'bot told me. "Allow me to take your jacket."

I shook my head.

"I can hang it up in here, sir. This building is warm and dry. For the horses, sir, when the family had horses. When your jacket is dry, I will return it to you."

"Not now. There were intruders in the house. Did you know that? Any of you?"

They all said no.

"Our hostess, Colette Coldbrook, was there as well. You must have been aware of that."

The maid said, "I was, sir."

"They, and she, have left," I said. "You're a housemaid, I believe. What are you doing out here?"

"My mistress told me to wait here until I was summoned, sir."

Of course I wanted to know why, but she had no idea.

I told her, "We're your mistress's guests. We would like to contact her as soon as possible. Please keep that in mind, all of you. Will you do that?"

The gardeners said, "Yes," and the maid, "I will indeed, sir." That was when I caught on that it was more verbal than they were. With 'bots, verbal always means smarter.

"The intruders grabbed your mistress and made off with her," I told them. "There's a slim chance that they may be hiding in one of the outbuildings. I'm ordering you four"—I indicated the four gardeners—"to search all the buildings on the property except the house. We will be in the house. If you find the intruders, your mistress, or both, you are to screen the police immediately. Then come into the house and tell us. If you do not find them, you may return here. Is that clear?"

It was not and I had to do some explaining, but I am going to skip all that. When they understood, I told the maid 'bot to come with us.

When we had run through the rain and into the house through the back door, the maid offered to make us a simple supper. I had more questions for it by then, but I was too tired, too wet, and too hungry to turn a hot supper down. I said to go ahead, and to let us know as soon as the food was ready.

"I am not a chef, sir. I hope you are aware of my shortcomings. My software permits the preparation of simple meals only."

"Soup and sandwiches?"

"Yes, sir. Also certain salads and simple desserts. I believe we have the requisite ingredients here. Will those do?"

Nodding, Mahala gripped Georges's arm. He said, "Yes, for both of us."

When we had left the 'bot and gone into the sunroom, Georges asked, "Are we going to go upstairs and try to break in to those locked rooms?"

I shook my head, and fell into one of the chairs around the largest table.

Mahala looked a question.

I gestured to them both to get them to sit down. "There's maybe one chance in fifty that we could pry open one of those steel doors tonight," I told her. "After that, maybe one chance in twenty that they're actually in there. After that . . ."

She was printing on her pad, so I shut up and let her do it. When she held it up, it read: THE CAR?

I nodded. "The ground car would make it appear that they're still here, I agree. It seems pretty doubtful, but we can't write it off. That's why I instructed the gardener 'bots to search the garage, the greenhouse, and the rest. It may not be their ground car, however. If it is theirs, they may have left by some other means. It's possible they stole one of the flitters, for example. Or that another ground car came here to pick them up, and they abandoned the one we found because it was stolen. There are automatic cameras everywhere in every city, or so I understand. They image ground cars and check the images against reports of stolen vehicles."

Georges cleared his throat. "You've got to change their appearance in a way that will fool the screens that vet—"

He stopped talking because I had held up my hand. I said, "Before you go on, I'd better warn you." I was keeping my voice down. "There may be listening devices in this house. There may even be surveillance cameras. You were saying . . . ?"

"I . . . well, I used to know a ground car thief, and that's what he told me." Georges waited for some comment; when I had none, he said. "There are a lot of things you can do."

"I'm sure there are. I was going to finish by saying that if we could break through one of those doors tonight, which seems unlikely, and if they're in there, which seems terribly unlikely, I'd say we'd have about one chance in a thousand of getting Colette away from them. When I saw them in Colette's apartment—I don't think I've told you about that."

"You haven't," Georges said, "and I'd like to hear about it."

"Later, perhaps. The point I wished to make was that when I saw them they had guns, which they drew as soon as they had entered. Pistols or handguns, or whatever you call them."

"Missile pistols?"

I shrugged. "I don't know. I don't know much about modern weapons, I'm afraid."

"Were the muzzles belled, flared like the end of a trumpet?"

I tried to remember, to picture them. "Now that you mention it, I think perhaps they were. Slightly flared."

Georges leaned toward me. "Those were missile pistols. We civilians aren't supposed to have them, but some of us do. They're stolen from the military, or from the plants that make them."

I said, "I see." I knew it sounded dumb, and I sure felt dumb when I said it.

"When the missile's fired, it's traveling about three hundred meters a second. As soon as it leaves the muzzle, its own propellant starts burning, doubling or tripling its speed. When it hits you, it penetrates and explodes."

It was not easy to smile. "That sounds fatal."

"It is, in most cases. If you're wondering about the belled muzzles, the bell is to keep the hot gases from the burning propellant away from your hands."

Maybe I nodded. If I said anything else then, I do not remember what it was.

"You think our chances of getting this Colette away from the men who have taken her are a hundred to one. That's even if we find them."

"Yes, I suppose I do. I just said so."

"Assuming you really believe that, why are we looking for them?"

"Suppose they'd taken Mahala."

Georges clammed up for a while after that. Finally he said, "I see what you mean."

The maid 'bot announced supper, and we went into the dining room to get away from the drumming rain. The table was big enough for two football teams and a jury, but the three of us sat together at the end nearest the kitchen. I asked the maid 'bot to have a seat and answer a few questions for me.

"I would much prefer to stand, sir. I would not be comfortable sitting in the presence of humans."

I was tempted to tell it I was not one, but of course I could not do that without losing Georges and Mahala; either they would go, or Georges would start bossing me. So I told the 'bot it could stand if that was what it wanted to do, and asked who had bought it.

"Mr. Coldbrook, sir."

"There were two of them," I said. "Do you mean Conrad Coldbrook, Senior, or Conrad Coldbrook, Junior?"

"Mr. Coldbrook, Senior, sir. He purchased me shortly before Mr. Coldbrook, Junior's, death."

That jolted me. I shoved it back to think about later and said, "I'm surprised he didn't hire human servants—a human maid and a few human gardeners. I've been told that he preferred those."

"My programming cautions against repeating anything I merely overhear, sir. However, Mr. Coldbrook, Senior, is no more."

"That's correct." I made it as firm as I could. "He is dead, and I would like to know exactly what it was you overheard."

"Mr. Coldbrook, Senior, told Ms. Coldbrook that we did not gossip or pry, sir. He was quite correct. We do not."

Georges asked, "What was it he was afraid you'd gossip about?"

"Nothing, sir. He knew I did not gossip."

I tried, "Suppose that he had told you not to speak of something. What would that topic be?"

"There was no topic about which I had been told not to speak, sir."

"That's good. There's nothing you know that you will not tell us. Is that correct?"

"Yes, sir, it is. Upon what topics do you wish to be informed, sir?"

"Did you ever hear Mr. Coldbrook, Senior, instruct anyone else to be silent upon a certain topic?"

"Yes, sir, I did."

"Good. What was the topic, and whom did he caution not to speak of it?"

"The topic was the death of Mr. Coldbrook, Junior, sir. Mr. Coldbrook, Senior, cautioned Ms. Coldbrook not to speak of it."

"Yet you yourself were not so cautioned, or so you said. Is that correct?"

"Yes, sir, it is. Your soup is getting cold, sir, if I may be so bold."

I nodded and sipped a spoonful. "Very good."

"Thank you, sir."

"What do you know concerning Mr. Coldbrook, Junior's, death? He died in the front hall, didn't he? That's what I've been told."

"I believe that is correct, sir."

"Did you see his body?"

"Yes, sir. I did, sir."

"Had he been strangled?"

"I couldn't say, sir. I have been given no medical programming, sir."

Georges asked, "Was he bleeding?"

"No, sir, I believe not. If I may speak, sir?"

I said, "Go right ahead."

"After Mr. Coldbrook, Junior's, body had been removed, I cleaned the floor, sir. I waxed and polished it as well, sir. I saw no trace of blood, sir."

I sipped more soup. "If there was no blood, why did you clean, wax, and polish the floor?"

"Mr. Coldbrook, Senior, told me to, sir."

"I see. Had Mr. Coldbrook, Junior's, traveling bag been searched?"

"I don't know, sir."

"Was it open? Were its contents scattered over the floor?"

"Yes, sir."

"You picked them up?"

"No, sir."

"Why didn't you? It would seem to me the natural thing for you to do."

"I agree, sir. But I did not, sir. I thought it best to inform Mr. Coldbrook, Senior, first, sir."

"What did you tell him? Your exact words, please."

"I said, 'Your son has come home and is lying in the front hall, sir. I believe, sir, that something may be amiss.'"

"Did he go to look?"

"Yes, sir, he did."

"And afterward?"

"He had me summon an ambulance, sir."

"Eventually someone must have screened the police. Do you know who that was?"

"Not specifically, sir. It was one of the medtechs, sir. If I may make a request, sir?"

"Certainly," I said. I had the feeling it might ask for a little time off, but I knew 'bots never do that. "What is it?"

"The soup remains upon the stove, sir. In a thermery pod, sir. If no one would care for more, I must attend to it, sir."

Georges said, "I would like some more."

"Shall I leave this gentleman to serve you, sir?"

Georges looked his question at me, and I told the 'bot to go ahead.

As soon as it had gone, I asked Mahala whether she was familiar with screens. She nodded energetically.

Georges said, "She's really very good. Much better than I am."

I gestured. "There's a screen over there, Mahala. Would you please go over and search for a company called Merciful Maids? I don't know whether it's local or worldwide."

I watched the screen while I ate my sandwich. Mahala tried eight or ten approaches. Maybe more. Finally she cleared the screen, which announced, "No such company," in a pleasant, feminine voice.

"Then here's another one. This is strictly local. Look here in New Delphi for a lady named Bettina Johns, please."

That took about as long as it took me to bite, chew, and swallow. Mahala turned around and pointed to the screen. I said, "See if you can get her, will you? I'd like to speak to her."

Mahala nodded. That one took longer, maybe half a minute before she rose, clapped to get my attention, and motioned for me to sit down there.

"My name's Smithe," I said, as soon as Bettina Johns had said hello. "You're a friend of Colette Coldbrook's aren't you? She said you were."

"I certainly am. How is she?" Bettina Johns was blond and attractive, about Colette's age.

"I don't know. To tell you the truth, I'm looking for her. I'm a friend of hers, too, and she was well the last time I saw her. I have to ask you a question, but I don't want you to think I'm prying. I'm not—I'm just trying to locate Colette. Did you recommend a company called Merciful Maids to her?"

Bettina Johns shook her head. "I never heard of it."

"Anything like that?"

"I don't think so. What was this for?"

"To clean up the house, following her brother's death."

"No . . . they had servants for that. After Colette's mother died, I mean. A housekeeper, maids, a cook, and so forth. I don't know how many."

I may have said something in reply. I do not know. Maybe I just froze; anyway, I stood up and Mahala sat down again, her fingers blurring as they danced over the keys. On Bettina Johns's side one of the sweetest female voices I have ever heard said, "Mr. Smithe and I thank you very, very much, Ms. Johns. You've been wonderfully helpful."

Bettina Johns said, "You have a simply marvelous secretary, Mr. Smithe," and the screen went blank.

I must have looked ready for the meat wagon, because Georges said, "She can do that on a screen. You probably know about voice recognition. You just talk to the screen and never touch the keyboard. This is like that, only it goes the other way."

I said, "I suppose it gives you a lot of voices to choose from."

Georges nodded. "I'm not sure how many. Dozens."

Mahala held up her pad: 500.

The third floor was just about all guest rooms, each with its own bathroom. I took a small one with a screen and a door that locked. Georges and Mahala took another one, a lot bigger, with a big bed. Probably their door locked, too. I never found out. As soon as they'd gone inside I went into my own room, locked the door, and sat down at the screen.

The way I figured it, there would be about a million guys named Georges Fevre, but most of them would be in la République. There would not be a whole lot of people named Mahala anywhere, since I had never even heard that name until Georges introduced me to this one. Also I had the feeling that Georges might be really interesting, but Mahala was sure to be.

That last was right. Her last name was Levy, and she had been institutionalized because of what the screen called incurable hysterical paralysis of allocution, but she had escaped. There was a small reward. I knew already that people who had really serious stuff wrong with them, like they were blind and could not be fixed, were tucked away out of sight so they would not ruin the view for the healthy and practically perfect fully humans; but I had figured that was okay. They could not see people and now people could not see them. Only now I knew one—heck, I liked her—and it was not something I could just let go of and not think about.

So I thought, and one of the things I came up with was that nobody on the bus knew except me, and nobody in the bus station here, and nobody in the van. She just seemed like somebody's wife or girlfriend who kept quiet and let her man do all the talking when they were out in public. Maybe you think that is okay and maybe you hate it like poison, but either way there is one hell of a lot of it and nobody notices much.

Another thing was that it explained something about Georges. He was a decent-looking guy and no dummy. Maybe he had no degree and maybe he had two or three, but either way he was a guy who could have landed a good job without much trouble. Only here he was, on the road with his lady, when it sure seemed like neither one of them had a scrap of money.

By that time I wanted to crawl into the sack so bad I could taste it, but I looked for Georges anyhow. There were two reasons for that. The first one was that I like to finish what I start. The second was that I knew I ought to take a bath before I turned in, but my body was arguing against it, and hard. I wanted to show it once and for all who was boss. So I did.

Like I had expected, there were more than a hundred Georges Fevres, but most of them were in France. Here, there were only four. One was three years past a hundred, one looked fat and worked in a winery, and one was twelve. I figured the fourth one had to be mine, but it was not. That last Georges Fevre was a left-handed pitcher, twenty-eight, and he had gotten both legs broken trying to pull off some fool stunt.

So no. Whatever my guy's real name was, Georges Fevre was not it. So maybe George F—? There would be hundreds of those, maybe thousands. I played around with it anyway, and what he was doing before. Suppose I just saw him coming down the street? Executive? Lawyer? Both wrong, but—cop! How about George Franklin, police?

Bang! There he was, good picture, full face, uniform, bars on his shoulders. Captain George G. Franklin of the High Plains

Police. Found not guilty but dismissed from the force anyhow. Divorced shortly afterward. Present address unknown.

I took my bath, darned near fell asleep in the sauna, and went to bed. I ought to say here what time it was by then, but I do not remember.

12

Behind Locked Doors

When I woke up I knew what I had to do. The room I had taken was not a corner room; but the one next to it was, and Georges (I kept calling him that because the way I saw it using his real one would be a double-cross) and Mahala were in another one across the hall. I washed up a little and got some clothes on, went into the empty one, opened a window, and took off my shoes and socks.

The rain had stopped. The sky was still sullen with clouds, but the window ledge I climbed out onto was almost dry. For a minute I wondered whether Conrad, Junior, had stood on a dry sill, and whether it had been this one. Then I stood up on my toes, got hold of the ledge above, and pulled myself up. He had not been all that much taller than I am, so it had been just about as hard for him as it was for me. Or anyhow, I kept telling myself that until I got one foot on the ledge above and was able to bring up the other and stand on that ledge.

Here let me stop and explain a couple of things. It was dangerous, sure it was; but it was not as dangerous as it sounds. If I had fallen I would have landed on the roof of the second floor, not on the ground. That would have shortened my fall quite a bit.

And the reason Junior had picked a corner room was that the third-floor corner room windows had fourth-floor windows directly above them. I had figured that one out the first time, when Colette and I had been there. The other third-floor windows did not. The third floor had a lot of windows; the fourth not nearly as many.

If the fourth-floor window I had climbed up to had been locked, I could probably have swung myself around the corner to another one, but I did not have to. Notint in a self-lubricating polymer frame works a lot better than the glass-in-wood windows we had. This one slid up smoothly as soon as I pushed. Climbing inside was a cinch.

It was a pretty small room and so full of equipment that for a minute I thought that was all there was. Then I saw a radiation sign and realized that the big round thing was a reactor. I had seen a micro pile once (which is what people generally call itty-bitty reactors) in the basement of the library, but that reactor had been one hell of a lot smaller than this one. My hands started to tremble; I had to wait until they calmed down a little (call it a quarter of an hour). Once they did, I got out of there fast and started working my way along the ledge until I got to a window I could see was not to the reactor room. I think that one must have been the one Junior had looked into. Maybe he opened it and stuck his head through, too. I do not know, but it makes sense.

Looking in, you did not see a room at all. You were seeing into a jungle or maybe some kind of greenhouse. At least that is what it looked like, a dark green jungle standing on edge. After a minute or two, I noticed a darker hole a little below the middle. At first I had not seen it because there were leaves and leafy branches and even some big flowers in the way. But behind them was this black hole. Back then, I figured it was probably the den of some animal.

Maybe Conrad, Junior's, window did not open. Maybe it did. I don't know. This one had, just about like the last one. It took me a long five minutes to get my nerve up to go in. I was standing there with my feet on a kind of shelf about as wide as my hand that sloped, barely holding on by my fingernails and breathing that air—warm, magical air full of water. It was like you had your nose in the groin of a flower, but I was not half as scared of falling off as I was of going in there.

You know what did it for me? If you were to guess, I doubt you would get it in a year. I finally looked off to my left, and there was a door there. Nothing special, just a door that looked like regular ponticwood standing there in the jungle all by itself. No wall on either side, no floor under it. Just that door.

When I saw the door, I climbed inside. There was a wrench, like you might feel on a really rough carnival ride. It felt like my guts were being stirred up with a spoon (or maybe somebody's fingers), and my brain was rolling over.

I fell on flowers, big leaves, and wet dirt. It was like falling into a flower bed that had just been watered, except that I was retching and gagging like I was going to turn inside out and there were little critters in among the plants that scampered off too fast for me to get a good look at them.

When I finally got up, I still felt sick and my head still hurt, but nothing was half as bad as it had been. I looked around for

the window I had fallen from, but I could not even see it. I felt
for it, too, but there was nothing there. I was in this new, hot, wet,
growing place; and there was nothing there that was even the
tiniest bit familiar except that door. It was still right there, and
it still looked exactly like ponticwood, just like it had before.

So I walked over to it, stepping carefully and so shaken up that
I thought I might fall any minute. When I started I was plan-
ning to knock, then I decided that might be a truly bad idea.
So I just pushed down the handle and pulled.

It should have fallen over on me, and to tell the truth I had
my free hand up to catch it. Only what I really thought was that
it would swing toward me like any other door, and that is exactly what it did. It moved slowly because it was so heavy, but I
had expected that.

What I saw then was what I expected, too. It was the fourth-
floor landing, with the stairs coming up, and the lift tube doors,
and the other doors, one to the room where the reactor was, and
the other one to what had been Conrad, Senior's, office and lab.
I knew that if I stepped out and shut that door, I would have to
climb through windows if I wanted to get in there again; I was
about to try to figure out how to reset the door so it would not
lock when a new thought hit me, and it hit me hard.

If I did it, it would mean that anybody else who came up here
and tried that door could just open it and walk into the jungle.
As if that was not bad enough, he might even leave the door
standing open behind him, probably because he would be afraid
it might lock if he closed it.

That would mean that anything in that jungle could get out
and come right down the stairs even if it did not know about
tube lifts. No sweat, just walk through the doorway. Animals

would be bad. Bugs might be a lot worse. So I did not reset the door. I just walked out onto the landing and shut it good and tight behind me, which took a good hard pull. I tried it, too, bearing down on the handle and shaking it. It was locked as solidly as ever, a thick, probably steel door that somebody who knew what he was doing had painted to look just like stained and varnished ponticwood. By that time I was breathing Earth's air again and glorying in it. It was the same air that I had been breathing ever since the day I had been pulled out of the incubator, air that knew warm golden light, birds' wings, and good cooking. The air of home. I got into the lift tube.

When its doors clanked open, I was about to go back into the room I had slept in, but I got stopped. It was Georges. "Ah! There you are, Mr. Smithe. Mahala's in the kitchen helping the 'bot make breakfast, and I've been looking around for you."

Thinking fast I said, "I'm afraid I haven't shaved. If you'll excuse me, I'll join you as soon as I shave. You're in the dining room?"

"No, no! In the sunroom, where all the pictures are. Just take this lift tube—"

"I know where it is."

"Hurry up before your breakfast gets cold. Mahala, well, she gets angry."

"I'll shave as fast as I can," I promised. Which I did, ducking into the corner room to put my socks and shoes back on, then taking the lift tube to the second floor and finding a bedroom that must have been Junior's, with a shaver on the basin counter and almost a dozen nice clean shirts hanging in a closet; these were the usual thing, all colors, with a deep V-neck and no buttons. I picked a blue one with green sleeves.

Georges and Mahala were sitting down and eating when I came in, but Mahala did not look angry. She just smiled and pointed to all the food. There was a beautiful fruit salad, a platter with a big pile of bacon and another with a big pile of sausages, plus scones and clotted cream to spread on them. When I said, "This is a feast!" she gave me a happy grin.

Georges said, "The 'bot will make you an omelet, too, if you want one. They're quite good." He was eating one himself.

I told him this was more than enough to satisfy me, and helped myself to a little of everything, beginning with fruit salad and ending with bacon.

"So what have you been up to?"

"Not much." I could not help smiling.

"You were outside your room without shoes? I'll bet you thought I didn't notice. If you were listening in on Mahala and the 'bot, you can't have heard much."

Mahala giggled.

"I wasn't." I tried to make it light.

"I didn't think so." Georges was having none of that. "What was it?"

I chewed and swallowed a bite of fresh pineapple. "I've been trying to decide how much to tell you."

"Meaning that you're not going to tell us everything?"

I had made up my mind. "You wouldn't believe me if I told you everything, so we're going to leave it at this: I have been exploring the house."

"But you're not going to tell us what you found?" Georges raised an eyebrow.

"That's right, because I want to show you and not spoil it in advance." I stood up and picked up my plate. "Besides, you wouldn't believe me."

"Try me."

"I won't, but I can show you something good right now. See that table out on the patio? What do you say we eat out there? Yesterday the rain kept us inside all day. I don't know about you and Mahala, but I'd like to go out and get a breath of fresh air."

It took a few seconds for Georges to nod; but he did, and when he looked at Mahala and touched his ear I knew that he was all over it. We took our cups and plates out and told the maid 'bot to carry out the rest of the food. Then Georges said, "This ought to be safe. Going to tell us about it now?"

"Absolutely not. In order to be believed, I've got to take you both into those rooms. How much do you know about electronics?"

He shook his head. "Very little, actually."

"Small nuclear reactors?"

"Enough to build one, maybe. Not enough to improve what we've apparently got."

That came as a surprise, and I had to take a moment to digest it. "You could run one? Operate it?"

He nodded. "And make simple repairs. That was what I did when I got out of the university. I fixed them. It was interesting for the first year or so, then I got bored with it. Eventually I quit and went to—what do you want to know?"

"I want to show you one, and get you to tell me a little about it. Teach me." I smiled. "Just a quick course."

"I'll be happy to. They're very safe, really. There are all sorts of safety devices built into them to prevent them from overheating."

"It won't explode?"

"Not the way you're thinking. Not if it's a standard model—they're not bombs. When a commercial reactor goes out of control, it overheats and there's a steam explosion. No mushroom cloud and nothing like the power of a nuclear bomb." Georges paused. "I see I've lost you."

"I'm afraid you're quite correct. I didn't know about the steam."

Georges sipped iced kafe. "Something like ninety-seven percent of all reactors power generators. They heat water in a sealed system, and the steam drives a turbine. Clear?"

"I think so."

"When one goes out of control—somebody's got to disable several safety devices for this to happen—it heats up, getting hotter and hotter. Steam pressure builds. There's a relief valve, of course, but for an explosion we've got to assume that valve's failed somehow. Meantime, the boiler's weakened by all that heat coming off the reactor, so you get a steam explosion. I've never seen this happen, you understand. Only seen film."

"No nuclear explosion?"

"Right. If you're lucky, the steam explosion wrecks the reactor so that it quits overheating. If you're not, it continues to heat up. That starts fires and melts steel, everything collapses, and inside the collapse you've got a loose collection of radioactive material. Dangerous but not catastrophic."

My mind was so full of thoughts that I wanted to stand up and pace.

Georges grinned. "Want to show me what's got you so interested, Mr. Smithe?"

"I do, only not now." I took a deep breath. "There are two things we absolutely have to find. You can guess the first pretty easily."

"No, I can't. Not unless you mean the woman who owns this house."

"Two things we have to find before we can find her. The first one is a card that will open those doors. Imagine yourself in the place of Colette's father—of Conrad Coldbrook, Senior. You've put something, or found something, enormously valuable behind one of those doors. Would you have just one card for it?"

"Wait up! Are you saying you've been in there without a card?"

I nodded. "What about that second card? Would you do without one?"

Georges considered. "I might, but probably not."

"Why not?"

"All right, I might lose one, or one might quit working. Quit if I got it near a strong magnetic field, for example. I've told you I don't know a lot about electronics, and I don't. But a friend who did told me once that would wipe a card. It's what hotels do. Do you know about that?"

"No. Please tell me."

"They give you a card when you rent a room, and they like to get it back when you check out. If they do, they wipe it. They send a signal that recodes the door, and they can recode your card to whatever room they want. A strong field wipes, a varying field recodes. They don't need a backup card because they can code any card they've wiped to open that door. In general, a private person had better have a spare."

I thanked him.

"Wait up. I said the father probably wouldn't do that. I said it because I've seen his lab. My guess is that he coded his card himself, and some screen will have a record of the coding. If his card were wiped or lost, he could code another. Or maybe he could wipe the doors and recode them, then code himself a new card, like the hotels. That way, if somebody found his old card, it wouldn't work."

I sighed. "This morning we're going to search the house for a couple of things. One is the spare card, if it exists. Colette's father probably had a card on him when he died. If he did, she will have gotten it and the people who took her will have it now. The second is a weapon, or weapons. Her father must have had some, and we may need them. We'll take missile pistols or ordinary pistols, and hunting weapons might be even better. Anything that we can find."

Mahala held up her pad: BIG HOUSE.

I nodded. "It is. I've been thinking about that, and it seems to me Colette's father would hide things—we'll assume that he had things to hide—in one of three places, places nobody else was likely to spend much time in. I'd like you to take the laboratory upstairs, Mahala; I'll show you where it is. I searched it superficially when I was here with Colette, but I found nothing. Will you look? A card or weapons. Possibly the coding for a card, or a means to code cards."

She stood up and gestured. Georges said, "Do you want her to go now?"

"No. She should know where you and I are. I'd like you to look for the master bedroom. It's probably on the ground floor, but it could be on the second. Will you do that, and search it thoroughly?"

He nodded.

"I'll be searching the library. That's on the ground floor on the other side of the house." I pointed. "This patio is on the south side, and that's where the sunroom is. The library's on the other side, the north side. It doesn't seem likely that he'd hide weapons in there, but it's possible. Behind the books and disks, under the floor, or whatever. On the other hand, it would be the perfect place to hide a card, or that's how it seems to me."

"Hollowing out a book is an old, old trick." Georges rose. "You just cut the center out of a lot of pages. If it's a big book you might easily put a missile pistol in there. Are you sure he had physical books? You don't see those much anymore."

I stood, too. "Colette told me once that all the books in the library had been pulled off their shelves. That may not actually have happened, and to tell the truth I don't believe it did. But I don't think she'd have said it unless it was possible to do it." I said "to tell the truth," only I was not; not the whole truth, which was that I had been in the library and seen her father's books when Colette and I had come.

Now I went back, and I must have pulled down thirty or forty books before it hit me. At first I was mad at myself for being so stupid, but after that I had to laugh. Right! That second card *was* hidden in the library, exactly like I had thought it might be. Only I was the one who had hidden it there.

Toward the back of the room, there was a freestanding bookcase a little more than half full of books with plastic bindings. I went to it and pulled out *Murder on Mars*.

What I wanted next might be in the kitchen or it might not. I went back there wanting to ask the 'bot, but it was off somewhere. So I poked around in the cabinets and eventually found what I wanted in the broom closet, small but powerful and, according to a built-in meter, all charged up and ready to go. After trying it out to make sure it worked, I dropped it into a pocket.

Georges was making enough noise that I had no trouble find-ing him and the master bedroom. He looked at me as I came in and said, "Nothing."

I motioned for him to follow me and led him to the lift tube. Up in the fourth-floor lab, I asked Mahala to do me a favor, if she could. "Find a site where people advertise for domestics. Make it a blind ad with a box number, if you can. We want an expe-rienced housekeeper, and we want to see references. Salary negotiable. Can you do that?"

She gave me a confident nod and handed me a sheaf of pa-pers before she went to the screen. I read the first two or three, riffled through the rest—there were a dozen or so—saw they were all pretty much alike, and put them in my pocket.

Georges had found a spare chair. "You don't want to talk."

"You're right. Right now I've got too much to think about." I had started pacing up and down, passing the book from hand to hand.

"Fine. I'll leave you alone."

It took me two or three minutes, but I finally got it. Colette had mentioned emeralds when she told me about her brother bringing her the book.

Mahala stood and pointed to the screen.

Georges said, "She means she's done. I doubt you'll get any answers today. Tomorrow there might be some. Want to tell me why you want to hire a housekeeper?"

I said, "No," and motioned for both of them to come with me.

Let me admit right here that what I was doing was dumb. If I had good sense I would have gone up there alone first and tried it out before I got Georges and Mahala; the trouble was that I had felt certain I had the whole works figured out. But by the time I stood in front of that door holding *Murder on Mars*, I was trying to think of what I would say when the door would not open.

First the back. Something clicked, but the door would not open. Then the spine, which got me nothing. Then the front cover.

That brought another soft click, but I could not be sure I had not imagined it. I felt like throwing myself against that steel door hard enough to break my shoulder, but I shoved down the handle and gave the door a good hard push instead.

It swung back, and I walked in and took a deep breath; the wrench was still bad enough to make me feel sick, but I guess I was a little bit used to it by then. I filled my lungs with that air, and wow! Home was good, sure it was—but this was magic and I could have floated away. I had not motioned for Georges and Mahala to follow; I knew what I was going to do if they did and what I was going to do if they did not. I had both those all worked out, and the book had done the trick, and I was on cloud nine.

Behind me, one of them gasped. I still have no idea which it was. I turned around to see whether both of them had come in, and told Georges to shut the door.

"You're going to want to have a look around," I told them. "Do it, but don't go so far you get lost. I'm going to climb that rock face. Maybe I can spot a good place for us to talk."

Although climbing was easier than it would have been on Earth, I climbed slowly, stopping pretty often to look around. Also, I was trying to spare Junior's shirt and wondering if his pants would fit me. Whether his shoes would, as far as that was concerned. There had been six or eight pairs in his closet.

After ten or fifteen minutes, I reached that dark hole in the rocks I had noticed before. I took a good look at it, and one of the first things I noticed was that you did not have to climb like I had to get to it. There was a steep little path off to one side. Another was there were no bones or anything like that around the entrance. Sure, it still might have been the den of some animal, but now that seemed less likely.

When I got back down as far as the hole, I took the path the rest of the way. Maybe Georges or Mahala noticed; I do not know.

If Georges had, he did not say anything about it, just asked what I'd seen.

"Over that way," I pointed, "I could catch glimpses of what looked like water and some white stuff that might be a beach. Let's go over and have a look."

He nodded, grinning. "Good news! There's water here. Wherever 'here' is."

"There has to be." I pointed again, up this time. "That's a blue sky. Must I tell you what makes the sky blue?"

Mahala giggled, and Georges said, "Water vapor, isn't it?"

"Correct." I started walking. "On Mars the sky's red with dust. There's water on Mars, but not much—or anyway not much left. Probably it would be better to say it like that. Earth still has a great deal, because Earth has more gravity." I have already said how I feel about the way I have to talk, and I felt that way more than ever just then. I said, "Do I sound like a professor?"

Behind me, Georges said, "You sure do. I was starting to wonder if you really were one."

"I'm not, and I wish to God I could learn how to stop sounding like one. We're on an alien planet, an Earth-type planet of another star system. Had you already figured that out?"

"I wasn't sure." After a moment Georges added, "You know, I feel lighter here."

"In the book—Did I leave that behind? How stupid can I be?"

Georges said, "Mahala picked it up," and she tapped my shoulder and handed it to me.

I thanked her. "I remember now—I laid it down to climb the rocks. Maybe we should leave it behind, in the house somewhere."

"That house can't have a door that opens on another planet." I heard Georges gulp. "Much less on a planet in another system."

"It does," I told him. "It will have as long as the circuitry that connects our world with this one runs. Now where should we hold our meeting?" We had reached a rocky beach.

After a couple of false starts, Georges and Mahala sat side by side on a driftwood log and I rolled another into position and sat down on that. "First question, and this is an important one. While you were searching, did either one of you find a camera or a listening device, or anything that might be one?"

Mahala shook her head. Georges said, "No. Nothing. How about you, Mr. Smithe?"

It had been no dice for me, too, and I told them so. "The people who kidnapped Colette brought her here. I know that, because I know it was she whom we heard speak, then scream, when I opened the door. While she was here, she may have left some sort of note—some clue that might tell us where they were taking her. Did you find anything like that?"

Mahala shook her head again. Georges said, "It seems to me they did, if they left that ground car. There could be a note in the ground car, and there ought to be things that will tell us where it came from. The license plate, registration card, and so forth."

"You're right. As soon as we get back to the house, we'll look; but while we're here I want to tell you about this." I held the book up. "Colette had it when I met her. She told me it was found in her father's safe when it was opened after his death. She said it was the only thing in there."

Georges said, "But you're not sure she was telling you the truth?"

"Correct, I'm not. Perhaps you can imagine yourself opening a safe that belonged to your late father. Might you not find things either too important or too personal to reveal to a new acquaintance?"

They nodded, Mahala reluctantly.

"One of the things I want to do while we're in New Delphi is to find the person who opened that safe for her and ask him or her what was in it when it was opened. A screen ought to give us a city directory. We'll talk to all the locksmiths listed. With luck, we may locate the right person."

Georges said, "You want to talk to a housekeeper, too—or do you really want to hire one?"

I shook my head. "I want to talk to the one who used to work here. After Mrs. Coldbrook died, her husband hired several human servants. I haven't been able to find out just how many there were, but it would appear there were at least three. My guess is that they had a cook, a maid, and a housekeeper." I waited for Georges to speak, wondering how much ultraviolet there was in the white sunlight, and grateful for the steady breeze that ruffled the glowing sapphire waves.

"You think the housekeeper will know something that may help you."

"Correct. It might be any servant, of course. But a housekeeper is apt to know more than a maid or a cook—or so I imagine. Almost certainly, a housekeeper will know who fired her."

Georges shrugged. "I can't see how that'll help you."

"It may help me learn who's taken Colette; if I knew that, I'd have a better chance of guessing where they've taken her. I hope so, at least. Have you anything more valuable to suggest? Believe me, I'll listen; and if we can do both, we'll do both."

"I'll work on it."

"Good. Here's my next question. I'm going by what Colette told me about her father, Conrad Coldbrook, Senior. She called him brilliant and a minor executive. He held executive positions, apparently, in several different companies here, not keeping any of those positions for more than one or two years. I don't know whether he was fired or quit."

Georges nodded.

"Then he stopped working for other people. He began publishing a financial news bulletin—a tip sheet. I don't know much about those, but apparently their readers pay a good deal of money to receive them."

Georges nodded again. "A couple of hundred at least. Sometimes a thousand or more. Whether they're worth the money . . ." He shrugged. "You tell me."

"I can't. All I know is that Colette told me he had thousands of subscribers, and it sounded as though they brought him a considerable amount of money every year." I paused to think. "Electronic publication, of course, so his costs must have been next to nothing."

"Well, look at it. Say five hundred a year, and we'll be conservative and say he had two thousand subscribers. That's half a million coming in every year. A year of that would set you, or Mahala and me, up for life."

I was thinking. "I wish I knew whether he quit those jobs or resigned."

"Pretty often they call a guy in and tell him they're letting him quit, but if he doesn't they're going to fire him. Naturally he quits, and that muddies the water—you know what I mean?"

"I do, and I wish that I could talk to a few of the people who worked with him."

Mahala raised her hand, and Georges said, "She thinks she can locate some for you. Want her to try?"

"Yes, indeed! Please do, Mahala." I stopped again to think. "I've never seen one of these expensive financial news bulletins, Georges, but you seem to know quite a bit about them."

"I used to subscribe to a couple. This was back when."

"I won't ask when that was. Wouldn't it take years to build up a substantial list of subscribers? I'm asking because from what Colette said, her father appears to have done it quickly."

"Depends. Say that the guy putting it out was a financial journalist who'd been reporting two or three nights a week on some news show. If he'd made right-on predictions there, he might get eight or ten thousand subscribers for his first bulletin."

"What if he himself had made profitable investments?"

"If he was a big investor—we're talking millions—sure. If he had the rep, that would do it. Want to tell me what's up?"

I shook my head. "It's still too nebulous. I think I'm getting closer, but . . . no. Not yet, and perhaps not ever. I'm about finished. Have you got anything we need to talk about?"

"Mahala wasn't through in the lab, and now she's going to be looking for the father's old pals from work. I've about finished searching the master bedroom. I'd like to suggest we check out the mysterious ground car as soon as we get back to the house. Are we still hoping to find a few guns?"

"Yes. For listening devices, cards, and weapons, in that order. Have you noticed the trees over there? On the horizon?"

Georges hadn't. He stood up to look, saluting this new planet's white sun.

I said it again, "On the horizon."

"You're right. Those are treetops, and there's a little white cloud over them. There's an island over there. The cloud's not very big, so the island's not very big either."

"Agreed. We've been here for a while, and we haven't seen anything much bigger than insects. Certainly nothing bigger than mice. Or at least I haven't. What about you two?"

Georges shook his head.

"I think this is an island, too, and not very large. If so, it's unlikely to have large animals. Of course, I may be wrong on either point, which is why I'd like you to keep looking."

Mahala got up and started down the beach, motioning for us to stay put.

Georges said, "She's heard something. She has good ears, that girl."

I got up and went after her. She motioned for me to stay back.

Pretty soon, I heard what Mahala'd been hearing; it sounded like a big kettledrum being beaten in a regular, monotonous rhythm. *Boom! Biddy-boom! Biddy-boom, boom, BOOM!*

After that, I was out in front and thinking what a jerk I was.

Georges was three or four meters behind me, with Mahala right behind him.

We smelled smoke, and Mahala wanted to go back. In a whisper I told her she could go back to the door if she wanted to, or go through it into the house. She shook her head and held Georges's arm. It meant where he was going, she was going.

He whispered, "I'm sticking with Mr. Smithe. You go on back, honey. Finish searching the lab."

It was no go. She stuck with Georges.

We went quite a way farther before we saw them, and it was like nothing I'd ever seen or even heard of.

13

Rented in Owenbright

Except for their tails, faces, and fangs, they looked more like people than I would have expected, but they must have been forty or fifty centimeters over two meters tall, with arms, legs, and necks not much bigger than broomsticks. My first impression was of four eyes, two widely spaced and two narrowly. All the eyes were small and may not really have been eyes at all.

So many thoughts flashed through my mind when I saw those creatures that I know I cannot possibly give them all here. For one thing, it would probably take me days to write them all down. For another—I guess this is the important one—I know I could not remember them all. I will try to give some idea, though, of the ones that have stuck with me. I cannot even make a stab at getting them in order. They came too fast for that.

One was that I wanted to call them aliens, only I realized that they were not; that we were the aliens there. They looked weird to me, but we would have looked weird to them if they had seen us. (I did not know then that they were about to.)

Another was that we were watching some kind of ceremony.

I could not even guess what it was about, they could have been getting in touch with God, or calling up the spirits of their dead, or making them stay dead, or maybe swearing in a new mayor. Only it was probably something else, something I would never have understood even if they had tried to explain it.

Another was that I was glad we had never found any guns, because if we had we might have ended up shooting two or three of them, and we had no more business shooting them than a burglar has shooting the owner of the house he is robbing.

Here is one that hit me hard, although I cannot say why. It was that Colette's father had probably seen them and they had probably seen him. Maybe he had made friends with them, but maybe they had been enemies; and it would be good to know that but I could not think of any way I could find it out.

Maybe that had something to do with his being gone so long that his kids had thought he was probably dead. That had been a mistake; he was really just off doing something that had taken him quite a while. That mistake may have been at the root of all the problems. I thought of that, too.

One more and I will quit. It was that they did not live here on this island. That could be wrong, but somehow I did not think it was. I was pretty sure the island was small, and there were an awful lot of them. This was a sacred place, a place they went to for secret ceremonies. It meant that if we could just pull back and go home, we could probably come back later and find nobody here.

They had lit a circle of smoky fires. One was standing in the center with his arms above his head. Another held something long and black up against his chest and seemed to be listening to the other end. Eight or ten were beating the ground—two clubs each. Georges, Mahala, and I watched them for a few seconds before one saw us and pointed. The rest jumped up, and a two-headed spear spun past my ear, missing me by about one and a half fingers.

We ran like three rabbits, me holding the book in one hand; and I must have waved it pretty much at the door without realizing it. That is the only way to explain what happened next, which was that Georges grabbed the handle and jerked it open. I dove through, and he and Mahala got in some way, because they were there when I looked around and stood up. They were panting worse even than I was.

(Right here I would like to stop and explain how the door worked; it took me a while to work it out, but there was nothing complicated about it. Each side had its own locking mechanism. The front, facing the house, was controlled by a chip in the front of the book; and the back, toward the jungle, by a chip in the back of the book. Unlock the front, and the front lever worked— you could press it down, open the door, and go in. The door would lock behind you. Unlock the back, and you could go out. The side you had unlocked remained unlocked for about two minutes. To go in *and* come out, you had to have two cards, or the book, or something else like that. Why do it that way? I think I know, but I'll leave it up to you to figure out.)

The door was shut, and Georges was holding the handle to keep anybody on the other side from pushing it down. He stayed right there holding it while Mahala and I rummaged around in the lab for some way of securing a door that swung away from us. Eventually Mahala found a tool chest, and we settled on big pliers with toothed jaws that would clamp and hold the handle. When they were tight on it, we locked them down, then taped the whole lashup to the door. After that, we sealed the door with tape, too—that was at Mahala's insistence.

While we were taping, I said, "Did they try to come through? You would have felt them trying to push down the handle."

Georges shook his head.

"Then I doubt that they will."

"That makes you a lot more confident than it does me. What would you say to a drink?"

"No. And go away."

"Well, I'd like one." He turned to Mahala. "What about you, honey?"

She shook her head, then pantomimed writing on her left palm and showed us her empty hands.

"No drink," Georges said, "but she dropped her pad. Shall I go back in and look for it? We'll have to pull off all that tape."

I said I did not think that would be necessary. "There must be paper in here somewhere, and pens, too."

"Fine. I'd still like a drink. Okay if I ask the 'bot?"

We asked, but not before I had opened the door to the other room and showed him the reactor. "This is a Westhaus M-9," he told me. "That's a standard setup. This one's probably five or six years old. In here"—he tapped the metal shell—"you've got uranium. There has to be enough for a reaction. That's what you want, but you've got to control it. You do that with carbon rods. The carbon rods damp it down. Lower the rods and there's less reaction, which means less heat. Are you following this?"

I nodded.

"Raise them, and you get more reaction and more heat. This here"—he pointed to a black box—"is a controller. You're powering a generator. If that's not putting out as much juice as you need, the controller raises all the rods a little, which gives you hotter steam and more steam. That should fix things. If it doesn't, the controller sounds an alarm."

I nodded again, listening hard and not even trying to hide my interest.

"What probably happened is that your uranium's getting exhausted. It wears out eventually, then you've got spent uranium; but for a long time the controller can compensate for depletion by raising the rods."

"Wouldn't they wear out, too?" I asked.

"Good question! Yes, they do. They're soaking up radiation, and eventually they get saturated. The operator has to watch out for that." Georges walked to the screen and said, "Got any hot spots?"

NONE appeared on the screen, and it said, "Everything normal."

"Show the heat surface."

An almost level plane appeared on the screen, slowly revolving and turning over. It was dotted with yellow numbers.

"That's heat throughout the reactor," Georges said. "The hills are hot, the valleys cooler. You want it pretty flat, but there's no advantage in having it perfectly flat. This looks all right."

I studied it.

Georges lowered his voice and stepped away from the screen. "Those numbers tell you where each rod is. Let's say you come into this room and there's an error message on the screen saying you've got uneven heat. You look at the heat surface and there's a steep hill marked number five. Say that you already knew number five rod was close to saturated. You tell the screen to pull and replace number five. Only on some setups, that's all automatic. Your screen will pull and replace number five, then tell you it did it."

I said, "He can't have spent much time in here, so I imagine that's what we've got."

"You're probably right. What would you say to that drink now?"

"In a minute. What would happen if there were no more fresh rods?"

"That could be bad." Georges rubbed his jaw. "Alarms would sound, to start with. The screen would try to shut down the reactor, putting all the rods in all the way. That would work for a while, at least in most cases. As far as I know it's never actually happened."

"Perhaps we should make sure there's a good supply of them before we go. Will the screen have that information?"

"Sure." Georges stepped over to a narrow black cabinet. "But we can check them for ourselves, too." He opened the cabinet door, revealing the round, dark ends of the carbon rods. "Don't worry about these. They're new rods, not hot and about as dangerous as the lead in a pencil."

"Eighteen." I had counted them.

"More than enough. I can't tell you how long those should last—I don't know that much about this system. But I'd think it's at least three years' worth, probably a lot more."

Downstairs, the maid 'bot showed us into a room I had never seen before, a cozy private bar off the dining room. Mahala and I had changed our minds by then. Each of us got a glass of white wine.

Georges made himself a stiff Scotch and soda. "You're not worrying a whole lot about those scarecrows coming in after us, are you?"

I confessed I was not.

"Fine, I'll bite. Why not?"

"In the first place, Colette's father wasn't. If he had been, he would have had that side locked. He didn't, or if he did, I have no idea how he did it." I had not realized then that the book had unlocked it.

"Another card, probably. Show it that card, and it locks from both sides instead of unlocking."

"Maybe, but if that's it, we haven't found it. We'll keep looking. Listening devices, cards, and weapons. I said that before."

"You still think this house is bugged?"

"Actually, I don't. It's probably clean, since there were three of us looking for them in three different rooms and none of us found anything. But if there are listening devices or hidden cameras, it's important that we find them. Would you like me to justify our searching for cards, too?"

"Sure. Let's hear it."

"As I said, I'm not greatly worried that the islanders will follow us through that door. To begin with, because they haven't tried to—not in all the time that we were looking for tools, taping up, and so forth. In addition, because it doesn't seem to have concerned Colette's father, as I said a moment ago. And lastly, because they would be stepping from their native planet onto a planet of somewhat higher gravity. I can easily see them falling down after a step or two and being unable to get up. I might do exactly that if I were set down on a new planet with more gravity than Earth. So might you."

"Right." Georges looked skeptical. "What does that have to do with cards?"

I sat down on one of the red-leather bar stools. "If there really are two cards, someone else may find the other one and go in there. That could be bad for half a dozen reasons; I'm not going to get into all of them. If there are two cards, I want us to have them both."

Georges nodded.

"The card I used to open the front door will open the hangar, too. I can guarantee that. It will probably open the garage as well, but it may not—we have yet to try it. The ground cars may require other cards, however."

"Usually there's a combination lock for the doors," Georges told me. "Once you're in, you can do everything by verbal commands or pushing buttons. You don't have to carry a car card. I'm surprised you didn't know."

"I'm afraid there's a great deal that I don't know. Couldn't there be locked cabinets or boxes in here that require different cards?"

"Sure, but what about the safe? It didn't take a card. I saw it when we were up there, and there was a combination lock, one of the tough ones with thirty-six buttons."

"Yes, I know. Colette's father was a wealthy man, Georges. Have you ever owned a house?"

Georges sipped his Scotch and soda. "What does that have to with cards?"

"Didn't you have money hidden somewhere in the house? Something for an emergency?"

"No," Georges said, "but I suppose a lot of people do."

"So do I." I pointed at the liquor cabinet. "That wasn't locked when we came in, but I'd be willing to bet that it has a lock, and that it was kept locked when there were human servants."

When Georges had finished his drink, Mahala got busy on the screen in the dining room and Georges and I went out to the mysterious ground car. First he tried the doors; I said, "When you lock one, you lock them all. Somebody told me that once."

He grinned. "Only when it's raining, but they're all locked. Come here and I'll show you something."

I came. The sky was as lovely a blue as that of the other world, if not better; our own yellow star, the star we call Sol, shone brightly.

"Some models have other locks." Georges pointed to a row of buttons just above the door handle. "But I'd guess that more than half have these single-row five-button jobs. See the letters? It's A, B, C, D, and E. The driver can change the code if he wants to. Lots of people think you've got to use a five-letter code, C, A, B, E, D, or something, but that's not true. Four letters will work and so will three. Let's say the guy calls his wife Babe." He pushed buttons and tried the door again. It was still locked.

I asked, "How are we going to get in? Break a window?"

"Nah, I can get into any ground car in under an hour. Ninety percent in under half an hour. That's without damaging the car or rocking it. If you break a window or rock the ground car it'll holler for help, only you can't hear it. About the time you're getting in it, the cop's getting out of his. A five-button lock like this gives you a thousand combinations, but most people use less than a hundred."

"And you know them?" It seemed pretty unlikely, and I was already wondering *how* he knew them—if he did.

"Sure. Initials are out for nearly everybody. Like yours are

E. A. S. You've got the *E* and the *A*, but you don't have the *S*. So no. If you've got kids, *D*, *A*, *D* or maybe *D*, *A*, *D*, *E*, *E*. I can look into your ground car and tell if you've got kids. I always try *D*, *E*, *A*, *D*, too. Undertakers use that a lot, and maybe somebody inherited the money. Real estate guy? Try *D*, *E*, *E*, *D*. Most people stick to simple stuff. *E*, *A*, *E*, *A*—something like that. When you buy a new ground car, it has some simple code that the whole dealership uses, like *D*, *C*, *B*, *A* or even *A*, *B*, *C*. That way, everybody who works there can open every car they've got."

The door did not budge, and he shrugged. "That one's always worth a try, because some people never change it. They're scared they'll screw it up and set some code they don't know themselves."

I said, "I understand."

"Or there's an agency called Ace Rentals. They code all the cars on their lot *A*, *C*, *E*, and—son of a bitch! It's a rental!"

It was something I had never even considered, and I said so.

"There'll be a rental agreement in the dash box." He opened it before I could reply. A moment later he pulled out a green folder and spread it on the hood. "This was rented in Owenbright to a Ms. Colette C. Coldbrook." He turned to stare at me.

"I have never . . ." I wanted to sit down, but there was no place to sit unless I sat in the ground car.

"Never what?"

"Never felt so utterly stupid. Never realized that I was such an idiot. She got away from them, just as I—" My watch struck one. "Well, never mind. May I tell you the whole story, Georges? I need to. I have to tell someone."

"Sure. I'd like to hear it. What do you say we go inside? Maybe the 'bot could fix us some lunch."

I followed him. When all three of us were sitting around the cheerful little table in the sunroom, I said, "Colette and I were together in Owenbright. I had no money—I have very little now, really—so she rented a suite for the two of us. Two bedrooms, two bathrooms, and a common lounge. We weren't lovers, you understand. Simply friends."

Georges nodded. "We've got it."

"We were going to freshen up, change clothes, and go out for dinner. I took a shower, changed, and waited for her in the lounge. It almost always takes a woman longer than a man."

Georges nodded. "Sure."

"After a while I realized there were no sounds coming from her bedroom. No water running in her bathroom, nobody walking around, nothing. I knocked on the door and asked if she were all right. There was no answer. Frankly, I got frightened. I thought she might be dead in there, or unconscious."

"This really bothers you, doesn't it?" Georges sounded sympathetic.

"I knew she had enemies, that people were spying on her. She had asked for my help. At first you think somebody's paranoid, but by then I knew she wasn't, that it was a fact." I tried to keep my voice steady; that was something I just about always did. "Now she was gone," I said.

The maid 'bot brought in a salad, lemonade for Mahala and me and a spritzer for Georges.

When the 'bot had gone, Georges said, "She couldn't have just walked out and left you?"

"No. A lamp had been knocked over and her shaping bag was still there. She would never have gone off without it. She kept everything in there, eephone, mad money, and makeup. All the things a woman carries."

Mahala tapped my arm and held up a yellow scratch pad and a pen: MAY I?

Georges said, "She found those up in the lab. Is it all right for her to keep them?"

"Yes. Yes, of course." I stopped for a moment to think. "What had happened seems to me reasonably clear. The people who'd been after Colette had entered our suite, subdued her, and abducted her, presumably while I was in the shower. You wouldn't have screened the police, I know. I did."

Georges nodded. "And . . . ?"

"They said they wouldn't even try to find her unless a relative had reported her missing and she'd been gone at least a full day. I tried to tell them that she had no family left, that her mother, her father, and her brother were all dead, but they wouldn't listen."

"And you're not a relative."

"Correct. If I'd known of a relative, I would have contacted that person and asked him or her to screen the police, but I didn't. Perhaps you took time out while you were searching the father's bedroom to do a screen search for the name Coldbrook."

"Wrong but right. It was before I started looking. You were in the library and Mahala was busy upstairs, so I thought why not me?"

I nodded. "What did you find?"

"Financial stuff. There were three companies with Coldbrook in their names. There was that newsletter. It was mostly stock tips, only he wasn't writing it anymore. Somebody else had it.

There was a family trust, and a bunch of bank accounts, broker-age accounts, and real estate holdings. Pretty good for a middle-management guy, I'd say."

I nodded.

"But no people except him, now deceased, the wife, also deceased, the son—it said he'd been murdered—and the dau-ghter, Colette Carole Coldbrook. She had two or three degrees, and she was teaching at a place called the Forest Glade Acad-emy in Spice Grove."

"No other relatives?"

Georges shook his head.

Mahala touched my arm and pointed to herself.

I said, "Yes, please look. If you find any, get in touch with them. Tell them I'm a friend and you're my secretary. Ask them to con-tact the police in Spice Grove. Tell them what I've just told you."

Mahala nodded, and wrote. When she handed me her new tablet it read: WIFE'S NAME?

"You're right, and I should have thought of that." I turned to Georges. "You must have come across it when you did your search. Do you remember it?"

"Yeah. I'm pretty good on that stuff. Joanne Rebecca Carole. That's 'Carole' with an *e*." He spelled it.

I said, "Meanwhile there's the ground car. Clearly Colette was able to escape her captors, probably without their realizing she was gone. She would have returned to our hotel, not only to re-claim her shaping bag but in the hope of finding me. Either her shaping bag was still in our suite, or it was in the hotel's lost and found. She had a leased flat in Spice Grove, but she also had an excellent reason not to return there. Perhaps there are commer-cial flights between Owenbright and New Delphi. I don't know."

Georges said, "She'd have had to fly to Niagara and get a new flight from there. But she wouldn't go to the airport anyway if she was smart. As soon as they found out she was loose they'd have had somebody there. What she did was a lot smarter."

"Perhaps. Still, they guessed where she'd gone, came here, and recaptured her. They may not have planted their devices in this house, but they knew of it." I paused to consider. "Couldn't she have hired protection? Armed bodyguards?"

"Sure, if she had the money and the time."

I nodded, mostly to myself. By then I was thinking of something else.

"Want us to go back to searching the house? Listening devices, money, or weapons?"

"I don't think so. I'd like Mahala to continue her screen search for Coldbrooks and Caroles here in New Delphi."

Turning to her, I said, "Remember what I told you. I'm Colette's friend. You're my secretary. She's been missing for two days. We'd like the relative to call the police."

Mahala nodded.

I stood, not the least bit hungry and anxious to get away. "Georges, I'd like you to search that ground car. You found the rental agreement in the dash box. Now see if there's anything else in there. Look in the trunk and under the seats—and in every other place you can think of."

He may have said something then; if he did, I paid no attention to it. I left the sunroom as quickly as I could and went straight to the lift tube. *Murder on Mars* was in the lab, where I had parked it after Georges and I checked out the reactor. I had shut the door of the safe, but since I did not know the combination, I had not locked it.

Opening the big steel door we'd been so anxious to seal took me fifteen or twenty minutes. I pulled off tape as fast as I could, scared that Georges or Mahala—or both together—would step out of the lift tube any minute. They did not, and I walked into the new world that Conrad Coldbrook had discovered, retched and nearly fell, took a deep breath, and looked around knowing I was going to pull it off.

After that, I tried the lever on the jungle side of the door. As I had pretty much expected, it was locked. When I had tested the book the first time, that door had been locked, both sides. I had waved the back of the book first, and heard the soft click of the lock on the back unlocking. I had unlocked it by accident when we dashed up to it, and it had locked again while Georges stood there holding the lever. We could have saved ourselves an hour or more of running around and taping just by thinking a little.

The steep path I had noticed earlier took me up to the dark hole in the cliff face. The little light from the kitchen was still in my pocket; I slapped it onto my forehead and switched it on and off a few times before I went inside.

The rocky ceiling was low, so low at first that a tall man like Conrad Coldbrook must have had to stoop. I did not. There was a permasteel fence about a dozen steps in, close-set bars as sharp as so many knives at the top; but *Murder on Mars* unlocked the gate, and I strolled in as if I owned the place. By then I had seen the rifle leaning against an old wooden table inside. That was the first thing I found in Conrad Coldbrook's mine, but not the last.

Not by a long shot.

14

Maxette, Money, Monsters, and a Moon

When Mahala came up, I was in the lab poking around and had just decided not to show Georges what I had found there. I expected her to show me her pad, but she used the screen to talk for her instead: "I found an Alice Carole. She was Joanne Carole Coldbrook's mother. I told her about her granddaughter Colette, and she promised to screen the police."

I gave her my best smile. "Good work!"

Mahala smiled back, and her fingers flew over the keys. "If you want her address, I have it."

"Not now. We may need it later, though."

"I found the housekeeper, too." The voice from the screen's speakers was brisk but sweet. "Her name's Judy Peters, and she'll come out so you can talk to her. All you have to do is set a time."

"More good work." I hesitated, trying to decide whether it would be better for us to question Judy Peters in her home or for her to come to this one. "Don't get back to her yet. We've got other things to take care of first. Do you know whether Georges has found anything in that ground car?"

Mahala did not, so we went downstairs to find out. He was still working on it, looking at the undersides of the floor mats. "I know you can drive," I said. "What about Mahala?"

She shook her head, and Georges told me that she could not and did not want to learn.

"In that case, you're going to have to teach me to do it." Naturally, I did not tell him the first me had driven twenty-first-century hybrid cars. I had not known how much of that would carry over; but it turned out a lot had, and modern ground cars were easier.

When I was sitting in the driver's seat holding the little wheel, Georges said, "The main thing is that you've got two parallel systems. It's just like a flitter. You know about flitters?"

I told him I knew a little.

"Same deal. You can drive by spoken command, or you can work the controls yourself. I like doing that, and so do quite a few other people. Then if you get tired, the car can take over. Some people go to sleep then, but I wouldn't advise it."

"I understand."

"Thing is, anybody can do voice commands. If you want to get a license, you've got to know manual. They figure you're not safe to drive if you can't do that."

I said, "Fine. How do I start it?"

"With a voice command or that switch next to the screen."

"All right, let's start."

"Look straight ahead and talk to the ground car, not to me. Loud voice, and clear, just like you were talking to a screen. I haven't found this car's name, if it's got one; but it's a Maxette, so 'Maxette' ought to work."

Facing straight ahead I said, "Maxette, start!"

There was no engine noise, but the screen came on, the sim a business-like guy in some sort of uniform.

"Now say 'manual.'"

I did.

"All right, you've got two foot pedals. The one on the right makes it go forward. The harder you push on that, the faster it goes. The one on the left makes it stop. The harder you push, the faster it stops. You already know about the wheel, right? Clockwise for right, counterclockwise for left."

I drove down to the road, stopped to look both ways, made a right onto the road, and drove down it for two or three kilometers until I found a good place to turn around. By that time I had seen a switch on the steering column that put Maxette into reverse, only you had to be at a dead stop or it would not move. When the road was clear both ways, I backed onto it and drove us back to the Coldbrook house.

"You were fine," Georges told me. "Just don't get too confident and you'll be all right."

I promised I would not, and told him that I wanted to try voice—only we ought to pick up Mahala first, if she wanted to come.

So we did, and after that she and Georges sat in back with him looking over my shoulder. There was a lot of that at first, then not much at all when he saw that I was not going to get into trouble. I kept the speed at fifty-five or under, and did not try to show off. One thing that surprised me and that I really liked a lot was that I could tell Maxette to go about as fast as the other cars on the road and it would do it. Then I saw what

I had been watching for the whole time, a floating sign for one of those rest-stop places. Loud and clear I said, "Pull into that rest stop and park, Maxette," and it worked like a charm.

Georges asked if I needed to go. They had restrooms there and some really advanced vending machines, plus four or five picnic tables under some trees. I said no, and got him and Mahala to go over to one of the picnic tables and sit down.

He said, "I get it. You're still afraid they might be listening."

I nodded. "Or looking. Or both. They knew about the Cold-brook house, and they knew pretty quickly when Colette got there, or that's what it seems like. I had the screen looking behind us. Probably you noticed."

"Yeah, I did."

"If we were being followed, I never identified them, but that doesn't mean they weren't there." I took the stones I had found in Conrad Coldbrook's mine out of my pocket and laid them on the table. There were seven of them; I said, "Look at these."

They did. Mahala nodded, and Georges picked up the biggest and held it up to the light. Finally he said, "Are these what I think they are?"

"Uncut emeralds? Yes, I think so."

After half a minute or so, he said, "Have you got any idea what they're worth?"

"Not really. A lot, I hope."

"It depends on color and whether they're flawed and so forth. Brilliance, and how big they are after cutting. I'm no jeweler." He put the emerald down. "Mind telling me where you got these?"

"You're right, I do—and I won't. Certainly not now."

"And maybe not ever. I get it."

"Good. You've been a great deal of help to me, both of you. I like you, and I'd hate to see our association end in a quarrel. I'm going to make you two mutually exclusive offers; you can take one or the other, but you can't combine both. Understood?"

They nodded.

"First offer. We've got seven stones. I'll divide them into three groups."

I spoke to Mahala. "You'll get to choose first, picking up one group. Those are yours."

I turned to Georges. "You next. You choose one of the two remaining groups. That one's yours. Mine is the remaining group. We drive into town, and I let you out at a jeweler's that bought emeralds from Colette's father. Mahala knows about that."

She nodded again.

"I drive away in the ground car, and when I do we have separated permanently."

After a moment or two, Georges said, "You're being generous."

I thanked him.

"Can we hear the other one?"

"Certainly. We stay together. We go to the jeweler as a group and get the best price we can for six of the seven. I keep the seventh, the smallest. When we've sold the other six we split the money three ways. I'll continue to search for Colette, and I'll expect the two of you to continue to help me in every way you can. Of course you may leave, taking your money, if you decide that helping me is too dangerous."

Georges whispered something to Mahala, and she nodded. He turned back to me. "We accept the second. Are there any more emeralds?"

"At the moment I don't have any more."

"When you do?"

I shook my head. "I can't say. I may never have any more; it will depend upon the circumstances."

"But you might?"

"Yes, I might. Certainly."

"Fine. Like I said, we're in and we'll stay in." There was more talk, and Georges and I decided on what we were going to tell—and what we were not going to tell—the jeweler.

After that, we went to a place named on several of the receipts. None of us knew where it was, but I gave Maxette the name, and it announced the streets we took and the turns we made till the shop was in sight and it had parked itself.

In the shop I told one of the clerks we wanted to see his boss and it had to do with Conrad Coldbrook. He was gone for five minutes or more, then came hurrying back and told us to follow him.

The boss was a porky man who looked about sixty. He hid his clever eyes behind lenses so thick they looked bulletproof.

There were only two chairs besides the one behind his desk. I took one and Mahala the other. Georges stood behind her. The boss told him, "I can have another chair brought in if you like, but I don't think this will take long."

Georges said he was fine.

I said, "I take it you know that both Conrad Coldbrook and his son are dead."

The boss nodded. "A great loss. Is that what you came to talk about?"

"One of the things, yes. Did you know Conrad, Junior, well?"

"I didn't know him at all. His father had mentioned him once or twice. I never met him."

"Did you know that he was murdered?"

From the way the boss reacted, I might as well have said, "Lovely day, isn't it?"

"Was he? I remember seeing in roundvid that his death was under investigation. Nothing more than that."

"How did his father take it?"

"I have no idea."

For a second I thought about that one; then I said, "I believe you saw him after his son's death."

"Yes, I did. We had business to transact, and we took care of it. Mr. Coldbrook didn't talk about his personal affairs—not to me, at least."

"Yet you said he had mentioned his son."

"Once he said that his son was waiting for him out in the shop. He asked my assistant to tell him he was going to be engaged for an hour or more."

"Was he?"

The boss shook his head. "I don't recall."

"I suppose you were haggling over the prices of various stones."

"Possibly. As I said, I don't recall."

I sighed. "He sold you uncut emeralds."

The boss said nothing.

"You gave him receipts. I've got some of them in my pocket. Would you like to see them?"

The boss said, "Are you from the government?"

"No. Did you know that Coldbrook had a daughter as well as a son?"

"Did he?"

"Yes, he did. We're friends of hers. We're acting for her."

"Really?" The boss sat up straighter and pulled his chair closer to his desk. "I'm surprised she doesn't act for herself."

Georges said, "We'll tell her that the next time we see her. Meanwhile, you'll have to deal with us—if you want to deal at all."

"You're aware that this is a jewelry store. Are you also aware that my clerks and I are armed?"

"Hell, yes." Georges was grinning.

I said, "We don't want that kind of trouble, and I'm certain you don't, either."

The boss seemed not to have heard me; he glanced at Mahala. "Is this Conrad's daughter?"

I said, "No, she's my secretary."

"Doesn't she ever talk?"

Georges said, "No, she doesn't. Maybe you could learn something from her."

The boss spoke to me. "What do you want?"

I got out the smallest emerald. "What will you give us for that?"

There was a lot of haggling, and once we got as far as the front door; but in the end we agreed on prices for all seven. I put that first one back in my pocket and told the boss we would sell him the others but we were keeping that one. He did not like it, but after a bit of argument he went along. Then he got out a card and said he would have the money transferred to our account.

I put the rest of the stones away and told him we wanted cash.

"If I withdraw that much in cash, there'll be someone investigating this transaction tomorrow. I wouldn't want that. Would you?"

Georges asked, "How did you handle things with her father?"

"If you've read those receipts you claim to have, you will have seen that he never sold more than three stones at once. It was usually just one or two. I transferred my payment to two or three of his accounts. He had half a dozen that I knew of, and I split it up."

There was a good deal of argument after that, but I will not give it here. In the end we had him write three checks on three accounts, a check for each of us. He and two of his clerks came with us when we went out to cash them, because we insisted on him and he insisted on the clerks. The three of them took the boss's car, and the three of us went in Maxette. We went to three different banks, Georges and the boss going into the first bank and cashing Georges's check, the boss and I going into the second, and Georges and Mahala going into the third with me, the boss, and his two clerks to cash hers. For the moment at least, Georges, Mahala, and I were rich.

All of this took quite a while. When we came out, it was getting dark. I handed over the stones, the boss gave me a receipt for them, and he and his clerks went back to their jewelry store. When they had gone, Georges asked, "What's next?"

"Dinner and bed," I told him, and at that time I honestly thought I meant it.

"Tomorrow?"

I had a couple of dozen vague ideas, but I said, "We'll talk about that then."

So that would have been that if I had not gotten up in the middle of the night. I was curious about the length of their days in the world behind the door, so I opened it. It was nice bright daylight in there, which of course woke me up.

The first thing I did was to go back into the mine and get the rifle. When I had carried it outside into the sunshine and most of the way down the path, I sat down on a stone and figured out what the various levers and buttons were for. One was to let you take the magazine out, which I did. It was a little rotary job you could not have replaced with a bigger box magazine unless you were a pretty good gunsmith and had a shop with all the right tools. It held five cartridges and was fully loaded, which did not surprise me a bit. There had been two cartridge boxes inside the mine. I had not looked, but my guess was that one was full and the other not.

The first me had not known a whole lot about hunting rifles, but he had known enough for me to recognize one when I saw one. Except for a couple of things, they had not changed a whole lot, and one way of looking at it was that both those things were really the same thing. The first was that some parts that would have been steel in the first me's days were something else now. It was black, and it had to be a lot harder and tougher than any plastic we had back then. The trigger guard, the trigger, the cocking handle, and the bolt were all made of this new black stuff; so was the receiver. So were the cartridge cases, for that matter. The barrel was slender and a bit shorter than my arm, made of the black stuff with a thin liner of bright rifled steel. The stock was ponticwood, as near as I could tell, but I may have been wrong about that.

The second was that the rifle was not as heavy as it should have been. Not as light as a wooden mockup would have been, probably, but quite a bit lighter than I expected when I picked it up.

On the one hand, I wanted to shoot it at least once and maybe a couple of times. On the other, I would not be able to clean it. I had no bore cleaner, no cleaning rod, no oil, and no patches. Not even a rag. What decided it was that I knew darned well that it might not be easy to get more cartridges. Sure, I had a lot of money now, and money never hurts; but I might not be able to get any more, and I did not want to blow a wad on cartridges I might never need.

So no shooting.

After that, I went down to the beach and found the place where Georges, Mahala, and I had sat to talk. I sat there for maybe ten minutes or more looking out at the sea and thinking about what we had said and what I had not said.

Next I wanted to go looking for the place where the scarecrows (which was what Georges and I called them when we talked about them) had sat in a circle drumming on the ground. It was a really stupid thing to do, and I knew it; but I swore up and down that if I had any trouble finding it I would give up and go back.

Besides, I had already given in on firing the rifle, and it was time I won one.

Finding the right place was pretty easy, because I knew it had been out of sight of the sea and a piece of level ground with no trees and no bushes. It had not been far away, either—so even though it was not exactly a piece of cake, you could call it a sizable cookie with chocolate chips. No scarecrows there, awake or asleep, and if they had left anything behind, I did not find it.

After that, I went back to the beach and sat looking out to sea again. The rifle had some kind of an optical sight. I think there must have been a switch in the butt plate, too, because every time I put it to my shoulder the sight came on. That sight was always focused on whatever was in the middle of its field, projecting a green hoop on the image to show you where your shot was going to hit. At first I thought the wind could blow that green hoop around, which seemed crazy. Then I realized it was telling me where the bullet would hit for sure, including the correction for wind speed and everything. So that was a very classy sight indeed.

If it had been my gun, I would have put a sling on it, but that is the only change I would have made. As it was, you could not sling it on your shoulder like I kept wanting to. You had to carry it. Like I said, it was not heavy, but it took one hand away, just the same.

When I was through playing with the sight, I decided to walk down the beach a ways to see how far it went. I wanted to take the rifle because I did not know what I might run into, and I wanted to leave *Murder on Mars* where it would be safe because I had been carrying it in my left hand. If I needed to fire the rifle, I was going to have to drop the book; and if it was gone when I tried to come back for it, I would have to stay here for the rest of my days.

I kept thinking about burying it in the sand. But if I did, I knew darned well it was going to take me a week to find it. Finally I realized the driftwood log I had been sitting on was hollow. I figured I would recognize it for sure, so I stuck the book in there as far as I could reach and took a good, long look at that log; then off I went, walking down the beach and turning to look back at the log every three or four steps.

Eventually I had gone so far I could not see it anymore, and there was nothing to do except keep walking until the beach ended. It was white sand (which maybe I have written about here before) and pretty coarse. For some reason I felt sure the water would get deep in a hurry if I waded out from the beach; it was probably the blue color of the waves that fooled me. Pretty soon I found that was dead wrong, and that I could have waded out for a country mile before the water got higher than my chin. I ought to have remembered sitting on the bank with Colette when all this began, and how blue the little stream we had splashed in had looked. Rivers that are not carrying a lot of mud and stuff out to sea, rivers of pure water, generally look blue like that.

The beach went on and on, wider here and narrower there; but I would glance at that little white sun (which was getting low now) every few minutes, and I could see that the beach kept curving around to the right. It made me surer than ever that this was an island—and not a real big one, either.

When my shadow was taller than I was, I decided I had better turn around and go back. That was when I saw a funny shape out to sea that stopped me dead; it looked like a big black rock, kind of rounded but bumpier and lumpier than most rocks.

And it was coming right at me.

It was not moving very fast, but as it got closer and closer I could see the little wave at the front where it was pushing through the water. I kept watching it and backing away from the place where it would come to land and telling myself I had the rifle now—which was right—and that I could run off into the jungle. Which was right, too.

Only I kept getting scareder and scareder just the same.

When there were at least three meters of it sticking up out of the water, I caught on that it was not really swimming like I had thought. It was walking on the bottom, and there could not be as much of it under the water as I was seeing above it. Something that waded on the bottom could probably walk on the beach, too; so I kept backing off and telling myself that it could not chase me if I ran between the big trees a little way inland.

They were pretty close together, and it looked way too big to have gotten through.

All that was dumb as it turned out, but if you had been there you might have thought the same thing.

About then I saw something smaller and flatter but still pretty big out in front of it. It was there for sure, but every so often it disappeared under the water for half a minute and then came back. It was black, too, or maybe just dark gray. When whatever it was, was still about thirty meters out, the whole thing began to heave up out of the water. It must have been eight or ten meters across and five or six high, meaning two or three times as high as a tall man. And that was just the part that was above the water.

By then I was pretty sure it was an animal of some kind. I did not want to shoot it; for one thing the idea of killing something just for the fun of it always makes me want to hit somebody. For another I was not one darn bit sure that I could kill something as big as that with what was basically a deer rifle.

Back when people still killed elephants, there were a few who could kill an elephant with a deer rifle, and did; but those guys were dead shots, and they knew a heck of a lot about killing elephants. The first me had shot with a rifle some, but I had never actually done it myself. When it came to killing elephants—well, maybe you could tickle them to death.

The sky was getting pretty dim by the time the animal I had been watching heaved completely up out of the water. It was still lumpy bumpy, and it looked about the size of a small house. It also looked like it had no head at all, so I told myself that just because our animals on Earth had heads it was dumb for me to think that animals here needed them. That was not really all that dumb, but what I did next was; in fact, it was maybe the dumbest thing I have ever done in my whole life. I got a little closer so I could see it better.

When I did, all the lumps and bumps started moving. I would have watched them better if I had not been watching something else. The head was coming out, a flat stone-ugly head that only looked small because the rest of the animal was so big, but was really about the size of a washing machine. If it had eyes, I never saw them; but it had a beak sort of like a hawk's or an eagle's, and it was white on the inside—so white that it practically glowed in the dim light.

One of the lumps dropped off onto the sand. Then another and another. One that had been high up slid all the way down. By that time, those that had dropped off first were coming for me.

No, I did not shoot. I ran, and fast. Forget what I said about the trees being too close together; these things were small enough to go between them. So I ran, and once I ran into a tree, hard. I dropped my rifle and fell down, and it hurt like all hell and just about knocked me out. When I sat up, I scrambled around and found the rifle. By that time, one of the lumps was almost close enough to touch.

It opened its mouth, and that was what really let me see it. I had found the safety back when I was looking at buttons and levers, a sliding button where the stock curved down. When the trigger would not move, I remembered the button and shoved it forward fast, and that beak and white mouth were about ten centimeters in front of the muzzle when I fired.

Maybe the recoil was bad and maybe the noise was—I would not know. I only know I rolled to one side without dropping the rifle, and one of the little monster's feet sort of brushed me. Then

I was up and running again. I think it was the light gravity that saved me; on Earth I would have been meat.

For a while I could hear them coming after me, then everything got quiet. I kept running for another minute or two, then I slowed down, gasping for air. I trotted for a little bit, stumbling a lot, and after that I trotted out onto the beach and waited.

The way I figured it, I had two big advantages. One was the rifle and the other was that I could outrun them. There was more light out on the beach, so I would be able to shoot better. What was more, the beach was perfect for running. I would not bump into trees or find anything to trip over worse than a few sticks of driftwood. All right, maybe the beach was perfect for them, too. Or they could swim faster than they could run; but they were going to have to prove it to me.

So I got out onto the beach again and jogged along for quite a while, looking behind me a lot. Nothing seemed to be chasing me, so after a while I slowed down to a walk. I want to say a brisk walk, but the truth is that there was nothing brisk about it. Maybe I have told you how I used to run up and down the stairs and do exercises after the library closed. All right, when I was walking down that beach I felt like I had gotten enough exercise to last me for a week.

Pretty soon I realized I did not know where the heck I was. Had I gone past the place where we had talked? Well, maybe. Had I not gotten to it yet? I liked that one a whole lot better, but what if it was not true? What if I walked clear around the island looking for it, and stumbled right into mama snapping turtle or whatever she was, and all her dear little bumps and lumps?

Then the moon, or whatever you want to call it, came up. It looked even whiter than ours, and when it was still on the hori-

zon it looked bigger than a cloud bank at sundown. Just seeing
it got me wondering about it, and I finally decided that the reason for that bright white had to be ice. So their moon has enough
gravity to hold on to quite a bit of water (this is what I decided)
but it is too cold for that water to be liquid. It is ice, in other
words, and that ice makes the moon look white—and bright,
too. There probably is not a whole lot of air. Since the ice
reflects heat and there is no air to warm, the ice stays frozen.
All that may be wrong, but it seems to me that it explains
what I saw up there.

Here in the library, one day when the library was closed and
I had nothing to do, I quizzed one of our screens about tempera-
tures on our own moon. The screen said it can get over 120
degrees in full sun. That sounds really hot until you find out that
when the moon is dark it gets colder than 180 below zero. And
oh my gosh! Guess what? There's surface ice on our moon, too.
Not much but some.

Naturally I did not know all that then, but it was the stuff I
wondered about when I was staring up at that big bright moon,
and I figure I might as well put it down here so you will know.

Finally I got so tired I sat down on a big piece of driftwood,
naturally facing back the way I had come. I pulled off my shoes
and socks and rubbed my feet, and thought of wading out a little
way, and finally decided not to because I would have to stand
up. You know. When I had put my shoes back on and had been
sitting there for twenty minutes at least, mostly thinking about
mama and her brood, and how much my cheek hurt, and how
close I had come to dying, and how little I had liked it, all that
got mixed up with thinking about the fire. By that I mean the
one they burn you in when you are just about worn out or if you

live on your shelf day after day and hardly ever get consulted or borrowed. I have never really been in it, but I know that it is in a special room in the basement. And I have seen it on a screen. I researched it, you know I did, and there was a neat little piece about it with some old worn-out guy getting burned. They had doped him so that he thought he was asleep, only he was really on this moving chain-belt. He was not tied down or anything because he was so out of it they had not had to tie him.

You go in headfirst, and I saw one of his legs move just a little.

15

SOME ERRANDS IN
NEW DELPHI

You have already figured out that the piece of driftwood I sat on was the one I had hidden the book in, right? So I am not going to tell about that. Besides, it took me quite a while, and it is embarrassing to be that dumb. And, no, I did not take the rifle back into the mine. I brought it home to Earth and New America and stood it in a corner of my room. I guess I should have gone back to bed then, but I did not. For one thing, it was light outside already. For another, I was not sleepy. Just tired and starting to get hungry.

So after I had shaved and finished sneering at this old face they have pinned on me (something I do every time I see myself in a mirror), I went downstairs and told the maid 'bot to make kafe, and talked to it about what the three of us might like for breakfast. I am a big fruit eater whenever there is good fruit to be eaten, so by the time Georges and Mahala came downstairs for breakfast I was eating peaches in cream and drinking kafe. Also running through all the stuff I wanted to get done. For one thing, I wanted to get an eephone.

After Georges sat down, I said, "If you've got an eephone on you, they can find out exactly where you are, right?"

He nodded slowly. "Mostly, yes. It depends."

"Tell me."

"If you get a regular one, you sign a contract and show identity and leave a thumbprint. Then they know who's got that phone and what the number is. They can monitor any calls you make—that's done on screens—and get a fix on the phone's location. Your friend Colette had an eephone, right?"

I nodded.

"So if the cops started looking, they could find out where her phone was. No sweat."

It had been in our suite, in her shaping bag; but I just nodded again. Then I said, "Let's say that I want one, but I don't want anybody to use it to find me. How would I do that?"

"Piece of cake. You go to any store that sells that kind of stuff and say you want a temp. They give you one—it's free—and you have to pay for so many minutes, maybe a hundred or two hundred. Three hundred. Whatever; it depends on the store. The clerk shows you how to code it with your number. Are you thinking you'll put somebody else's number on there and get their calls?"

I shook my head.

"That's good, because you can't. If you try, it'll tell you to try again."

Mahala touched my arm and pointed to herself.

"She means she can get on a screen and find you an unused number. It'll be a lot quicker than you trying to find one on a phone."

I said, "How will people know to use that number if they want me? Will the screens have it? Is there a directory?"

"They won't, not unless you tell them. But once you call them, they'll have the number."

I was thinking of watching mama monster come up out of the sea. "Suppose we went through into that world where we saw the scarecrows. Would an eephone still receive calls? Could I make calls from there? What do you think?"

"I don't think, I know," Georges told me. "It would if we left the door open, but not if we shut it. And it wouldn't matter whether it was locked or not. That door's steel. Do you want your eephone to work in there? If you do, change doors. Take that one off the hinges and put in a polymer door or a wooden one. A steel door with a slot would work, too, but not solid metal, which is what we've got now."

"I see. What happens when I've used up my hundred minutes?"

"You throw it away. At that point, your eephone's junk. It can't be loaded again."

"Really?"

"Yes, really. They used to make them reloadable, but some smart hackers figured out how to do it and make hundreds of free calls. So you can't. Could you take one apart and use some of the parts to build your own eephone? Sure, if you were a genius—but you'd need some other parts, too. Maybe you could buy those. I don't know."

Georges paused; when I did not ask another question, he said, "Suppose I wanted to know what you want an eephone for. Would you tell me?"

"Yes, certainly." I chewed and swallowed a chunk of fresh peach while I formulated my answer. "Here I can use Colette's screens to make my calls, but I'm not going to be here forever."

"Right. Also you're afraid the cops will be looking for you."

I smiled. "They and others. Those others will be looking for me already, I'm afraid. The police may be looking for me, too. I really can't say. Let's just say I'm not where I'm supposed to be."

Mahala held up her pad. NO MORE?

I said, "If that means no more questions, no. If it means no more on that topic, yes. I've told you as much about it as I intend to."

She folded back the sheet. WHAT?

"What should we talk about? What we plan to do today. I intend to buy one of those temporary eephones Georges told me about, for one thing. Another—which should probably have been the first—is to return the ground car Colette rented. My reasons for wanting to do that should be pretty obvious."

"She rented it just a few days ago," Georges told me. "They don't start looking until you've had one for two weeks."

I nodded like I had known that all along. "But the longer we keep it, the higher the bill will be, and if we find Colette, she'll be stuck with that bill. I'd rather pay it myself and be done with it—that's if there are ground cars in the garage here, and we can use those instead."

There were, and we could—a classy limo, a sleek red convertible, and a big alterrain. I told Georges that since he would be driving he could take whichever one he wanted, expecting him to choose the alterrain. He surprised me by picking the convertible.

When he had driven it out of the garage and closed the door,

I asked Maxette to take me to the nearest Ace agency, and it did. No sweat. I explained to a 'bot there that Colette had asked me to return her car, said to charge the account she had provided, and that was that. Mahala was riding in the front seat of the convertible with Georges, so I got in back.

Getting my eephone was no trouble either. After that, I told Georges I wanted to talk to the housekeeper, Mahala screened her and told her we were coming, and off we went as smooth as wrap.

While we were going there, I made up an eephone number using the birthday of the first me, and a few other numbers like that. (Strictly speaking, I personally was never born, so that seemed like the best way to do it.) The store's clerk 'bot had showed me how to code my new eephone with my number; it was so easy that I could have worked it out myself in two or three minutes. I tried the number I had made up, and it was accepted—meaning that nobody had it already.

The housekeeper had a little prefab on the south side of New Delphi, a pretty long drive. Later I found out that she'd been renting; when she'd worked for the Coldbrooks, she'd had one of the third-floor bedrooms.

She was a middle-aged lady, kind of heavy, with smart eyes. Those eyes told me right off I was going to have to be careful and stick just as close to the truth as I could. Nothing fancy; they made me glad I had told Georges to keep a low profile.

"Mrs. Peters? I'm Ern A. Smithe—that's Smithe with a final *e*."

She smiled. She had a nice smile, and I was glad to see it. "Come right in, Mr. Smithe. I'm happy to see you. All of you come in, and please sit down."

I said, "This is my secretary, Ms. Levy. I believe you've already spoken with her."

That brought another smile. "Yes, indeed!"

"And this is my associate, Mr. Fevre." Everybody took a seat after that, Georges on the couch on my right, and Mahala in a chair to my left. The three of us made Mrs. Peters's front room kind of crowded.

"As I understand it, you've worked for the Coldbrooks in the past. Is that correct?"

"I did, Mr. Smithe. For three years."

I nodded and smiled. "I'm afraid I'm going to have a good many questions, Mrs. Peters. If you feel I'm becoming too intrusive, just say so and we'll go."

She smiled back. "My life is an open book. That's something my mother used to say, Mr. Smithe, and it means there's not a single thing in there I'm ashamed of or afraid to talk about."

"Then let's begin with Mr. Peters. Are you still married?"

Her smile vanished. "In my heart, yes. Jim died six years ago. We had fifty-seven good years."

"I'm very sorry to hear that. Most sincerely sorry. You have not remarried? You're still a relatively young woman."

Mrs. Peters shook her head. "I doubt that I ever will, Mr. Smithe."

"Were there children?"

She nodded. "Our daughters, Spring and Summer. Good girls, both of them—although Summer could get pretty hot, if you know what I mean. Spring's a teacher now, just like dear Ms. Colette, down in Nuevo Dinero. Summer's a surgeon now, if you can believe it. She's up in Kokolik City, but she travels a bit. Going where they need heart surgery, you know."

"Both your girls have done very well for themselves, I would say."

"So would I, Mr. Smithe. I was a housemaid, back before they were born, and Jim was a gardener. From the beginning, we made it clear to them that we expected them to rise above our station, and they were going to have to make such fine grades that the government would keep them in school. At first we tutored them—that was reading and arithmetic, mostly—and later they tutored us. The years flew by and they did it, both of them."

I nodded some more and got down to business. "You mentioned Colette Coldbrook," I said. "She's not here at present. I'm a friend of hers who is acting for her. Perhaps my secretary told you about that?"

"She said something about it, Mr. Smithe. I imagine Ms. Colette has mentioned me to you?"

I ignored the question. "Did you and she get along well, Mrs. Peters? Would Colette be smiling if she were here? Assume that I'm utterly ignorant of whatever may have passed between you. Frankly, I don't care whether you liked or disliked her; but I must know whether she liked you."

"We were friends, Mr. Smithe. You may not believe it, but we were. I knew my place, you understand, and I kept to it. But we chatted and gossiped as friends when the two of us were alone. She showed off her new clothes to me, and told me things in confidence about various people she knew."

"You said you worked for the Coldbrooks for three years."

For a moment I thought that Mrs. Peters was going to cry. "About that," she said. "Yes. It seems, well, far away and bright now, Mr. Smithe. Something wonderful that happened a long, long time ago. Since Jim died . . ." Her voice trailed away.

Mahala went over to stand beside her, patting her shoulder.

I said, "I understand, believe me. Who hired you, originally?"

She swallowed audibly. "It was Mr. Coldbrook, Senior. He engaged me because they needed—would you like me to explain the situation? How things stood in the family back then?"

I said, "Please go ahead. It may save us quite a bit of time."

"Well, Mrs. Coldbrook had passed away not long ago. While she was still among the living the family had no servants, although they needed several in that big house and could afford good ones. Mrs. Coldbrook hadn't wanted them, and Mr. Coldbrook had let her have her way. So Mrs. Coldbrook and Ms. Colette had taken care of the light housework, with the cleaning service coming in once every four weeks. Master Conrad had taken care of the ground cars, and there was a service—"

"How many ground cars were there then? Do you remember?"

"Certainly. There were two. One was a large sedan—quite the thing, if you know what I mean. Mr. Coldbrook, Senior, drove that one. Neither of the young people were allowed to touch it. The other one was a large alterrain. It was sturdy and reliable and could carry a lot. Both the young people could drive that; but it had a card, and I kept it. That was so I would know if it was gone and who had taken it. Where they had said they were going and so on. Then, too, once a week I drove it into town to buy groceries. I did all the grocery shopping."

"From what you've said, I take it there were other servants as well."

"Not at the time I was first employed, Mr. Smithe. Mr. Coldbrook had me interview maids and cooks—subject to his approval, you know. Eventually, we had two maids, a cook, and a scullery maid. I believe I interviewed for six weeks or so. Of course that wasn't the only work I did. That was the easy work, because I could sit down to do it; but it's terribly hard to find honest, hard-working girls these days. Of course the young men snatch them up. You know how that is."

I smiled and said, "I understand."

"The cook wasn't hard at all, because Mr. Coldbrook was willing to pay a lot for a good one, and he interviewed them himself whenever he was at home. He traveled a lot on business. Perhaps you know about that."

I said I did.

"Then he let the cook interview scullery maids because they were supposed to be her helpers. 'Assistants' is what we called them. That was at first, but Ms. Keck simply could not be satisfied; so after a lot of getting nowhere I had to do that, too."

Here I had Judy Peters name all the servants, with Georges taping the names and Mahala writing them down. I will not go through all that here. In the end, it did not matter.

Probably I ought to tell you that I let Georges ask some questions then. His were mostly about whether any of them had an arrest record, who gambled, whom she thought might have used drugs, did Ms. Keck steal groceries, and so on. That sort of thing.

Back to me now, when we were through with all that. "When you were discharged, Mrs. Peters, were you given a reason?"

"We were assembled in the kitchen, Mr. Smithe. The maids, the cook and her assistant, the chauffeur, both the gardeners, and me. Mr. Coldbrook told us he had decided to go to an all-robotic staff. Everyone would be given a good character reference and a severance bonus. But we were to leave at the end of the week, all of us."

"How long ago was that?"

"Oh, let me think. Well, goodness! Week eighteen of last year I believe it was, Mr. Smithe. I know it was in the spring. One of the gardeners was terribly angry because—because—well now, I don't suppose you care about any of this."

"Yes, I do." I was trying to get her going. "Please tell me."

"His bulbs were starting to come up. He'd planted a lot the fall before. Five hundred, I think it was, and he wanted to see how it looked. They're all gone, now. The 'bots took them out, I suppose."

"You went back to see?"

"No. No, not really. I—well, I was looking for work, Mr. Smithe."

I smiled and said, "Nothing wrong with that, Mrs. Peters."

"One of the girls we'd had . . . her name's Ella-Jean. She'd gone to work for Span & Spic. That the cleaning service they had. They hadn't been in since Mister'd got the 'bots, only Master Conrad had told them to come again. So Ella-Jean told me about that. Mister'd gone away somewhere and Master Conrad thought he was dead. Only the law said he couldn't be declared dead by a judge for years and years."

"I understand."

"But they thought he must be dead. Master Conrad did and Ms. Colette, too, she said. Everybody else that knew about it, the same. I talked about it to some others, you know, afterward. He'd been gone for half a year, and nobody had heard a word from him."

"You must have hoped you'd get your old position back."

"Yes, Mr. Smithe, I did. Well, Ms. Colette was off teaching. She'd gone, Master Conrad said, before Mister'd disappeared.

That was how he talked, 'disappeared.' Only I know he thought he was dead. Everybody did. He hadn't told Master Conrad he was going anywhere, or packed a bag, or taken a ground car or a flitter, or anything. I talked to one of those 'bots, too, while I was there. That was while I was waiting for Master Conrad to see me. He was busy with something for an hour and over. I don't know what it was. Probably that girl he was going to marry had screened him, or else he'd screened her."

"Go on."

"Well, Master Conrad was just as nice as could be, when we talked, and what he said was the same as what the 'bot had told me. One morning Mister'd not come down for breakfast. Master Conrad thought he was working in his shop upstairs. He did that sometimes, and I would've thought the same thing most likely. Only after a while the cook 'bot wanted to know what he'd like for lunch, and Master Conrad went to see. And he wasn't in there, or his room, either."

I nodded.

"Master Conrad was very nice to me, Mr. Smithe, only no job. He was planning to get married and close the house. Sell it, only he couldn't now under the law. It was Mister's, you see. He promised he'd recommend me to people, only no job, like I said."

Georges asked, "What about his father? Did he ever come back?"

"Yes, sir, he did after Master Conrad passed away. You know he died, I suppose." Mrs. Peters looked from Georges to me.

I said, "We know something about it, but not as much as we'd like to. What can you tell us?"

"Somebody killed him is what they say. Those news reporters

do, only they can't be trusted, Mr. Smithe, the men or the women, either. They talk like they know a lot, but sometimes it's all wrong."

I nodded.

"Ms. Colette could tell you more, only I doubt she wants to talk about it. They were real close, her brother and her were. She told me once they'd fought like cats and dogs when they were little, and now they laughed about it and it was them against the world, you know."

"Against their father?"

"I wouldn't say that, Mr. Smithe, though he was a hard man. Hard and quiet, you know. So quiet it would frighten you. Only when he talked you'd better listen, because he meant every word and he'd back it up. Those 'bots suited him just fine, I'm sure. I hope—well, I don't suppose you want to hear my gossip."

Georges chimed in with, "Yes, we do."

I confirmed that.

"Well, I was about to say maybe he loved his wife. I hope so. She wasn't quite right, is what I heard, and that was the reason they'd never had servants. 'Bots would've been worse, I guess. They do pretty much whatever anybody tells them, is what I hear. But Mrs. C. wasn't exactly right sometimes, and I guess maybe she might have told one to kill her."

I said, "It wouldn't have done it, but basically you're correct. 'Bots might have done a great deal of damage if she had ordered it."

"It seemed like he'd loved her and taken good care, you know. I heard that various times from Ms. Colette and Master Conrad, too."

"But not his children?"

"Well, nothing that I ever saw." Mrs. Peters's voice fell. "Maybe you knew him?"

"No, not at all. None of us did."

"Sometimes all three—that's him and Master Conrad and Ms. Colette—would just sit at table and eat, and nobody'd say a word."

"What about visitors to the house?" I asked. "Can you tell us who came?"

"Nobody. That was the funny thing. Of course it was less trouble for the staff, but it meant no tips for us, too. There were eight bedrooms, you know, up on the second floor. That was six guest rooms and the children's rooms. Master Conrad's and Ms. Colette's, and all those guest rooms, too. But nobody ever slept in those. Not while I was there."

Mrs. Peters waited for me to ask another question, but I did not. I had been struck by an idea and needed another minute to facilitate it. After a second or two it came, and I stood up. "Georges, I'm sure you have more questions of your own for Mrs. Peters. Ms. Levy and I are going to go outside for a breath of air. We won't be gone long."

When we returned, Georges was saying, "On those trips, the short ones, where did he go?"

"Out of town, sometimes. I could tell because he always packed his suitcase for those. Then, too, he had a cabin in the mountains. He went up there pretty often. When he needed to think, is what he told me."

Georges asked, "Do you know where that was? It could be important."

"No, sir."

"What road his cabin was on?"

"I'm sure I never heard."

"Where did he go to buy supplies?"

Mrs. Peters shook her head. "I haven't any idea, sir."

I said, "I'm sure someone's looked into that by this time, and he's certainly not there now. Do you happen to know where he's buried?"

Mrs. Peters nodded. "In the Old Church Yard, I believe, Mr. Smithe. That's a new place somebody opened a few years ago. It's over on the west side."

Georges said, "I suppose we'll go over there to ask him a few questions."

I grinned. "You and Ms. Levy? I agree. I might send you both."

Mrs. Peters laughed politely, and I turned to her. "You're the person we need. I talked it over with Ms. Levy and we agreed on that. Would you accept a hundred and fifty a week?"

There was a good deal of bargaining after that, which I will omit; in the end, we agreed upon a wage. She would start on Monday.

When we were settled into the convertible's firm, fighter-flitter's seats once more, Georges wanted to know what I wanted with a housekeeper. I said, "I want the house kept, of course."

"I see. . . . All right if I ask what you and Mahala were really talking about outside?"

"Certainly, and she'd tell you in any event as soon as you two were alone. I wanted to know what the Coldbrooks had been paying Mrs. Peters, and I thought Mahala might have seen it as she was going through the father's records. She had. It was two hundred a week. Knowing that, I was able to make a low offer that was not insulting."

"For a housekeeper we don't really need."

"We won't need her as long as we remain in the house, I agree. But I want someone there I can rely upon to apprise me of developments, if there are any. Suppose that Colette returns, for example. She may escape from the people who have her, or they may free her or bring her back. If that happens, Mrs. Peters will screen and tell me. Or if the police come looking for you, or a dozen other possibilities."

Georges laughed. "Believe me, they don't want me. They've had me, and they're through with me."

I did not believe a word of it, but I said, "Glad to hear it."

"Where do you want to go now? Shall we visit the grave?"

I had been thinking about that. "Not yet, and perhaps never. How many funeral directors would you think there might be here in New Delphi?"

"Eight or ten. Could be more. You want to talk to them?"

"I may. Yes. Can Mahala use this ground car's screen while you're driving?"

"Sure. I could drive manually."

"Suppose we tell the car—what's its name, by the way? Do you know?"

"Geraldine. Somebody had a sense of humor."

"Junior. I don't know that, but it seems almost certain. If you give Geraldine a destination, can it take us there while Mahala's using the screen?"

"Sure. Where do you want to go?"

"The coroner's office. It may be called the medical examiner's office. Try them both."

Again, I reached over the seat to touch Mahala's shoulder. "I'd like you to find out which mortuary prepared the body of

Conrad Coldbrook, Senior, for burial, if you can. He probably died last year, but it could be early this year. I realize it may be impossible to find that out, but please try."

She nodded, unhooked Geraldine's little keyboard, and went to work.

Georges said, "Medical examiner. We're on our way," and I thanked them both.

At the medical examiner's office, I explained to a smiling young woman that the three of us were collaborating on a biography of Conrad Coldbrook.

Her smile vanished. "You'll have a difficult time of it, I'm afraid. He was a man of mystery."

"He was indeed! That's what makes him so interesting. What was your guess, Georges? Fifty thousand hits?"

He said, "Forty-seven thousand. Eventually you'll find out that I was very close."

"I hope so."

I turned back to the young woman. "May we see the result of the examination? It should be a matter of public record."

"It will be if there was one. Have you searched?"

"Not yet," I told her.

"Then I will." She spoke to her screen, "Conrad Coldbrook. Any record."

Her fingers flew across the screen. "This is his son. Do you care about him?"

Georges said, "Hell, yes. Anything that bears on his father's life."

"He was strangled. I'll send you the whole thing. What's your address?"

Mahala wrote on her pad, tore off the sheet, and handed it to the young woman.

The young woman spoke to her screen again and turned away.

I said, "What about the father?"

"No examination. No reason for one. Do you want the attending physician's report? It's cardiac arrest."

"If that's all there is, then we want it. I was told that the law required an autopsy whenever someone under the age of one hundred died."

"That might be a good one," the young woman said, "but it's not the law. It messes up the body, you see, and you've got to have a closed-coffin funeral. The families hate that. We do an autopsy whenever there's reason to suspect foul play—that's at public expense. We'll also do one if the next of kin requests one, but the next of kin has to pay. There's one or two of those in most years. Otherwise, when the doctor certifies natural causes, that's that."

Back in Geraldine, Georges said, "What are you smiling for? You didn't get a thing there."

I said, "You're quite correct. By rights I ought to weep. Later I may. I hope not, but I may. May I ask how Mahala's progressing with the mortuaries?"

She turned in her seat to give me a thumbs-up.

Georges said, "She's enjoying herself. This is fun for her. For me, too, in a crazy kind of way."

I said, "You know a great deal, and in fact you've been a fountain of information and sound advice. Can you tell me whether there will be a written report on the death of Conrad Coldbrook, Junior?"

"On the son? Sure. You looking for the police report or the

medical examiner's? There'll be both, and if you want the examiner's we could've gotten it back there."

I shook my head. "I want the police report, if we can get one."

"We can, but there's two glitches. The first one's not too bad—there'll be a fee. Nothing that will break the bank." Georges paused, looking thoughtful. "The second one's likely to get really rough."

I said, "I think I can guess."

"They'll want to know why we want it. Plus who we are and where are we staying. Show some ID. So count me out. Mahala, too."

"I understand. Let me out two or three blocks from police headquarters, please. Where can we meet when I'm finished in there?"

"How about the bus station?" Georges looked worried.

16

Him Again

Maybe three minutes after I left headquarters, I caught on to the fact that I was being followed. I had kind of expected it sooner or later, but it was a jolt just the same. The first me had told his readers how you can tell for sure in *Nine Dead Women*. You make three right turns. If he is still back there after that last turn, you have a shadow.

I had a shadow. Now what?

Two things bothered me straight off. Number one, I should not have spotted him so quick. The cop I had talked to mostly—that was Detective Serody—had been friendly and cooperative. No one had questioned the false ID that had been Colette's father's. Could Serody have arranged to have me tailed when I left? Well, of course, even though he had not sounded like he would want to. But that tail would have been a pro, right?

Also the tail would have been a cop, and cops are generally pretty big, even the women. This was a little guy in a black raincoat and a black rain hat—in July, when it had not rained a drop since the day our bus got to New Delphi.

So something really funny was going on, and maybe the Cold-brook house was actually bugged.

That is what I was thinking when I walked past a classy de-partment store, the kind of place where you can buy a 'bot, a bassoon, or a bottle of perfume. Stores like that are always on corners; maybe you've noticed. Hey, if the store is going to take up half the block, are you going to put it in the middle? I stopped, looked at the stuff in a window, and saw that the little guy had stopped, too. Which tied it.

I went in, made a quick left, and went out another door onto a side street. Swell, only if I had just gone around the corner, he might not have gone in yet. Heck, we might have been almost nose to nose, and I wanted to get around behind him. So I made a right instead of another left, walked around the block fast, and went back into the department store through the same door I had used the first time. My tail was too short to spot easily; but there he was, smack in the middle of women's clothing, looking around for me.

Now I wanted a good look at his face; so I bumped him a little and said, "Pardon me." Then I bumped him again, harder.

He spun around and said, "Hey!" then snapped his mouth shut.

As soon as I saw his face I had him. I said, "Come on, I want to buy you some hot chocolate. A sandwich, too, if you'd like one. There's probably a restaurant in here somewhere."

He sort of froze, so I took his sleeve. "Besides, I owe you three hundred, remember? Only if you won't have a sandwich with me and a little quiet conversation, I won't pay you back."

When I said that, a guy behind him who'd been looking at embroidered breast boosters turned, stuck his hand into the black raincoat's side pocket, and whispered, "Do what the nice man tells you to and I won't lift your pocket rocket." It was Georges.

A 'bot stationed by the lift tubes told us we could get lunch at Alice's Tea Room, on the fifth floor. It was a little bit too lady-like for three guys, maybe, what with the faux-linen tablecloths and napkins, the expensive-looking tableware, and the polished crystal wineglasses; but we got a good spot near a window and not too near anybody else. When we had ordered I told the little guy, "You're a friend, or at least you and I were friendly the first time we met. Today you were following me. Want to explain?"

Georges added, "While you talk, I'll be watching your hands. Keep them outside your coat."

My tail nodded.

I said, "What's your name?"

I could see him trying to decide whether he should tell the truth. "Chick."

"Your full name, please."

"It's Chick Bantz." Chick hesitated again, sucking air. "Probably you'd like to see some ID. Smooth, I got my license and some other stuff—only I'll have to reach inside my coat to get it."

I shook my head. "I just wanted to know what to call you, Chick."

Georges said, "Your ID would be fake anyway, so what's the point? What do you want with us?"

"Nothin' with you," Chick told him.

I smiled, wondering whether Chick's fake ID would be as good as you could get with the app I had turned up on Conrad Coldbrook's screen. "With me, then."

"Remember the first time, when you were in that place with all the screens, and people on the wall like stuff in a store?"

Right then I started trying to figure out some way to get rid of Georges; if this went any deeper, he was bound to figure out that I was a reclone. I said, "The place in Owenbright? The one with all the screens? Certainly I remember it."

"That's the one. My boss wanted to talk to you then, only he said be nice, no rough stuff, an' you wouldn't come along. I tried, an' I figured I'd come back later and try again. I did, only you were gone."

He had stopped talking. Wishing I could shut him up, I said, "Go on."

"Then him and his girlfriend come down here. That big house belongs to her, or that's what he told me. Maybe you saw 'em there."

Trying to digest "his girlfriend," I shook my head.

"Well, he seen you. That's what he said. They both heard your ground car and went over to the window, and you got out with some other guy and a woman. That's what he told me."

The wait 'bot returned with kafe for Georges, hot chocolate for Chick, tea for me, and a plate of pastries Georges had ordered.

It had given me a little thinking time—time I needed pretty badly. "You gave us your name," I said when the 'bot had turned away. "What's your employer's? His full name, please."

"No ducking," Georges added. "No dodging. What is it and who is he?"

"He's a government cop." Chick stirred his chocolate. "I'm talkin' about the big one in Niagara. Do you care?"

I raised my eyebrows. "Should we?"

"You better. You're thinkin' you can hand me over to those cops you talked to if I don't play along, only I'll walk. Want to try? I'd like that."

Georges said, "You mean that your boss will spring you, but he won't like having to since he'll have to report it. You'll catch hell for getting yourself booked. Also what did you tell us? He'll know you talked, but he won't know how much and he'll have a lot of questions. Some other people may have questions, too. You sure you want to go that route?"

"You remember how it was that time in Owenbright, Mr. Smithe? Remember how nice to you I was? You were flat— anyway you said you were—an' I fronted you three hundred. Three hundred for nothin'! Are you an' me goin' to shank each other now?"

I shook my head. He was scared and it showed, but probably not half as scared as I was. I said, "I'd like us to remain friends, Chick. Georges here is a friend of mine. If you're a friend, too, he won't have any reason to get rough with you."

"Listen up! I can get rough myself!" His voice quavered.

"I'm sure you can. Please don't. Why were you following me?"

"'Cause you come out of headquarters! I wanted to find out what was up. If you'd been me, you'd have done the same thing."

"I doubt it. You told us that your boss is an officer of the law."

"He is! He's Continental, too. These guys are just local, and he can pull rank on them. Think they'd like that?"

Georges asked, "Who does he work for? What department?"

"It's the Continental Government, and that's all I know."

"How'd he get you—"

The 'bot was coming to our table. I said, "We're fine. I don't believe anyone wants anything more just now."

"Are you Mr. Fevre, sir? I have a screen." It held up an eephone.

"I am." Georges reached for it. "You turn the damn thing off and this is what you get." With the eephone at his ear, he said, "Fevre."

He listened, his face serious; then he said, "Hold it," and turned to us. "Excuse me a minute. This is private."

I said, "Certainly," and he hurried out.

Chick grinned. "Your buddy's got problems."

I nodded and tried not to look as relieved as I felt. "Don't we all."

"Now that it's just you an' me, we can settle this like pals, right?" Chick picked up a pastry, took a bite, and followed it with a sip of hot chocolate.

"Yes," I said. "I hope so."

Chick gave me a lopsided grin. "To start, look at where you're sittin'. Your buddy was sittin' up close and watchin' my hands, all set to grab me anytime I went for my burner. You're not. I could draw, shoot under this table, an' you'd be rocket wrecked before you knew what happened."

I smiled. "But you're not going to do that."

"Right. I'll make you a deal. You want my boss's name, right? Well, I'll tell you—his first name an' last name, an' planetwide. Only you got to tell me what you were doin' in headquarters." For an instant, Chick hesitated. "An' you got to go first."

I said, "Fine, I will. How familiar are you with the house that your boss and his girlfriend were in when they saw us?"

"I never seen it, but I know where it is. He told me."

"Good enough. Did you know that there was a murder committed in it a few weeks ago?"

Chick looked a trifle surprised. "I never heard nothin' about that. I didn't do it, an' I don't know who did."

"There was. A young man named Conrad Coldbrook, Junior,

was killed. Presumably you've seen your boss's girlfriend. Perhaps you've even spoken to her."

I waited until Chick nodded.

"The victim was her brother, and the case is still unsolved. The police report on that murder is a matter of public record, available to anyone upon payment of a small fee."

The report was in an inner pocket of my jacket. I took it out, unfolded it, and held it up. "I went to that police station to obtain it. Here it is. Would you like to read it?"

Slowly Chick nodded. "Look it over anyhow. That smooth with you?"

I said it was and handed him the report.

"A 'bot found the body an' told his pa when he got back? That must'a been rough." Chick returned the report. "What's it to you?"

"That goes beyond our agreement. I've told you why I went to the station, and shown you the document I obtained there as proof. That fulfills my half. What's your boss's name?"

Chick finished his pastry and sipped hot chocolate. "You going to drink that tea?"

I sampled it obediently.

"You got me bothered a little. Maybe you can see it. See, I can tell you what my boss says his name is, an' I think it's the pure. Only I don't know for sure an' can't prove it. Dane van Petten is what he says. The other cops call him Dane."

It took some prying to get Chick to describe van Petten, but eventually he did.

Georges returned and sat down. I glanced at him, and he said, "Later."

"Fine." I turned back to Chick. "How long have you been here? In New Delphi?"

"Since yesterday."

"How did you get here?"

"None of your business."

"I know," Georges told me. "He came on the bus."

Chick's eyes opened a trifle wider at that.

"Your boss sent you here," I told him. "Or anyway, so I'd guess. If he didn't . . ." I shrugged. "I think he must have had a job here for you. If I'm wrong, you can laugh in my face. But if I'm right— and I believe I am—we may be able to help you accomplish it. You'll be able to report back to him proudly, and presumably you'll be well paid."

Georges said, "His boss may have a stronger hold on him, be able to send him up whenever he wants. Something like that."

I shook my head. "He was generous with me once in order to win my friendship. Clearly he was well paid."

I turned back to Chick. "I'm in your debt, as I just said, and I'll help you if I can. What is it you're after?"

"Couple of things. The first one is find out what you're doin' here an' who that guy and the girl are that he seen with you. The other one is find out how you found out where him an' the girl was."

Georges chuckled.

I glanced at him. "Your call, was it urgent?"

He nodded. "Fairly."

"You may see to it, if you wish."

"If you've got things to say to him"—Georges jerked a thumb at Chick—"that you don't want me to hear, just say so, and I'll go."

"No, not at all. I admit that what I'm going to say to him next will sound so weak that I'll be discomfited. Truthful answers to his questions will be embarrassing, in other words; and I'd prefer not to be thus embarrassed in your hearing." I sighed. "No doubt it will be salutary, however."

"You're a village cadet." Georges was still grinning. "Clean as snow."

"If you say so."

Chick selected another pastry. "You come for the fruit festival?"

"I'm afraid not. Basically I came because I was terribly concerned about Colette. That's your boss's girlfriend, I take it."

"That's what he calls her, yeah."

"You have to understand that I didn't know then that she'd been arrested. This was in Owenbright. The bed was mussed, a lamp had been knocked over, and she had left her shaping bag behind. At that time, we supposed that van Petten and his confederate were criminals."

"Cops? Yeah, they all are. Just dig down a little."

"I had been arrested myself, taken to a safe house, tormented—tortured would be too strong a word—and questioned for hours. I had escaped. I hoped to find Colette and help her to escape as well."

Chick nodded. "I got it."

I finished my tea, which was getting cold. "Where to look? She and I had seen them in Spice Grove. She had been kidnapped, as I then thought, in Owenbright. When I had been in New Delphi with her, she had clearly been convinced they were there as well. There, perhaps, more than anywhere else. That they had planted their listening devices in the family home, for that matter."

"So you come here. I got it."

"Correct, I did. Everything seemed to revolve around the fortune Colette was in the process of inheriting, and that fortune—her father's fortune—around the murder of her brother. Thus it seemed quite possible she had been taken here; and that if only I understood the fate that had overtaken Conrad Coldbrook, Junior, I might understand the entire affair."

Chick was watching me sidelong; he said, "Smooth. Do you?"

I shrugged. "Not yet, but I'm trying. That's why I went to the police station and paid to get the police report. You wanted to know why I was here and who the couple who had come with me were. Now you have the answer to your first question. The second is not at all complex. Georges?"

"Sure, if you want me to."

He turned to Chick. "You came here on the bus. So did we. It's a long drive and there are stops—you know all about that now. We met Mr. Smithe on the bus and got to talking with him. We liked him, and it looked to us like he liked us. It was raining buckets when we got here."

Georges waited for Chick to speak, but he remained silent.

"He asked where we were staying, and I told him we didn't have anything lined up. We'd have to wait till the rain stopped, then have a look around. He said he had a card for a mansion, and we could stay there with him until we got settled."

"Yeah. What's your name?"

"Georges Fevre."

"What about the lady's?"

"Ask her."

"Yeah, I will. I'm supposed to believe all this turdticky?"

"It's true," Georges told him, "and I don't give a busted bucket whether you believe it or not."

Chick spoke to me. "You got him and the lady helpin' you? That's all it is?"

I nodded. "Georges is an acute observer and the lady with him is much better on a screen than I am. If they're willing to help me, I'm happy to have them. I'll be happy to have your help as well. What about it?"

Chick was silent.

"If you're willing to join us, we'll welcome you. If you're not, Georges will confiscate your pistol and we'll turn you loose. Which is it?"

Chick cursed under his breath.

"Please understand, we won't be confiscating your pistol as some sort of punishment. I simply do not want to be shot."

"Only you want to be pals?"

"Exactly." I smiled.

"Smooth. I'm in, Mr. Smithe. What you want me to do?"

"You have funds, I know. I want you to find the main public library here. Ask if they have the poet Arabella Lee. Not her books, the person."

"On a shelf, like."

"Exactly. If they have her, check her out." I considered. "For a week. That should be enough."

Reluctantly, Chick nodded.

"If they don't have her, tell them you want her. Ask them to borrow her from another library for you. You'll have to get a library card, to start with. I'm sure you understand."

Chick had thought of a new objection. "What if she won't come?"

"Come back and tell me why she objected, and anything the librarians may have said. I doubt that we'll be here. We'll probably be at the Coldbrook house, the country house you call the mansion. Bring her there if you get her, and come there alone and report if you don't. There's a 'bot. It will let you in. If we're not back yet, it will make you comfortable while you wait for us."

Chick rose. "Sounds like candy. Be seein' you in a couple hours."

He walked away, and I told his back, "Good luck!"

Georges waited until he had gone. "You wanted to get rid of him."

"I did. What did Mahala say?"

Georges nodded. "You're right, it was her. Somebody there let her use a screen, I guess. Either that or she found one nobody was watching."

"Or several other things. What did she tell you?"

"She'd seen that picture in the sunroom, the one that shows the Coldbrooks, the whole family. You pointed it out to us one time."

I nodded.

"Maybe she found some other pictures, too, while she was searching. Anyway, a young woman came into the bus station looking for somebody. Brunette, pretty tall and fashionably dressed, expensive clothes. She went around looking at people, then she left." Georges took a deep breath. "Mahala's seen those pictures in the sunroom, and she's pretty sure this woman was Colette Coldbrook."

I got up and walked to the big window at the other end of the room. We were five floors up, and the ceilings were high all over the store. I stared down at the spotless sidewalks and orderly traffic, and up at the pure blue and almost cloudless sky until my watch struck the hour.

Georges was still at our table when I returned; I had half expected him to be gone. He wanted to know what I had been thinking about.

"Motivations," I told him. "The reasons why people act. Motivations are always important, and I haven't been thinking nearly enough about them. Not principally about yours or Mahala's, but I'm going to start with those. You suggested that we rendezvous in the bus station. You were afraid of the police; and I suppose you suggested we meet there mostly because all three of us knew where it was and there were places to sit down, buy food, and so on. People can wait there without arousing curiosity."

"Sure." Georges sounded impatient. "Now you're going to ask me something. What is it?"

"You and Mahala have been together ever since I met you on the bus. Why did you leave her in the bus station, and where did you go?"

He grinned. "I can tell you, but I doubt you'll believe me. I guess you thought I was afraid I'd be arrested."

"Yes. I did."

"I'm not. I told you once the police have already seen more of me than they ever wanted to. You shouldn't have doubted me."

"I see." I waved the wait 'bot over and asked for more tea.

When it had gone, Georges said, "It's Mahala they want. She can't talk, and that makes her a defective. They want to lock her up."

I knew that already, but this did not seem to be the time to discuss it.

"We've got money now, both of us, thanks to you. We need new clothes and at least one more suitcase to carry them in. We decided I'd come here, buy a few things I need pretty badly and another bag, and she'd wait in the station in case you came. We could both go shopping when there was less pressure and more time."

"I see. How did she know you'd be here, in this restaurant?"

"I didn't ask her about that, but knowing her I can give you a good guess. She would have tried Menswear first, then Luggage, then maybe Lingerie and Women's Wear in case I was buying something for her. After that, all the other departments. She'd have turned up a list of those somewhere, probably alphabetized. This tearoom is called Alice's."

It made sense, and I nodded. "Have you bought what you need?"

"Not yet. I parked Geraldine and walked Mahala into the terminal, and we sat around for a while. When I came in, I saw you and that little guy."

"Chick."

"Right. What are we going to do about the woman that Mahala saw? About Colette?"

"That's the least of our problems. She will almost certainly go out to the house. This time we'll get there first and wait for her. Who was she looking for in the bus terminal?"

Georges considered. "That's a good question. You want a guess? Chick."

"I doubt it. A better one would be his boss, van Petten, but I believe there's another that's better still."

"What is it?"

I shook my head. "I'm going to reserve that. It's a mere guess, but it's mine until we know more. Why did they come here?"

"Ah! I think I know that one. Chick has money, so he'll have an eephone for sure. He spotted you coming out of police headquarters, and he saw a chance to score points with his boss. While he was tailing you, he texted him and told him he'd seen you. . . ." Georges paused. "Wait up! That won't work. If his boss and the girl were out of town, they can't have gotten here that fast. Not even in a flitter."

"Correct. But they probably did fly in."

Georges rubbed his chin. "She came by car before. We found that rented car. You turned it in."

"That's understandable. She was afraid to return to her apartment building in Spice Grove to get her flitter. Whether they were watching it or not, she would have thought they were. From what I know of her, that is a certainty."

"She has a private flitter?"

I nodded. "A small red one, a two-seater. I've flown in it."

"You said 'they.' Do you think van Petten's with her?"

"I do. Or she's with him. That might be more precise."

"Suppose she's here alone?"

"Then I will have been proven wrong. She will have returned to what she believes, perhaps correctly, to be a hotbed—"

"And shown her face in public in the bus stations. I get it. You're probably right. Do his superiors know he has her?"

By that time, I was thinking of something else. "I don't know," I said, "and I doubt that it matters. Here's something that does. Let's assume they're together, which I think likely. Assume, too, that van Patten was with her in the terminal. Mahala wouldn't have recognized him, and it doesn't seem probable that he'd let Colette go off on her own—or that she would want to. What brought them to New Delphi?"

"Damn it, I need more kafe." Georges waved at the wait 'bot and held up his cup.

"Also time to think." I sipped what remained of my tea. "Go ahead. If you come up with something I haven't thought of, I'll be happy to hear it."

"You know, I ordered these and I've hardly touched them." Georges pushed away the pastries. "I thought I was hungry."

"You've eaten two," I told him. "One before your screen and another after. But please go ahead. Have a third."

"Kind of you." Georges grinned. "I'll pick up the check."

"I assumed you would."

The wait 'bot poured his kafe, collected the whitener jug, and set a fresh one on the table.

"All right," Georges said when it had left. "You want to know why the girlfriend came here. As I see it, it had to be one of two things. Here's the first. One of the 'bots back at the house was under orders to screen her if we showed up, and did. Probably the maid."

"Possible, but I doubt it. What's the other?"

"Chick called in yesterday. Not just to tell van Petten he'd gotten here, but something else that made Colette and van Patten move fast." Georges paused. "By the way, are we on their side? Or are we going to try to get her away from him?"

"I don't know. We'll find out when the two of them come to the house—or so I think."

17

ESCAPE

"M s. Coldbrook and her guest are waiting for you in the sunroom, sir." The maid 'bot opened the door all the way and stood aside.

I wanted to say, "Sure"; but what I really said was, "You needn't show me in." I was alone. Like somebody I had been thinking about, I had paid off my cab and walked up to the front door. Unlike him I had rung the bell, though I had a card for the door in my pocket; and it had come to me while I waited for somebody to answer it that I was going to have to get used to being alone again. When it did, I realized that I had known it ever since Georges and Mahala had left me to shop, with instructions to meet at the bus station. I have a subconscious, just like you and everybody else, and now and then mine shows me that it is a lot smarter than I am.

Colette stood up and hugged me. Probably you will laugh, but her hug has stuck with me. Also you will probably think Colette is a witch when you finish reading all this clear to the end (if I ever get to the end), but she is not and I could never think of her that way if I tried. The luck of the draw plays some really nasty tricks on a good many of us, and if you do not understand that, there is a whole lot about life that you do not understand. Take it from me; I am on my second, and I know. Destiny is what the cruel twist in my brain would make me call it if I wanted to say it out loud. God is playing a board game with himself, or that is one way to look at it. He shakes three dice and throws, and two of them are Destiny and Chance. It was a good hug from a fully human who smelled glorious and looked even better, and it was warm and long.

Van Petten—I had already guessed that he was the tall young cop who had tied us up in Colette's apartment—held out his hand when she let me go. I could see he knew I was just a re-clone, but he made himself do it. So I shook his hand quick and hard, and said thank you; by the time we let go, which was maybe less than one half of one second, I had given up wondering what he wanted; I knew I was about to find out.

I should have guessed it by then, because the answer was really easy.

"Have a seat, Mr. Smithe," van Petten told me, and sat down on the couch; you would have thought he owned the house.

Colette was already sitting there, close enough that their elbows touched. "I've still got you checked out, Ern." She smiled.

I explained that I had returned myself when I thought she had been kidnapped. I did not tell her it had been a prize mistake, that I ought to have known better, or that I was still ashamed of it.

The smile got a little bit brighter, if anything. "I understand, but I didn't return you; so I've never gotten my deposit back."

"In that case, I'll return myself again when they find out you haven't really been kidnapped." I was smiling back at her. "When I do, the library will be happy to refund your deposit."

"I don't want it, Ern. They sell you—sell reclones like you, I mean—don't they? When the library no longer wants them? I've bought disks like that."

I nodded and braced myself, knowing what was coming.

"Wonderful! They'll sell you now. You're practically new, so they'll want more money. I'll pay whatever they want, and I know the president of the Friends. She can put a little pressure on them if we need it. I'll get you and I plan to keep you. Wouldn't you rather sleep in a nice bedroom than live on a shelf?"

I nodded again.

"Has anybody checked you out besides me?"

Two nods are all right, but three are too many. I said, "Two officers of the law." I had tried to say "cops," but that would not work. "Two detectives" [ought to be: "dicks"] "from the Spice Grove Police."

I turned to van Petten. "Their last names were Payne and Fish. I have never known their first names. Possibly you know them?"

He shook his head.

Colette asked what they had wanted.

"They wanted you. You're a prominent resident of Spice Grove, and you had been taken from our hotel suite in Owenbright. Kidnapped by criminals, or so they—and I—believed. They thought, just as I did, that you might be somewhere in Spice Grove. Since neither they nor I had any idea where you might be, Spice Grove seemed as likely a place as any. Failing that, it might be possible for them to learn where you were and inform the Owenbright police. In either case, Payne and Fish would receive a great deal of credit, as would the entire Spice Grove department. They hoped I knew where you were, or if I did not that I knew something that might point them toward your correct location."

Van Petten grunted. I could see that he was taking all of it in, but I could not guess what he planned to do with it.

Colette said, "I'd think they could've asked you about that without checking you out."

"They asked me scores of questions by which they hoped to elicit information of value, and struck me whenever they thought it might make their questioning more effective. I was forced to describe your mother, for example, although I had never seen her."

"Did they know about the book?"

There it was.

"Only what I told them about it." Remembering those hours hurt. "Also that it was very rare. Fish tried to use a screen—there was one in another room—to locate a copy. He could not."

"But you know about it," van Petten said. "Tell us about that."

"Indeed I do. The title is *Murder on Mars*. Colette had her father's copy in her shaping bag when she consulted me. She showed it to me then, and allowed me to examine it after she had checked me out. For some reason her father seems to have valued it. Surely she's told you."

"I checked you out," Colette said, "and you say these policemen checked you out so they could question you. Was there anyone else?"

"There was another man who tried to check me out when I was in Owenbright." I was still talking to van Petten. "Short, blond, and fairly young. His name's Chick, or at least that's what he calls himself—Chick Bantz. He's an employee of yours or says he is."

Van Petten nodded. "He works for me off and on."

"The Owenbright Library could not permit it, since I was not theirs and they had not received me as an interlibrary loan. May I ask why you attach so much importance to this?"

"I don't," van Petten told me. "Colette does. But anything that's important to her is important to me. I think she wants to see if you've been checked out by other women."

"I do not!"

I said, "The answer is no. Only by Payne and Fish, and both are men."

Van Petten said, "Let me be blunt. I won't threaten you, because that's not something I do. We want you on our side. You know the library will burn you if there isn't a lot of demand for you."

I nodded.

"For them it makes sense. You have to be fed every day, from time to time you need new clothes and so on. Colette checked you out. Fine, but she's one of us. Chick would have if he could, but he's one of us, too. Payne and Fish won't check you out again once they find out Colette's no longer missing. You know how the library operates. She and I have only a vague idea. Suppose you go back now and nobody else checks you out. Nobody, ever. How long would you say you'll have?"

"How long will I live?"

Van Petten nodded.

"Fifteen years, barring unforeseen circumstances." I was stretching it.

He leaned forward. "And what might those unforeseen circumstances be?"

"Suppose that someone visited the library regularly to consult me. He didn't check me out, you understand, but he and I went to a table and conversed for an hour or more each time. I might get a considerable extension in that way."

Van Petten nodded. "Are there others?"

"Certainly. They would try to sell me before burning me. If I were lucky, someone might buy me. Do you want more?"

"Suppose you were sold. Could your new owner burn you?"

I should not have smiled, but I am afraid I did. Van Petten was thinking exactly as I had feared. I said, "Of course. You knew that."

"I did, but I wanted to confirm it." Van Petten might have been talking to a chair.

"As you now have. You invite me to join you. As soon as I do, you will want to know where the book is and what I've learned about its secret. A bit of experimentation will show you that you've learned all that you really need to know. So the fire for me, or the shredder. Whatever you choose."

Colette said softly, "I wouldn't let him, Ern."

"You couldn't stop him," I told her.

After that I think van Petten said she would not have to, but I was not paying much attention. From the front of the house, I had heard a woman's voice and footsteps; and I thought, *Oh my God, it's Chick bringing Arabella! What have I gotten her into?*

A second or two later the maid 'bot appeared in the doorway carrying a beat-up suitcase. Behind the 'bot, I saw Mrs. Peters.

Colette jumped up. "Judy! It's Judy! I can't believe it!"

Van Petten was looking at me; but I ignored him, getting up and going over to the two women, who were hugging and whispering.

Colette turned to me, radiant. "You got her for me! Ern, you're wonderful!"

I nodded. "I try."

Mrs. Peters was beaming. "I know I wasn't going to start till Monday, Mr. Smithe, but I—well, I didn't have anything particular to do today, and I thought it might be good for me to have a look at things here to find out what I ought to do first when I went to work. I hope you don't mind."

I said, "Of course not. It's actually quite admirable, Mrs. Peters."

When she had gone, van Petten said, "You've been busy. Who authorized you to do this?"

"No one. Are you considering a lawsuit? As a nonhuman I cannot be sued, but I suppose you might sue the library. You'd have to show the court that my actions have resulted in injury to you, of course."

Colette said, "I want to keep her, Dane. Won't you agree to that? For me?"

"I suppose you want to keep Smithe here, too." He had made his voice softer, but I could see it took effort.

"I do." Colette paused, looking from him to me, then back again. "You have to get used to him and he has to get used to you, that's all. I love you, and he's very nice. He's useful, too, and loyal and clever. You should be glad I've got something like him."

"You told me once that he knew where the book was, that he'd hidden it here, in this house, before the two of you went to Owenbright."

"Yes, I did." Colette turned to me. "You did, didn't you, Ern? I think you said you were going to."

"I doubt that I said it. We were very much afraid of their

listening devices then, and it would have been less than prudent. Or at least, it would have seemed so. Did Mr. van Petten here really have listening devices in this house?"

He shook his head.

"I thought not. I found one in Dr. Roglich's office and smashed it. He had found it earlier, clearly, but he'd been afraid to touch it."

Van Petten nodded. "That one was a decoy, actually. We let him see us install it."

That jolted me, though I tried not to show it. "So a working device remained there?"

Van Petten nodded again.

"In that case, I'm surprised that you didn't plant a few here, in this house. It was Roglich's conversations with Colette's father you wanted to overhear? I've been assuming that."

"Yes, of course. If I tell you about the listening devices in this house, will you tell me where you hid the book?"

I shook my head. "I will not, since it isn't yours. It belongs to Colette, however, and I'll tell her. Will you agree?"

"Yes, agreed. We put three bugs in this house. One in the laboratory, one in Coldbrook's bedroom, and one in this room. He found all three."

"And destroyed them?" My eyes wanted to wander around then, but I kept them on van Petten.

"No. Just watched what he said, and said very little."

"In which case, they're still here."

Van Petten grinned. "Do you want to look? Have fun."

"You think I won't be able to find them. You're probably right."

"You won't be able to find them because they're gone. We caught on eventually and took them out to make him think we were no longer interested in him."

Maybe if I were smarter I could say here that his eyes told me he was lying, or that they told me he was telling the truth. All right, this is the truth. His eyes told me a little less than a snake's. They said that I should not like him or trust him, and the less I had to do with him, the better off I would be. But I had guessed most of that already.

So I talked to Colette. "Do you want to know where I hid your book—your copy of my book, actually—before we went to Owenbright? If you do, I'll tell you. Either here and now, or in some private—" I heard the doorbell ring, and stopped.

The 'bot spoke, a man muttered, and a woman insisted, her voice shrill. A moment later steps, with the woman's *tap-tap-tapping* ahead.

I stood up.

Have I described Arabella already? Well, probably, but I am going to do it again. If you already know, you can skip this part. Long dark curls flying, cast-a-spell dark, dark eyes open wide, and tiny mouth open wider. An old-gold complexion that made you want to run your hands over every square centimeter of her, then push her skin up against yours.

Got it?

Very, very hot. Pocket-sized. High, high heels, perfect legs, hula-hips, narrow little waist, and tits to die for.

"Ern! He said you were here but I couldn't believe it." Kiss-kiss-kiss. "Ern, you freezing son of a bitch, aren't you going to introduce me?"

I wanted to pinch her bottom, but I knew where that would get me. Had I seen a styptic pencil in the brother's bathroom? I did not think so. "Colette, this lovely girl is the famous poet Arabella Lee. Arabella, this kind and beautiful lady is my patron,

Ms. Colette Coldbrook. The gentleman is Dane van Petten. Mr. van Petten is some sort of officer of the law, and someday I hope to find out just what kind."

Van Petten cleared his throat. "Strictly speaking, Mr. Smithe, I'm not a policeman of any kind, even though I'm authorized to wield various police powers. I am an enforcement specialist in the Continental Office of Emolument."

"I stand corrected," I told Arabella. "He's a tax collector."

Van Petten spoke to Colette. "She is . . ." He paused. "Somebody whom somebody else has checked out of a library. No doubt you've realized that already."

"Me," Chick said. "I did it." By that time he was standing in the doorway.

I added, "He had offered to do me a favor, you see. This was the favor I asked."

"I ordered Chick to come here to New Delphi and find out what Mr. Smithe was up to," van Petten told Colette wearily. "He seems to have taken the shortcut of asking him."

"They made me," Chick explained. "So I got friendly with them and got them talking."

"They?" Van Petten's eyebrows were up.

"He has a pal. George something."

"Georges," I said, and spelled it. "'Zhorzh.'"

"There was some guy and a woman with him today," Chick said. "I told you. George was the guy, probably. Smithe says the woman was his secretary. It looks like we've got her already."

Arabella shook her head. "I haven't seen Ern in ages."

I said, "That is almost literally true. I could explain who Georges and the woman were, but is that what you really want to know?"

Van Petten held out his hand. "First, give me the money, Smithe. All of it."

I shook my head. "We not fully humans are not subject to taxation, nor is there a tax on property possessed by municipalities. If there were such a tax—"

"Shut up!"

"—the Spice Grove Public Library, to which I belong, would be responsible for paying its share. Or so I'd think. Not me."

Van Petten had gone pale. "I could kill you."

"Of course you could. You have a weapon, I'm sure. Perhaps even one of those pocket rockets? A missile pistol? Chick has one, and I think that's what they call them."

Colette was holding his arm.

"It would be as easy as throwing a book into the fire. You could put my body out with the rest of the garbage." I spoke to her. "Is that how you dispose of your garbage out here? Or do you have to take it to a dump?"

She shook her head. "There's an incinerator."

"Easier still. Just shove me inside and switch on the fire."

"He was a horrid husband," Arabella told van Petten, "one who nearly drove me mad; but if you kill him, I'll kill you."

For a second or two he stared at her, then he laughed. "You won't have to, and two dozen of you couldn't manage it. But it might be fun to watch you try. Looking at you, I wish I could."

Colette asked, "Have you had a great many husbands, Ms. Lee? I've never been married." I could tell that she was trying to change the subject, and it made me like her better than ever.

"About four." Arabella held up fingers. "Ern was my first, and if I'd known what the other three were going to be like . . ."

"'About'?" Colette looked interested.

"Sometimes it can be hard to tell." Arabella turned to me. "You don't like this man, do you?"

"We circle and snarl," I told her, "largely because Mr. van Petten fails to understand the natural respect and affection I have for my patron. When he does, things will become a bit more friendly."

"He could check you out after she returns you, Sugar Pie. It might be—"

I nodded. "Less than pleasant. I know."

"He couldn't because I'm going to buy him," Colette protested.

Van Petten ignored her. "I could leave you out in the rain, Smithe. That's what one does, I believe. What would you do then?"

"Get wet, of course."

Chick had found a chair. "You said to get her, and I did. You got anything else for me?"

I shook my head. "Not at the moment. No."

He spoke to van Petten. "How 'bout you? If it's somethin' you don't want 'em to hear we can go somewhere else."

"Later. Did they take your gun?"

Chick shook his head. "We got friendly. I said that. Hell, we still are."

"Watch your 'luted tongue!"

I said, "Thank you, Chick. We need more friendship here."

"I agree," van Petten told me. He still sounded angry. "You're friendly with Ms. Coldbrook, or say you are. You say that she's your patron, and that the book belongs to her."

"Correct. She is and it does." I made it just as sincere as I could, which is pretty close to titanium alloy.

"If you and she could speak privately, would you tell her where it is?"

"Where I hid it before we went to Owenbright? Why yes, I would if she wanted to know."

Van Petten stood up. "In that case, the rest of us will go into the lounge. You and she will come in there when you're finished. Agreed?"

"Not by me. Ms. Coldbrook and I will go wherever she chooses."

Colette said, "We will, Dane. I take it that's what you want."

Van Petten, Arabella, and Chick left together, and I said, "May I suggest we go into the garden?"

"You're still worried about Dane's listening devices, aren't you?"

"Yes. The one I destroyed in Dr. Roglich's office was a decoy, or at least Mr. van Petten said it was. He may have been telling the truth. If so, the one they removed from this room may have been a decoy as well, or so it seems to me."

She nodded and we went out. When we had reached the dry fountain and sat, she said, "You're looking terribly glum, Ern."

"I suppose I am." I could not meet her eyes. "Would you like to hear it? All cobwebs and moonlight, I assure you."

"I doubt that. Tell me."

"I have the mind of a writer. I won't call myself a writer because I'm not permitted to write. There's little demand for fiction these days, in any case."

"That will change."

"I hope you're right." I glanced at her and looked away. "You're wonderfully patient."

It was a whisper: "I try to be when I see real pain."

"This place reminds me of the one in which we talked ten

days ago when we met—the ruined garden with the two stones to sit on and the waterfall. Remember?"

"Of course."

"The writer I used to be would like to have our last conversation take place there, but I don't see how I can possibly arrange it. There will be no formal closure to our story, Colette, only a brief and brutal final chapter of the kind this life generally supplies."

"I'll help you if I can, Ern."

I thanked her, knowing all the time what I would have to say to her.

"Please tell me about the book now. If you don't, Dane will always think you did and I wanted to keep the information for myself."

"As you wish." I stared at the dry fountain. "Before we went to Owenbright, I hid the book among the other books in your father's library." Sometimes I feel terribly guilty when I lie; but what I feel when I lie is nothing at all compared to the guilt I felt then, when I had told Colette the truth.

"I see. You know, you actually are very clever, Ern. I wasn't exaggerating at all when I said that. Is it still there?"

I shrugged. "I haven't gone in there looking for it lately."

"Of course you haven't. That would have given its location away."

I waited.

"You've been selling emeralds. Chick found that out yesterday. Dane says he talked to a clerk in a jewelry store, and this clerk knew all about it. It's why we came."

"I see."

"My father did that, and I think they must have been some of his. Don't you want to explain?"

"No. It will only make trouble." I waited. When Colette did not say anything, I added, "The result of my explanation would be bad for you and for me."

"I can't see that. Are you sure?"

"Absolutely. I'm not a fully human being. Not really. Can we agree on that?"

For a long moment Colette stared at me. Then she said, "Of course."

"But I used to be a human being. I was a real man who lived about a century ago." I paused to think. "You can see the house from where you're sitting. You don't have to tell me you can, I know it."

She nodded.

"From inside it looks quite different, doesn't it?"

"All houses do."

It was my turn to nod, and I did. "Humanity is like that. Seen from outside, it's quiet and peaceful. Almost torpid. You'll agree?"

"I suppose I must." Colette sighed. "I've been to two universities. That may seem unlikely to you, but I have. I was a history major, originally. And I . . ." She shrugged.

"You were baffled by what you learned—baffled or sickened. Which was it?"

"Sickened. Yes, I was. You can study the history of women's fashions, if you want to. One of my friends did that."

I waited.

"Or there's the history of sports, or architecture, or dozens of other things. I wasn't interested in any of them. I wanted to learn real history, the rise and fall of empires and the history of human thought. And I found out that real history is largely the history of war, of people killing one another. The reasons for wars differed, but the result was always the same. Stones and arrows and spears and blood at first. Then bullets and shells and poison gas. Bombs, rockets, flying 'bots, and blood. And more blood, always more blood." Suddenly she laughed, but her laughter was empty and bitter. "Torpidity is fine with me, Ern. I like it."

"But why is it torpid? I used to think full humanity was tired, and there may be some truth in that; but it's not enough. There must be something more."

"There is, of course." Colette paused, staring off into space. "Imagine three farms. For centuries all three harvested rich crops. Each had wells that produced what seemed to be an endless supply of pure, clear water, and all their livestock were fine and fat and healthy. As long as those things were true, they stole from one another. They cheated one another, too, and each of them seized another's land whenever they could."

She stopped speaking. I said, "Yes?"

"In time their fields wore out, Ern. Their flocks and herds were poor and sickly, they had to boil their well water, and the wells went dry soon after the spring rains. The families that owned those three farms became no more honest, but they stopped stealing each other's land and livestock."

"I understand. It wasn't worth the effort."

Colette nodded and swallowed. "It was no longer worth the effort, and all three families were tired and weak. That's what has happened to the nations—to every nation all over this whole historic planet on which we live. Our governments know how

to manufacture terrible weapons—but they can no longer manufacture them. They haven't got the resources anymore—the resources and the technically trained personnel."

"Or the determination." I tried to smile. "So spears and war
clubs."

"They no longer inspire loyalty. We know they don't deserve
it, and the more thoughtful of us even suspect they never did. It's
a good time to be alive." Colette rose. "Let's go into the library,
Ern. You can show me where you put my father's book."

I did not stand. "Even if it will end that torpidity? Bring back
the bad old days?"

She stared at me. "Will it?"

"I think so."

"If that's true, I'll have to think about it."

Perhaps she did, but I did not. I showed her where I had put
the book. It was gone, and we both looked for it in case I had
forgotten exactly where. Naturally we did not find it. It was
hidden again, but this time up in the lab. All the time I kept
thinking I ought to have left it buried in the sand under the
driftwood. I could have done that, opened the door and blocked
it from closing with a stone, buried the book, stepped back into
the house, and shut the door forever.

Eventually Colette sent me away. Up on the third floor I talked
to Mrs. Peters, who was unpacking her suitcase. Georges and
Mahala had come, learned that van Petten was there, and gone
again. They had left a note, which Mrs. Peters swore she had not
read. It was simply an eephone number. I felt like I ought to mem-
orize the number and eat the note, but I did not really do either
one, just folded it back up and stuck it in my pocket.

18

My Watch Struck Midnight

I think I told you yesterday that the book was not really in Conrad Coldbrook's library anymore. I had put it in the safe upstairs, up in the lab that had been his. Now it was hidden elsewhere in the laboratory. Even though I could not be sure when I hid it, I felt certain now that Colette was not likely to look there; so I had picked the best place.

So thank you, dumb luck!

Also the worst. Dumb luck will do that to you. Van Petten took me up there and told Colette to go away. She had not even stepped inside, and I could see that it was music to her ears. She had beat it to the lift tube almost before he finished telling her to go.

He turned to me. "Think you can fight me?"

I shook my head.

"Right. You're twenty years older than I am, and I probably outweigh you by ten kilos. I'd grind you to dog meat, Smithe, and I will if you give me trouble."

Probably I should have been scared, but I was not, just tired of him. He could be nice around Colette, but it was an act. Get past the act and he was ugly, mean, and cruel. Get past that, too, and there was nothing else, just an empty suit and a bad smell. Maybe you will say I could not know that for sure, but I could feel it.

"You had emeralds, and I think you got them in here. Isn't that right?"

He wasn't my patron, so I nodded. No sweat yet.

"Show me where you found them, and it had better not be empty."

I shrugged. "In that case there's no point in my showing you. There were seven uncut emeralds in a drawer, and I took all seven. Did you expect an entire drawerful?"

"What I expected doesn't matter. He found a way to make them, didn't he? He could manufacture them. That has to be it."

There was a stool in front of one of the lab benches.

I pulled it out and sat. "Chick told me you work for the Continental Government. Is that correct?"

"Don't change the subject!"

"I'm not. For the Department of Finance, I suppose. The Department would love to know how to make emeralds. The Office of Emolument will be a part of that, I imagine. Making emeralds would be a lot better than just printing money, something the government can do, although your department can't. Am I right?"

"Keep talking." I could see that he was planning to knock me off the stool. He was just waiting for the right moment.

"I will. I'm going to try telling you the truth, and if that doesn't work, I have some good lies all ready to go. Here's the truth. Colette's father—let's call him by his name, Conrad Coldbrook—

didn't make emeralds. He found an emerald mine and mined them. It's just a small mine, and the emeralds are close to the surface there. One man could dig them and get quite a few in, oh, six weeks or less. Earlier they'd been a bit closer to the surface, so the time had been even shorter, but we won't bother with that now."

"Can you prove this story?" Van Petten's face was two fingers' width from mine; we almost touched.

"I can take you to the mine and even show you the drawer in which I found the emeralds. It's in the mine, close to the entrance." A new thought had occurred to me, and I paused to consider it before I spoke again. "I believe he must have been afraid his mine was worked out. He went back to it and dug there—it must have been extremely hard work—until he had mined enough emeralds to establish to his own satisfaction that it was not. There were seven. I believe I said that."

"Keep talking!"

"Yes, I'm nearly certain I did. Chick cannot have told you how many of the seven we sold. Of course he may not have known himself. The clerk he spoke with may not have known, or knowing, may have thought the fact not worth mentioning." Almost unconsciously I readied myself for the blow. "We sold six."

Van Petten took a step backward. "You're going to have to tell me about that. All the details."

"Certainly. I'll be glad to." I was fumbling in my pocket; by pure bad luck—there it is again—the seventh emerald was in the pocket with Georges's note; I was afraid the note would come out with the emerald and flutter down to the floor.

Eventually I fished the emerald out without the note, tossed

it in my hand, and passed it to van Petten. "Here is the last emerald, the one we didn't sell. Do you know a lot about gems?"

He shook his head.

"Neither do I; that one may be of the first water—or not. I'm
inclined to think it is, but I'm generally of an optimistic turn of
mind. Need I explain why I held back one?"

"Shit no. You kept it for yourself. I'm surprised they didn't
search you."

"Not at all. At that time it seemed likely that we would divide the stones rather than divide the money, which is what we
eventually did. Seven stones divided among three persons were
almost certain to foment quarrels, or so it seemed to me. Six,
however, worked out perfectly: each of us would receive two
stones. I wanted to avoid a quarrel."

Van Petten dropped the emerald I had given him into his left-
hand trousers' pocket. "You're not getting this back. I suppose
you know that."

"Of course. I anticipated it. Remember when you and a
confederate came to Colette's apartment in Spice Grove? You
stripped us naked and tied us to chairs."

"Sure." Van Petten nodded. "But he wasn't exactly a confederate. He's my boss."

"I see. You were looking for a book you knew must be in Colette's possession. It was the book her brother had discovered in
their father's safe, and at that time it seemed certain to all of us
that it must be in some way important."

Van Petten nodded again.

"As in fact it was." I slid off my stool. "I could ask now whether you would like to see it, but I will not. Whether you would or

not, I must show it to you in order to exhibit the emerald mine to you; and I know that you must be anxious to see that."

Van Petten drew his pistol. "If you're going for a weapon—"

"I'm not. I'm going for the book, which is a key, not a weapon." Crossing the room, I touched a screen. "Conrad Coldbrook's safe is behind this. No doubt you know."

"It's empty."

"It is indeed, unless someone has put something in it quite recently. However, it struck me that searchers who knew that the safe had been hidden there and that the safe was empty now would be unlikely to look behind the other screens." I took down another screen, not far away, and pulled off the tape that had held my book.

Van Petten said, "Ah!" My guess is that he had not meant to.

"Yes." I offered it to him. "*Murder on Mars*. I wrote it during my first life, while I was still legally human. There's a brief passage urging that space itself might be manipulated as other physical objects are. Conrad Coldbrook must have found it suggestive. Would you care to page through the book?"

Van Petten shook his head. "That's not much of a secret."

"You're quite correct, it isn't; but Conrad Coldbrook added something significant to my book, and it was that addition of his that motivated him to lock the book in his wall safe. Come with me."

I led him out of the lab and onto the landing again, then over to the door we had sealed once with tape. A bit of tape remained; I pulled it off and tossed it away, then waved the book at the door, pushed down the lever, and opened it. "The elder Conrad Coldbrook had a sense of poetic fitness that I find greatly preferable to his son's sense of humor. This book opens the door to a distant world indeed."

Van Petten stepped inside. "Wow! Is this the Southern Continent?"

"No," I said. "Not at all. We are on an island in a sea of another world, a world almost infinitely remote from our own." I pointed. "Up there on the cliff face, do you see the dark opening? It may look black from here, but it is really only in shadow. That is the entrance to Conrad Coldbrook's emerald mine."

Van Petten took a step forward. Only one, but a step.

"It's invisible from here, but there's a path up from the base of the cliff. It begins a bit to the left of the entrance."

He took two more forward steps, then broke into a trot. It was enough. I stepped backward through the doorway and pulled the door shut behind me and held the lever up until I heard a faint click, then pushed down on the lever to make certain the door had locked.

It had.

Back in the lab that used to be Conrad Coldbrook's, I found a new place to hide the book. It was pretty good, and in fact I thought it was probably better than behind a screen. I would not mind telling you where it was now, but if you knew it would not be worth squat to you.

This part hurts to write, so I'll make it quick. After that I went into the reactor room and moved all the spare rods into the lab. Hiding them was out; it would have been like trying to hide a dead horse. I just found a good out-of-the-way spot and stacked them there. It took three trips, carrying six rods each time. That done, I disabled the safety devices Georges had shown me. The reactor, I figured, would be good for a while, maybe until winter or even longer. After that it would overheat, go out of control, and quickly melt down. It would probably take out the garage and some other stuff as well as the house, and it might leave a crater; but with no one living nearby, there was a good chance there would be no lives lost. If somebody was inside then—well, that was a chance I had to take.

After that I changed clothes, showered, and went off to find Colette, which was pretty easy. "Is Mr. van Petten around?"

"Dane? I haven't seen him for a while." She didn't sound worried.

"Neither have I. I ran into the maid 'bot a minute ago and asked her. She hasn't seen him either. I'm going to venture a personal question. I can only hope you won't be offended." I hesitated. "Of course you need not answer if you find it impertinent, but does he have you under arrest? I get that impression."

Colette nodded. I kept quiet, and after a few seconds she added, "He's very nice about it. I'm sure he wishes me well—but yes, he does."

"In that case I'm going to offer unasked advice. I can only hope you'll consider the advice itself and not its humble source. I believe you ought to return to Spice Grove and engage an attorney. May I explain?"

"You think it's actually worth doing? That I stand a chance?"

"I do. Quite definitely."

"I've signed a confession, Ern. He made me." Colette leaned forward, eager for any ray of hope.

She had jerked the rug out, and I floundered around trying

to get my bearings. "Was it witnessed? Was there a roundvid re-corder?"

"No, nothing like that. He wrote a paper and I signed it. That was all there was to it."

I started breathing a whole bunch easier. "Was this here or back in Spice Grove?"

"Here, before you came."

"We may be able to disregard it. I'm pretty sure we can. Where is it, and what does it say?"

Colette took a deep breath; by that time I had relaxed enough to enjoy watching her do it. "Just that I'd known my father had some secret source of income, and that out of loyalty to him I'd refrained from telling the Continental Office of Emolument about it. That was all it was. Dane kept trying to get me to say something about emeralds, but I really don't know anything about them." Another deep breath. "Do you?"

Lying to your patron's just about impossible, but sometimes you can sort of ignore the question, which is what I did. "Your con-fession doesn't worry me, and I don't think you ought to let it worry you. Engage a good lawyer and let him worry, although I don't believe you'll find he worries much. What we must do im-mediately is leave this house and engage him."

Yet another deep breath. I wondered what was coming next.

"Is it all right if we take Judy?" For just a moment Colette's gleaming white teeth gnawed at her lower lip; I think it was the only time I ever saw that. "Ern, I want to close this place and buy a house on the coast. Can you understand that? A big one, but not more than two stories. And—and from my bedroom windows I'll be able to look out at the ocean."

Deep breath. This one was mine.

"I know you must think I'm silly. But it's what I'm going to do, and Judy can take care of it for me. She can keep it clean, supervise the kitchen and, oh, a dozen other things."

I smiled. "I don't think it silly at all. I think it's a wonderful idea. Will you go and find Judy and tell her she's coming with us? Explain to her that you're in charge, and tell her I'm wholeheartedly in favor of it anyway."

Colette nodded.

"I have to make a screen, and I'll tell the 'bots we're closing up the house."

My screen was to Georges, of course. I told him not to come back, for him and Mahala to get out of town and stay out of town. That it was dangerous for them here. I said he could take Geraldine if he wanted to, that I had fixed it, but to stay away from the house. I finished by saying that I might be in touch again later.

All right, I knew perfectly well that the reactor was not going to melt down in at least a quarter minimum—it's turned out to be more than two quarters—and the house would be safe until it did. I knew it, but just knowing about that reactor made me nervous.

Also I was afraid van Petten would find some way to get back. Right then he was up there looking at the mine, was the way I figured it; only sooner or later he was bound to realize that the door was locked, that there could be no easy walking back onto Earth. After that, maybe he would think of something I had not figured on; or maybe he had some sort of supercard that would open any door, and that was how he and his boss had gotten in to Colette's the first time I had seen him.

Only I figured I held a couple of aces, too. One was the rifle standing in a corner of my room upstairs. There was plenty of ammo in the mine, sure, but no gun. He had his pocket rocket, but no way would it shoot the same stuff as the rifle.

So my second was the locals and their spinning spears, or whatever you wanted to call them, and those things that had come up out of the sea. They had armor and on the big one that armor would be thick. How much explosive could a little rocket you shot from a pistol carry? About as much as a big firecracker, maybe. Sure, the explosive would be a whole lot more powerful, but still . . .

Add it all up, and maybe van Petten would get out before the reactor went *boom,* only maybe not. I was betting on not, a bet that left me with just one big problem.

That was Arabella. I knew she was around somewhere, and I had to get her out of there and back to the New Delphi library, or anyway, to some library somewhere. I was still mulling that one over when Colette came back. "Ern, I want to give Judy enough money to let her drive the alterrain to Spice Grove. How much do you think would be enough?"

That one sort of knocked me off my feet. To get a minute's thinking time I said, "Do you have money? I would have thought van Petten had taken it."

"I've got an account here. I'll screen a draft." Seeing my blank stare, Colette added, "She can pick up the money at the bank."

I nodded like I had known. "Yes. Of course. But couldn't she ride with us in your—no, it only seats two. I'd forgotten."

"I don't suppose you could take one of the others. . . ." Colette hesitated. "They're all mine now, after all. Dane and I came in mine. Or should I leave it for him? What do you think?"

That gave me a little time. I said, "Absolutely not. It's yours, and you should take it."

"I suppose he'll take one of the others. One was father's and the other was Cob's, but . . ."

I said, "They would've wanted you to have them, Colette, and they're yours now anyway."

"Then could you fly one back to Spice Grove for me? Just tell it what to do, like you'd tell a car. It's not hard at all."

"Certainly." I do not believe I have ever said one single thing that scared me more than that did, so I held it to one word, afraid that I was going to choke or start stammering.

"Wonderful! You'll fly yourself back to my apartment? I'm in Taos Towers, I'm sure you remember."

"I certainly do." I was getting it together now. "You still have me checked out. Can you give me the combination to one of the other flitters? They may be locked."

Colette nodded. "They probably are. It's *C-O-N-C* for both. The black one's Cat and the yellow one's Canary. I think maybe you'll need the names."

Here I tried to look thoughtful, and I think I pulled it off pretty well. "I'd probably better give you a headstart so that you can admit me when I get there."

Looking happy, Colette nodded again. "I'll tell Judy."

I hiked out to the hangar while Colette was in the kitchen looking for Judy. My house card opened the doors, just like I had expected. The locks on the flitters had thirty-six buttons in four rows, and *C-O-N-C* unlocked the door of the yellow flier. I climbed in and sat down in the pilot's seat, trying to look as though I knew what I was doing. Nothing happened, so I cleared my throat.

Maybe it worked; right after that the screen lit up, showing a ravishing blonde. I said, "Canary, about how long will it take you to fly to Spice Grove?"

There was a pause. "Weather clear, wind northwest at fifteen kilometers an hour. Estimated time to Spice Grove forty-three minutes at full speed, sir."

After I had waved good-bye to Colette and Mrs. Peters, I found Arabella in the library, which I would have guessed right away if I had any sense. She was deep in something, so I asked what she thought of Conrad Coldbrook's taste in books.

"Strange." She shuddered. "I've been reading the poems of somebody named Smith. Not Smithe, like you—there's no *e*."

"Pity."

"Yes, isn't it. He's terribly morbid, but good." Arabella paused, looking at something far, far away. "I doubt that they appreciated him," she said. Then she recited this:

Bow down: I am the emperor of dreams;
I crown me with the million colored suns
Of secret worlds incredible . . .

"Do you like that?"

I do not, but those lines are still stuck in my brain; probably you can guess why. Well, anyway, I told her that I did, that we were going to Spice Grove, and that she could bring the book with her if she wanted to. And she surprised all heck out of me by doing it. With women, you never really know.

Have I said already that Canary would seat six? It would.

Arabella surprised me again when we were nearly there. She saw the mountains in the distance and asked if we could fly over for a closer look at them. "I've read about them, but I've never really seen them myself. Not when I was alive the first time and not in this life either. So please, Ern?"

I told Canary to make a pass over the mountains for sightseeing, and it—Canary had a female voice, an octave higher than Geraldine's—said, "Yes, sir. I will amend our flight plan." After that it slowed way down, our cabin separated, and its wide, golden wing spread between the halves. We sort of drifted among snow-covered mountaintops and along dark, forested valleys for at least half an hour. I was keeping an eye on the instruments, but the screen showed Arabella whenever I asked; the mountains were really beautiful, and she was so darned thrilled she could barely sit still. I worried about wind currents, but I was thrilled, too. I had never seen the mountains up close like that, either.

After that we turned back to Spice Grove and set down on the roof of the Taos Towers. Arabella and I got out and Canary parked herself next to Colette's red flitter as soon as the hangar door opened. They tell me that flitters cost a lot and cost a lot to operate, too; it is probably true, but they sure are smart machines.

I had figured Colette would be mad because I had brought Arabella, but she was okay with it as long as Arabella and I stayed out of her bedroom, slept in my bed, and promised not to stay too long in the bathroom. I figured that with three women in the apartment there was always going to be a long wait, but the one time I went it was not as bad as I expected.

What *was*, was that I was going to have a chance to sleep with Arabella—only I was scared to death I would not be able to take it until we were both tired enough to drop. That was wrong, the way things turned out. Mrs. Peters stayed up talking about old times with Colette for quite a while, and then the two of them got going on the house on the coast that Colette was planning to buy for them—how big would be big enough, how big would be too big, what you could do to keep a house like that safe from storms, and so on and so forth.

So Arabella and I climbed into the sack early. For a minute I was afraid she would not want to do what I wanted, but it was just about the best I have ever had—better than I ever got in my earlier life. When we were finished, I let her use the bathroom to clean up first. She took quite a while, and I got to calculating how long it had been since the last time; it had been 137 years almost to the day. It felt like longer than that.

While I was in the bathroom myself—it did not take me nearly as long—I heard Mrs. Peters say good night and start getting ready for bed.

Back in our bedroom Arabella was asleep, or maybe just pretending for fear I would want to start in again. Only I think she was really sleeping. Because there were no other noises, none at all, I could hear her breathing. It was very regular and very soft. I kissed her cheek, keeping it as gentle as I could, and said goodbye in my heart.

As quietly as I could, I got my clothes back on and went out into the lounge. Colette was all alone out there, not sleeping or reading or even watching roundvid with earphones, just sitting on the couch and staring off into space. It was exactly the setup I had been hoping for.

I got a chair, pulled it up facing her, and started walking up and down the room because I was too nervous to sit. "I'm leaving now," I told her. "I've got to go." I got out my card and showed it to her. "Only you are going to have to promise me something before I go. I believe I've been a good friend. Do you agree with that?"

She said, "Yes, Ern. A very good friend." Her eyes were wondering what was up.

"Then I want you to promise you'll check me out next year, and every year after that. It doesn't have to be for as long as this time. One day ought to be enough, and if you get your card approved for reclones, you won't have to leave a deposit. So promise?"

She nodded, then held up her right hand. "All right, Ern. I will, upon my honor."

I said, "Fine," and held up my own hand. "If you keep that promise, I swear I'll never tell the authorities what I'm going to tell you now."

Let me stop right here to say that I never have and I never will. The reactor has gone up—it was on the news, and Millie Baumgartner told me about it, wanting to know if that was the place I talked about sometimes. I have been waiting for it, and now it has finally happened. Good-bye to the scarecrows, to the emeralds, and to the stars! So I am writing all this down, and I am going to hide it in the stacks. Someday somebody will find it there, but we will be dead and gone by then—or so I think. Nobody reclones a reclone, and if they reclone Colette, so what? It was the original who killed her father.

The armchair that I had moved would give me a good view of Colette's face, and after a minute or two I sat down. "I've never been sure about the best way to tell this, but I'm going to start by saying you warned me early on. You told me women lie a lot before you lied to me. It made your conscience feel a little better, no doubt, and it made me like you. I still do, and of course you've been my patron. That has always made you special, Colette. A very special person to me."

I waited, but she did not say one word.

"Then you lied to me, and it was a really fancy one. Too fancy, if you ask me. The way you told it your father had died, then your brother, Cob. That turned everything over on its head, and as long as I believed it I'd never even get close to the truth. It was as cunning as two foxes, sure; but it was too cunning, if you know what I mean."

Colette said, "How much do you know, Ern?"

"I'm telling you. What really happened was that your father disappeared for a long, long time. I don't know how long, but I imagine it was at least two quarters. Perhaps you assumed he was dead."

She shook her head, the motion so slight I nearly missed it.

"All right, you didn't. But Cob did and that is absolutely certain. Thinking your father was dead, he searched his laboratory, and when he found the safe he brought an expert in to open it for him. Did he really tell you there was nothing in there but the book? I've never been sure of that."

Colette nodded, her face expressionless but those dream-deep eyes bright with tears.

"That was a lie. He found uncut emeralds in there, too. Going through your father's files, he would certainly have found receipts that told him your father had been selling uncut emeralds, how much he had gotten for them, and who the buyer had been. He took the ones he had found in the safe to one of those jewelers and sold them. That may have been what sealed his fate. In his defense, we need to remember that he was convinced that your father was dead. In addition to the emeralds, he found the book, and here your story was simple truth. He had no idea why it should be in the safe. He hoped you might know, and when you didn't, he left it with you hoping you might discover some clue he'd missed. Then your father returned, probably with more emeralds. Do you know where he got them?"

"No. No, I don't. Are you going to tell me?"

"Let's say that I don't know; it will save a world of ill feeling and argument. He got them in the place where he had been when he had been gone so long. When he got back, he went into his lab and opened the safe, intending to lock them in it. The safe, which should have held the book and several emeralds he had not sold before he left, was empty. I don't know how he found out that Cob had done it, but I doubt that it was hard. For one thing, Cob seems to have put his own receipts into the file with your father's. If that wasn't it, he may have looked in Cob's room and found something that tipped him off, something else that had been kept in the safe, for example, or a bill from the locksmith Cob had hired."

Colette said, "He explained to the jeweler. He told me."

"That would do it. You weren't in the house at the time—the maid 'bot mentioned that when I questioned it; so Cob went to Spice Grove and gave you the book. You must have flown to New Delphi as soon as he left; and I admit I don't know why you did that, although I could venture several guesses."

"Father screened me. He had just gotten back from wherever it was he had been, and he was looking for Cob. He sounded angry, very angry. Cob . . ."

"Yes?"

"He was in my apartment when Father screened." Colette looked thoroughly wretched.

"But you didn't tell your father that Cob was with you."

"No. I didn't know why he was so angry with Cob; and I was afraid he'd be angry with me if he found out. He was—was truly savage when he was angry, Ern. Savage, and he held grudges. You didn't know him!"

"You're right, I didn't. Did he demand that you come home, come back to the house in New Delphi he'd bought for your mother?"

Colette shook her head. "No, Cob did. He asked me to go there and try to smooth things over with Father. So I did, and I thought I had done it. I went and explained to Father that Cob and I had thought he was dead, and why we had thought it. I told him how happy we were to find out we'd been wrong. I begged him to forgive me for thinking he was dead, and he did. He hugged me and told me not to worry. He was still furious about Cob's opening his safe and going through his files, but he hid it. He was like that, and I should have known."

I said, "You must have told your brother the storm was over."

"I didn't, Ern! I swear I didn't. I screened him as soon as I could and told him I thought everything would be all right in a few days. I told him to wait three or four days, then come and talk to Father. But he didn't! He wouldn't! He told me he was out of clean clothes and there were things he had to do in New Delphi, and he had a lot of money to give Father. He seemed to think that would make everything right."

I said, "So he came home, and your father strangled him."

She sobbed. I sat quietly, trying to figure out if Judy or Arabella was awake and listening. Finally I gave up and looked; neither of them was. I let Colette use my handkerchief and waited.

"I wasn't there when it happened, Ern. You've got to believe that. I wasn't!"

It did not matter just then, so I nodded like I did.

"Father saw Cob coming up the walk. There's an alcove for coats and things beside the front door."

I nodded. "I know."

"We called it the cloakroom." Colette sighed, and it was almost another sob. "Father waited in there. He didn't hide, he just stood there, not moving. Cob walked right past him."

"And his father caught him from behind and strangled him."

"He didn't use those words, but you're right. He did."

"You saw it, Colette. You watched him do it. You watched Cob die."

"No!"

"Yes, you did." I was keeping my voice down, not much louder than a whisper. "I don't know whether your father actually saw your brother come up the walk, but you did. You knew he was coming, and you wanted to be right there when he came in to make peace if you could. You'd probably watched him as he got out of the cab."

She stared.

"He did come in a cab, didn't he?"

It took her a long time to nod; when she had she said, "How did you know?"

It had been easy and I shrugged. "No one with money would drive from Spice Grove to New Delphi unless he were trying to evade arrest."

"Like me. I did, and you know that, too."

"Correct; you did it later. Your brother clearly came in the front door. The police report made that plain. So did the maid 'bot's account of finding his body. If he'd flown in a private flitter—presumably Cat or Canary—he would have come in through the kitchen door. Why not, when the house in New Delphi was his home? So he had taken a commercial flight. You no longer had a chauffeur. If your brother had driven out to the field and parked there, it seemed unlikely that he would leave his ground car in your driveway and enter through the front door. Garaging his ground car and coming in the side door or the kitchen door would be much more likely. Neither you nor your father had driven out to the field to pick him up, making a cab almost certain."

"I see."

"Also there seems to have been a slight delay before he entered the house. That delay gave your father time to get into position. Paying the cab would account for the delay."

"I've lied a lot." It seemed that Colette was ready to start crying again.

I nodded, and tried to be gentle. "We all do, I suppose."

"But I wasn't lying when I said I hadn't seen it. I shut my eyes."

"I believe you, Colette." That is what I said, because it seemed to be the thing to say.

"Are you going to tell somebody?"

"No. Not as long as you keep your promise. You must check me out for at least one day each year."

"I was going to buy you, Ern. Really, I was."

"Don't. I'll talk if you do. I don't want to spend the rest of my life worrying about what I eat."

She buried her face in her hands; after a while I got up and sat down next to her. "You were an instrument of justice."

She did not look up.

"There are a great many kinds of murders, Colette. Back in my real life, when I wrote mysteries, I studied murder. Studied it seriously, because making up fictional murders was a part of my profession. A lot of people are killed by people they don't know. A lot more are killed by enemies whom they do know. A few are killed by friends, and now and then murderers kill relatives from whom they expect an inheritance. That's what you did, and it's why this whole situation is so dangerous for you. You were an instrument of justice, and I know it; but if you're tried, the prosecution will never allow it. The prosecutor will say—will insist—that you killed your father to get his money. It's wrong, but a jury will agree and you'll spend the rest of your life in re-education."

I waited, but she did not speak. Finally I said, "That's if I talk. But only then."

She looked up. "He killed Cob, Ern. He really did. I—I saw it. He waited until Cob was past, then he got him by the neck and squeezed. I saw Cob's face, saw his tongue come out and the color fade, and I shut my eyes. When I opened them again, Cob was dead and Father was gone."

I nodded. "Your brother was killed by a tall man with strong hands. The police report made that clear. I don't suppose you know what the rarest of all murders is?"

She shook her head.

"It is the killing of a son by his father. That one almost never happens, which was one reason the police were disinclined to suspect your father. That, and your swearing that your father was away when Cob died. In addition to those two, his wealth and the fact that your brother's suitcase had been searched. Where was the money?"

"You—you know! You're frightening, Ern. Terribly frightening, and you look like such a nice man."

"I am a nice man, but I think. Your brother had told you he was bringing a lot of money. It was the money he'd gotten for the emeralds, of course. Where was it?"

"Hidden in his suitcase. There was a pocket in the lid. It would have been hard to find if it wasn't so full."

"Thank you. I had been thinking all along that your father had searched your brother's baggage for the book; but if that had been it, you would've seen him searching it when you opened your eyes. You didn't, showing that he hadn't searched your brother's baggage at all. So it was you, and you had the book already. You must have been looking for the money."

"You're r-right, I was. I did. May I tell you why?"

"Of course. Go ahead."

"It was because I was absolutely determined to bring Cob's murderer to justice. I didn't know how much money that might take, but I felt sure it would take a lot. As it was"—her shoulders rose and fell—"Father died of a heart attack before I could even begin."

I said, "A few days ago, it was a brain aneurysm."

She stared.

"Perhaps he had a bad heart, and the guilt of Cob's murder made it worse."

Back in control now, Colette nodded. "I think you're right. Certainly I hope you are."

I said, "However, you poisoned him."

"You—" She froze again, openmouthed.

"Will you tell me what you used? I'm professionally interested."

"No! No, I won't! Ern, I didn't poison him at all."

"You're good," I told her. "You need more practice but you're good. You have a lot of talent. Shall I tell you how I knew?"

She nodded without speaking.

"When you brought me to this apartment originally, you insisted that I stay out of the kitchen and your bedroom. Your reasons for wanting me to stay out of your bedroom were obvious; just about any other woman might have said the same thing. Your reason for keeping me away from your kitchen puzzled me and seemed out of character. When Arabella and I got here a few hours ago, you told us not to go into your bedroom but made no mention of the kitchen. That was when I knew. You'd had the poison in there, just in case you needed to kill me; but it's gone now. Did you use it up?"

Colette shook her head. "I washed it down the drain. I—I'd brought it here in case I needed it, and later I was afraid I would really use it again. Not on you, on Dane."

I nodded. "I won't ask where you got it. Several of the chemicals I noticed in your father's laboratory might do, and there may have been others. You seemed to have a horror of that laboratory, by the way, and now I—well, never mind."

I stood up. "With your brother and your father dead, you were alone in the world. Your father's fortune is coming to you in dribs and drabs. You won't get most of it until you're thirty. You won't get Cob's share of it until his murder is solved, which probably means never. You had the book, and you must have hoped it held the secret of your father's fortune. You couldn't find a clue in it, but you checked with the library—a natural approach for a teacher—and found that it had a reclone of the author."

I paused, but Colette did not speak.

"You asked how much I knew, and now you know. If you'd prefer that I didn't talk about it, you'll check me out for one day next year, one day the next year, and so on. I'm going to leave a complete account of your father's death where it will be found when I die—but only when I die. Do you understand?"

"Yes, Ern." Colette nodded. "Yes, I do." And then, "Are we still friends? I'd like that."

That one stopped me in my tracks. I said, "I hope so. I'd like that a lot."

"I won't ask you to trust me, or to believe everything I say."

I think I may have said, "Good," before I got out of there; but perhaps I said it only to myself.

Out on the street, I began what I knew was going to be a long walk. Cabs passed now and then and I was carrying a great deal of money, but I wanted to walk. I was still a kilometer or so from the Spice Grove Public Library when my watch struck midnight. It was July thirty-first, and I was overdue.

Persons Mentioned in the Narrative

Persons are listed by their surnames, if those are given. Thus Dane van Petten will be found under V, and Arabella Lee under L.

Bantz, Chick   A gunman employed by Dane van Petten.

Baumgartner, Millie   A library resource.

Coldbrook, Colette C.   The library patron who checks out the narrator.

Coldbrook, Jr., Conrad "Cob"   Colette Coldbrook's brother.

Coldbrook, Sr., Conrad   Colette Coldbrook's father.

Coldbrook, Joanne Rebecca Carole   Colette Coldbrook's mother.

Electric Bill   A 'bot belonging to the Spice Grove Public Library.

Fevre, Georges   A knowledgeable traveler who assists Ern A. Smithe.

Lee, Arabella   Ern A. Smithe's former wife, a library resource belonging to the New Delphi Public Library, the Owenbright Public Library, or the library of an unnamed university, depending upon the copy intended.

Levy, Mahala   Georges Fevre's mute paramour.

Peters, Judy   Formerly the Coldbrooks' housekeeper.

Roglich, K. Justin   An astrophysicist.

Smithe, Ern A.   The narrator, a library resource.

van Petten, Dane   An enforcement specialist; Ern Smithe calls him a tax collector.